Blank Canvas

GRACE MURRAY

FIG TREE
an imprint of
PENGUIN BOOKS

FIG TREE

UK | USA | Canada | Ireland | Australia
India | New Zealand | South Africa

Fig Tree is part of the Penguin Random House group of companies
whose addresses can be found at global.penguinrandomhouse.com

Penguin Random House UK,
One Embassy Gardens, 8 Viaduct Gardens, London SW11 7BW

penguin.co.uk

First published 2026

001

Copyright © Grace Murray, 2026

Extract on p. v from *The Complete Psychological Works* by Sigmund Freud

The moral right of the author has been asserted

Penguin Random House values and supports copyright.
Copyright fuels creativity, encourages diverse voices, promotes freedom
of expression and supports a vibrant culture. Thank you for purchasing
an authorized edition of this book and for respecting intellectual property
laws by not reproducing, scanning or distributing any part of it by any
means without permission. You are supporting authors and enabling
Penguin Random House to continue to publish books for everyone.
No part of this book may be used or reproduced in any manner for the
purpose of training artificial intelligence technologies or systems. In accordance
with Article 4(3) of the DSM Directive 2019/790, Penguin Random House
expressly reserves this work from the text and data mining exception

Set in 11.6/15.8pt Calluna
Typeset by Jouve (UK), Milton Keynes
Printed and bound in Great Britain by Clays Ltd, Elcograf S.p.A.

The authorized representative in the EEA is Penguin Random House Ireland,
Morrison Chambers, 32 Nassau Street, Dublin D02 YH68

A CIP catalogue record for this book is available from the British Library

ISBN: 978–0–241–76730–6

Penguin Random House is committed to a sustainable future
for our business, our readers and our planet. This book is made from
Forest Stewardship Council® certified paper.

Blank Canvas

'*Blank Canvas* is razor-edged and emotionally rich,
an unflinching portrait of identity and loneliness. Grace
Murray's prose navigates the desperation of loneliness
and selfhood with exquisite depth, rendering even the
quietest moments astonishing and haunting'

Lucy Rose, author of *The Lamb*

'Fantastically engaging, the kind of interior voice that ensnares
you . . . Brilliantly and satisfyingly off-key and absurd,
with a vein of tragedy running through it, it's the art college
campus novel I've always wanted. Grace is such an astute
observer of people (especially artists) and a sharp, bright
and hilarious writer. I can't wait to see what she goes on to
write next. She's one of those writers who you can devote
yourself to. I'm along for the ride of her whole career'

Claire Kohda, author of *Woman, Eating*

'A study in self-sabotage and yearning that crackles
until it erupts, *Blank Canvas* follows a listless art student
who constructs herself from lies. With prose alive to every
sting and silence, Grace Murray exposes the longing beneath
the performance, and the cost of connection built on deceit.
A debut that lingers – acidic, funny, and painfully astute'

Seth Insua, author of *Human, Animal*

'I loved this brilliant debut, compelled by the spiky interiority
of Charlotte, and her minute, cold observations of the world she
disdains yet longs to join. This novel is astute and absorbing,
whether in upstate New York, a riverbank in Italy, or
Lichfield, at all times asking and answering the question:
how far would you go to stop being lonely? Comic and
acerbic, with moments of real warmth and sorrow, we are
drawn into Charlotte's warped, misanthropic worldview
and the tentative relationships she forms, and are eager to
stay. I was enthralled; Grace Murray is one to watch'

Emma van Straaten, author of *This Immaculate Body*

'One of the best debuts I've read this year . . . I read the whole thing in one sitting, so enmeshed in Charlotte's life and lies that I simply couldn't leave her. A character eliciting the level of frustration and sympathy that Charlotte does in a reader is a mark of truly impressive writing. The middle act, set in Italy, floored me. Murray's writing moves between a New York campus, a terraced house in Lichfield and a work-away trip in Italy with the ease of a writer unencumbered – each setting, each relationship, and each conversation felt real, as if they were being recounted to the reader from memory. Grace Murray is a writer to watch'

Jodie Matthews, author of *Meet Me at the Surface*

'A campus novel painted with the most startling, profound hues. A portrait of queer love, loneliness and dark lies, *Blank Canvas* has a sharp, striking wit that cuts at the heart of what it means to be human . . . An absolute triumph of a novel'

Rupert Dastur, author of *Cloudless*

'The sharpest, meanest of prose in the best possible way. An outstanding debut from an author to watch'

Heather Darwent, author of *The Things We Do To Our Friends*

'Slick with spite, desire and intrigue, this is an exceptional debut. Charlotte is audacious and addictive. You'll race through it, breath held, skin prickling'

Celia Silvani, author of *Baby Teeth*

'*Blank Canvas* is a perceptive, witty and subversive exploration of honesty, relationships and identity. Grace Murray writes with such clarity and boldness achieving a refreshing, nuanced take on the campus novel'

Ela Lee, author of *Jaded*

'Oh no.'
Sigmund Freud,
The Complete Psychological Works

I

In my final year of college, I started to tell everyone that my father had died, very suddenly: Nightfall. The bedroom. Heart Attack. The words – he is dead – slid out quickly, rising from my throat, into the air. It was just a sentence, and it only took a few seconds, a brief dash in the conversation. It was easy. And it might have all been fine – I might have got away unscathed, with a little sympathy, a few hugs, and nothing else – had I not decided to tell Katarina first.

She was ugly, short, and had been burdened with a kind face and a terrible body. Her skin had the texture of gooseberries, all prickled and marred. The pimples started at her neck, in small raised red bumps which crept over the throat, the jaw, making their way to the centre of her chin. Imperfections were insulting: I felt that there should be a degree to which ugliness could no longer be acceptable, a line drawn somewhere, like with supermarket foods, yellow stickers on, tossed into the hands of the homeless. It bothered me. I usually looked away whenever I saw scars, scabs or untidiness of any kind, but, with Katarina, I just couldn't stop staring.

I found her at the centre of the room, LED lights hanging over her head. It was almost midnight, and they were playing Britney Spears, the tinny, trashy sound contrasting with the glow. Only a few people had arrived – there was just the host, a first-year and Katarina – and so I had to speak to her.

A bulb hung above her face, revealing the white and pitted marks over her cheeks. It swung as I walked towards her, and she ducked, then smiled.

'Hey,' she said, 'how was your summer break? Was it okay?'

I thought about summarizing everything that had happened within those two months, time stretched out and thickening like a divine punishment, and settled on a lie:

'Actually, no, it wasn't at all. My dad died.'

Her bloated and blistered face went slack; she looked at the window, then at the open kitchen door, then back to me, her eyes wide and panicked. It was an incredible display. I almost felt bad for her.

'I'm so sorry,' Katarina said. 'I had no idea. I'm so very sorry.' She seemed to have tears in her eyes – either that or the light above her head was getting to her. 'I can't even imagine what you're going through right now.'

'It's okay, honestly.'

It was fantastic, brushing her aside, playing the martyr. No, don't concern yourself with my emotions. I'm fine. It's okay. I smiled a little, and looked at the carpet, as though I were hiding a dark cavern of suffering she couldn't access.

'I'm so sorry,' she said again, as more people started to arrive, spilling into the room with bags of tortilla chips and vodka bottles.

Katarina put her arms around me, and held on to my wrist with one flushed hand. She smelled like alcohol, or a second-hand store, doused in old perfumes. Bitter and sweet all at once. It made my eyes water, which only contributed to the quality of my performance.

Still, it was nice of her, and it was the first hug I had received in a very long time. I'm sure my mother used to do it, after a cut or scrape of some sort. It was possible.

'Please, if you need anything,' Katarina said, 'come and talk to me, or text. Whenever. Seriously.'

'Thanks. That's so kind.'

I wondered how I appeared to her. My face must have been attractive, with its thin nose, turned slightly at the bottom ('a mini-slope', as my mother had told me, her arms weighing on mine), and the eyes, large, blue. I'm sure it was difficult for Katarina, having me there, so close to her. We were so different.

'I really do mean it,' she said. 'Just send me a message, any time. But I have to –' She looked at the new arrivals. 'I have to go now.' Katarina looked around again. 'I think that's – is that Amelia?'

She did a small, almost apologetic, dance away from me, until I could only see her hand, the soft inside of her palm, waving from the crowd.

I didn't stay long after that.

Outside, I stood on the street and watched the students dance, their shadows grinding against each other, all outlines and open mouths. One student grabbed her friend's hand and held it, triumphant, and it was almost too much, so that when I blinked, and stepped closer, I felt something pass through me – a desire to be like her, to have the house, the friends, the happiness. I wanted so much to be happy, there, that I felt as if I could hold it physically, in my hands.

But it *was* possible, I thought, watching the friends sway together; I could have it. My father called so infrequently that it was entirely possible that he could have died. And his death wasn't too much of a stretch – he had always been a sick man, a severe asthmatic, a type 2 diabetic, a hypochondriac. He was always announcing his imminent demise: at seven years old, watching him eat his shepherd's pie – 'I think I'm coming down with something, now' – at ten, finding bloodied tissues by his side of the bed, hearing his announcement that 'it doesn't look good, love'. I had been preparing for it for years.

And I was in a new town, in a new country: Pittsford, New York. Thousands of miles away. My father would never visit. He rarely left the house, let alone the town, and would often boast that it had 'everything a man could need', from the football pitch to the corner shop down the road.

I had no standards to live up to, either. I had never been particularly honest. Other people were good and kind – the rest were predestined for mediocrity, or cruelty. It wasn't my fault that I fell, through the random act of my birth, into the second category. If I ever woke up with an ungodly dread – that I could change it all now, turn around, and confess – I ignored it. I had never been good, and there was no point in trying now.

2

Lying was easier in America. They didn't have the same obsession with the past, with schools, the difference between St Paul's and Westminster, and they didn't constantly refer back, in a dredging up of old summers and football games and cycling holidays. At the institute, nobody asked if you knew Thomas's great-uncle's son, the one who went to Worcester College, and nobody would care whether you had seen mad Mary Sullivan in town, carrying her pet goat past the church. Instead, the students at the institute were obsessed with the future, the job posts and properties waiting for them in the city, and they would talk about starting salaries openly, without shame. The things you used to have were nothing, insignificant, in comparison to the things you might get in five years' time – and their friendships were organized around this ideal future. They were the perfect conditions for a liar. In the beginning, I didn't even have to worry about getting my facts straight, because nobody would ask. It also helped that none of them knew any places in England. If I was ever asked, in a lazy, drawling tone by one of the many unidentifiable American accents, where I was from, I told them: 'London.'

The morning after the lie – that my father lay in a coffin, not safely tucked up in bed – I walked into the cafeteria.

Katarina was by the cashier, ordering food while Tamsyn, her roommate, hovered by her shoulder. She spotted me, in my grief-stricken state, by the door. Tamsyn looked nervous, and slipped into my accent, her high, grating American vowels sliding away. She blushed and doubled-down, as her voice became Dick Van Dyke adjacent. She talked about her latest hair extensions, which were disjointed, in a rat's tail at the back of her head, and her UTI, which was 'brewing right this second'. It was several minutes before she asked if I was 'okay, after – you know'.

'I'm fine,' I said. 'Or as fine as I can be.'

'Of course.' She made a sympathetic noise. 'I can't believe we haven't met before. Were you in Fine Art 3B last year?'

'Don't think so.'

'Right. Well, it's nice to talk to you anyway.' She asked why I had come here, to Pittsford, of all places. The Everett Institute wasn't known outside of the US, and it was a long way to travel for 'a few walls'. Tamsyn leaned against the exposed brick of the cafe as she waited for my answer, her leopard-print bag hitting her knees.

'Well,' I said, 'I just wanted to get out. The city can get *dreary* after a while.' I drew the 'dreary' out, elongating each syllable, like an affectation from the royal family.

'I understand the feeling.' She smiled, and then turned away, tapping Katarina's shoulder. The pair of them launched into a fast-paced, rippling conversation which, in their enthusiasm, isolated the students in their vicinity.

I walked up to the counter, thought about buying one of their muffins – lemon, with crystals of sugar on the top – before resolving not to. They were four dollars and fifty cents. Walking back to the table, I wondered if the others thought that I had some kind of disorder, and then felt the pulse of my own intrigue at the very idea.

As I sat down, Katarina and Tamsyn continued their conversation. I watched Katarina's hands, consumed in the task of splitting her pastry in half, the flecks getting everywhere, on the table and the side of her mouth. She looked over at me often, and smiled, almost apologetically, when the others spoke. While Tamsyn lamented the 'bathroom facilities', Katarina slid part of her pastry towards me in silence. It was new, this attention. The woman seemed to be concerned, to an almost inappropriate extent, with my wellbeing. She stood up as I left, her arms outstretched, as if to give me another hug. It was an aborted attempt: her left arm fell, she waved once – a slightly pathetic action – and sat back down.

I returned to the studio. The space was bare, and the large windows in front of me looked impossibly cool, the light emanating from it dull, uncomfortable. I had set up a canvas on the floor the previous morning, on top of a cream sheet, to collect the stains of the paint. I sat down and crossed my legs, as if I were about to start meditating, and thought about the easy way Katarina and her friends had communicated – had moved, even – looking back at the room.

In previous years at the institute, I had laughed at joint projects, those who had worked together on their art for a showcase, believing them to be like nursery-school tasks, tiny hands sticky and immature. I did not discriminate in my distaste. I did not like many people. They had trivial concerns, trivial desires and terribly proportioned faces. They were shallow, their tasks artless, their tastes even more so. I saw my hometown through a similar lens of discontent, watching others in the street, or from my window, with a slight wrinkle of the nose, like a cartoon villain. It was easier to withstand home if I attributed its greying, faded atmosphere not to myself, but to the people around me. My mother had always insisted that I 'thought I was better', to which I would shake my head, while believing it to be entirely true. There was no problem with wanting more.

The canvas was still empty. I considered pissing on it. It wouldn't be that far off from the 'art' I had studied: Duchamp, at sixty years old, burning with controversy, and the lust of a man who had not been laid in weeks, ejaculated onto his work, called it *Faulty Landscape*, and got exactly what he wanted. I started to fill in the corners of the soon-to-be painting with black paint, straight from the tube, no water of any kind.

That evening, I walked the distance between my bedroom and bathroom entirely naked, skipping past the kitchen window, which was wide open, despite the rain, the strangely hot air.

I looked down. It was so rare, to be completely confronted by nakedness, without distraction. There the fingertips, shrivelled up and pruning under the hot water, the rising chest, a little loose skin, the extra roll of the lower stomach, inherited from the twelve-year-old standing at the edge of the sea, yellow towel over the chest, waving off everyone else into the water. Go on, without me. Go on. Blue veins, more than ever before, dark hair from the wrists to the upper arm. I had my mother's hands, her thighs, too. This thing, this meat-casing with limbs and nerves, and God knows what else. Odd to think. Most days, I felt like a floating mind; or, better still, nothing at all. This idea, of going beyond the flesh, as Father Stuart used to say, could be rudely interrupted by physical pain, as it was then, gushing water stinging the skin. What would it even look like, to be comfortable? I thought about Katarina, the way she pressed her palms into the table when she got up, the way she laughed, entirely unselfconscious, as though perfectly at home. How was it that we could be made from the same material? I looked at my own body again, still under the heat of the shower, and imagined it was hers, softer, kinder, changed by proximity.

In the morning, motivated by images of grieving children – the Bambis, Oliver Twists and Simbas of the world – Katarina sent an email. They were usually contextless, arriving in my junk folder, with links to discounted concerts, events from visiting lecturers and institute showings like a little bot. This one, however, was personalized: 'got a spare ticket to this exhibition, and was wondering if you'd like to go together.'

'Why not,' I replied, 'does 11 work?'

She sent a 'yes!!!', followed by another email, where she had included her number – 'i realize that I told u to text me if u needed anything, but didn't actually give u my number (classic), so here it is!!!! and also this is weirdly formal, so texting would be nice. see u at 11!'

There was nothing artful about the buildings which surrounded the journey into campus. Each one boasted at least three storeys, and, as we moved past, the sky was broken by their height, morphing the little people who scuttled around them, going about their silly tasks – preening their lawns, knocking on doors, crying on their porches. I listened to folk music on the way, the plink of guitar strings serving as my personal accompaniment. Swaying with the gentle movements of the bus, the faint scent of coffee, and the picturesque, all-American lie of modern life, modern homes, I thought that if I could prove my happiness through a series of aesthetics, I would be doing very well indeed.

The bus stopped at a community centre, and a woman walked on. Her hair was loosely tied back, and fell limply to one side, smaller hairs decorating her black top. She had a child with her: red-faced, teary, sucking on two fingers. The woman was around my age (young, bewildered, in her early twenties), and her body jerked when the bus took a turn, hitting her side on an occupied chair. She sat down. I gave them both an unwilling smile. The child was a weak, pale thing.

'She's sixteen months,' the woman said, as if I had asked.

I nodded.

'Seventeen, actually, in a few weeks.'

The woman obviously wanted someone to rejoice at the fact that her daughter had made it through this harsh world, full of suffering, cot-death and coughing men on public transport.

'That's great,' I told her, in a tone which indicated the very opposite.

'It is. She's getting on well with her walking.'

'Is she?'

'She really, really is. I thought to myself – well, I thought that I was doing something wrong, being so young. You know how it is,' she looked at me, appealing to our shared age as some kind of understanding, 'but it's all fine.'

'Good for you.' I put one headphone in.

The woman looked up and started fiddling with the fan at the top of the bus. 'Do you mind if I adjust this?'

'Go for it.'

The woman was sweating so much that the liquid took on its own form, the dampness lacing through her clothing, her forehead. She wiped it away, careful not to touch her child with the same hand. Her glorious sixteen-month-old was hoisted on her side, towards me. The child squealed.

The woman, having an obvious allergy to silence, started talking about her dream wardrobe, entirely unprompted. 'Guess how much this cost,' she said, pulling her shirt closer towards me. It smelled like cigarettes and cheap body spray.

'Three dollars.'

'It's *Urban*, come on.'

'Ten.'

'No. You're so bad at this.' Her child was crying again. 'So, where are you going, anyway?'

Given that whatever I might answer would be brought back to some item of hers – 'Shoes? Six dollars, thrift' – the pair of us settled into silence, the only noises being the classic, open-mouthed coughs of her child, and the overhead fan which puttered about while the kid cried between breaths.

All three of us were heading towards the same stop, like a tortured family. I got up first, as I was closer to the aisle, and heard the woman struggling to get all of her bags behind me, a series of wails, cellophane movements and iterations of 'fuck' being expelled at my back.

*

There was a chill air about the avenue, which gave way to a hill, the incline so gradual that it would go unnoticed until, quite suddenly, a visitor would find themselves wheezing, hands on their knees. Buildings with brown, dirtied bricks had been placed around the site, like relics, while the gallery, Brutalist and barbaric, stood out from the very bottom of the hill. It was early (eleven o'clock), and a few students milled about, necks bent downwards, looking at their phones. The place knew outsiders, and was armed against them. All signposts led to campus buildings and overpriced coffee shops: nobody could just 'walk by' without advertising they were not one of us. The woman on the bus had turned away from me the minute we got off, as if she were about to be contaminated by the space and its opinion of her.

There was a square opposite the entrance to the gallery, and a fountain, the water, clear once, now tinged with yellows and browns. An older woman teetered near the edge, a greasy paper bag in one hand. The hem of her jacket dipped further into the bowl with every swaying movement. There was a sign at her feet. I walked closer, to see if it had a message ('Help me' or 'Change'), written in pencil. But there wasn't one. No coins were laid at her feet.

At some point, the woman saw me. She tilted her head to one side, as if to say something, and, in that gesture, she looked so much like my mother that I had to turn away. I thought about her greying hair, and that stained bag, as I moved back, towards the brownstone gallery.

The exhibition was called 'Portrait of the Nudist as a Young Woman'. Hoisted onto the walls were several images, all cut off at the head. The artist believed in 'transgression', the placard told us, and 'there is nothing more transgressive than the female body'. Each photograph was dedicated to a body part – in full colour, no impressionistic angles, no filter, no mercy. Beneath the description, there was a little headshot of the artist herself: the missing head. I did not know where to look, or how to look appropriately, and I channelled all my discomfort into resenting her. I found the 'artist' herself inches away from the scene of her crime, watching attendees, as if she could scoop something out from their expressions. When I turned around, she was there, iPhone in hand, staring at me. I made sure to look repulsed; I did not want to add to her complex.

I had fifteen minutes before Katarina arrived, and I became bored of looking at the flecks on the floor – dried gum, brown grit and crusted paint – and had no choice but to settle on staring at the artist's right nipple. (This piece was aptly titled *Right Nipple*, and sat beside the equally imaginative *Left Nipple*.) I looked at it so much, I almost forgot what it was. It was a strange thing. The cracks in the woman's pinkish skin became cavernous, like the space between land. It certainly wasn't erotic. When Katarina found me, startled, she asked if I was enjoying myself.

I looked back at the artist, still there, scrolling on a phone the size of her face. 'I hate it.'

Katarina nodded, almost solemnly. 'That's the point.'

She laughed, and devoted the rest of our time in the gallery to convincing me to go to lunch. Katarina took immense pleasure in my embarrassment, and insisted on visiting each piece, 'as the artist intended'. My case was not helped by the institute's heating, which attempted to justify the cost of tuition by blasting the space, bringing in the flies and making me sweat. All of it – the presence of the artist, clothed and unclothed, Katarina's comments about the incredible shade of my cheeks – made my acceptance of her lunch offer easy, and almost relieved.

On our way to the cafe, Katarina walked uncomfortably close to me, and talked incessantly. She was the internet's poster child, endlessly weighing-in, and there was nothing she couldn't discuss. Tennis leagues, her uncle's psychosomatic limp, student elections. She gave summaries of global conflicts, regurgitated from ten-second videos, then launched into descriptions of her brother's room, how it smelled of damp, the black mould growing along his wall. 'It's still like that now,' she said, as if she were offering crucial information for my wellbeing.

At the cafe, she ordered for us both, and read a limerick she had made from AI. 'I asked it to write about my dog entering *Drag Race*,' she said, leaning over the table to give her performance: 'There once was a Dane called Doug/ Who found RuPaul stunning and smug.' She waited for me to laugh, before saying: 'Of course, the whole thing is very funny. Until it isn't.'

Katarina was often surprising. She seemed to enjoy disrupting someone's comfort, knocking their elbow. It was simultaneously exhausting and exhilarating.

On the walk back, she gave an account of her constant chatter – 'I just realize,' she said, 'that you're probably after a distraction.' We were beside an ice-cream shop, towards closing time, and parents, holding their children's shoulders, rolled down the street, bringing cries of laughter and sticky chins. 'I know I would be, anyway,' she said.

It took a moment too long, and a glance at one of the father's hands, before I remembered what she was alluding to. 'Oh,' I said, stepping away. 'Thank you.'

'No problem.'

She started smiling on the street, almost madly. It was insane, to be that happy, looking at me. Katarina touched my arm, and her sickly smell – it must have been in her washing powder – drifted back in with the wind. 'I can listen, too,' she said. 'I know I seem bad at it, but I can. I actually got little stickers for it in school.'

I must have looked incredulous – and who could blame me, having watched her mouth move for several hours? – because she said, 'Well, maybe not too many, if I'm honest.'

'How many?'

'Two.' She scratched her neck. 'In my defence, the teacher didn't like me very much. Had something against me.'

'Probably all that talking you were doing.'

She let out a short laugh. 'You're right. I did try, though.'

'I bet.' I mimed talking with my hand; she swatted the gesture away with hers. By the time she had asked me about what I had been like as a 'kid' – 'We're talking six or seven, here' – I had told her the truth: that I had been painfully shy, apologetic, avoidant of almost everything, including potential friends. Her reply – 'Not much has changed, then' – was met with a light kick to her shins. She kicked back, and there we were, almost wrestling on the street, her hot breath against my neck. And in all of this, the laughter, and the touches to the forehead, I had forgotten about the lie completely.

3

At first, I thought Katarina was taunting me with her ugliness. I just couldn't get rid of her. She appeared to me at night, like a warped gargoyle. The hair which grew on one side of her lip. The nasal passages which flared when she spoke, giving her voice its grainy, American quality. And the softness of her – the sweeping stomach, the rounded chin. The flat-footed walk. All of her. I imagined her in different states: going shopping down the road, choking on a cigarette, collecting little prescription pills for her face, returning to her apartment, changing into a soft pink shirt. And I couldn't help but feel something – the trimmings of disgust, then annoyance, and then, finally: desire, sizzling away like fat off the bone.

The next day, I expended most of my energy trying not to think about any of those things. Which was difficult, given that we had a seminar together. On seminar days, we all had to present a work related to an emailed topic: 'destruction', 'tiredness', 'charity'. The sessions included people who worked in different mediums: one woman, a sculptor, had the unfortunate task of hauling her project over to campus each week. The institute's central tagline for these groups was that they 'encouraged collaboration', allowing us to see our own mediums in 'unconventional ways'.

Katarina was already there when I arrived. She sat at the centre, listening to Lars, whose artistic specialization was entirely unclear. He was doing a great deal of talking, leaning against the wall in corduroy trousers and a cream shirt. Katarina moved her head up and down occasionally, and opened her mouth, like a fish. It was an entertaining battle of wills: her incessant desire to talk; his refusal to let her.

Men liked Katarina. They wanted to take up her time, to sanctify it. They must have seen a rawness in her features, in the arch of her nose, the roundness of her face. Her clothes, too, were often hyper-feminine: long, flowing shirts and dresses. When she twisted her head a certain way, or breathed out, that quick rising of her chest, I thought I saw it too, the shadow of their attraction to her.

There were two empty seats; I took the one closest to Katarina, by the window. Whenever I looked at her, Lars was still talking, gesticulating in the space. He often made grand proclamations about the state of the world in white text, and posted them to his Instagram in order to make himself more popular with the opposite sex. 'It's just not fair,' last night's story read, 'and it makes me so angry.' By 'it', he meant some vague and unnamed female struggle. 'We just need everybody to be treated the same,' the next slide said. Lars liked to masquerade as Jesus in other areas of his life, too, and wore his hair long, past his shoulders, or tied up in a bun.

We had been placed in the same class the previous year, and after our first seminar together, he had asked me out for a drink. I had accepted. At the end of that dingy, sticky evening, he had moved his hands to my underwear, and pressed downwards, rooting around as if in search of the lost Ray-Bans he had posted about that day – 'Guys, whichever fucker took those, I swear, I will end you.' Now, a year after that catastrophic date, he ignored me in group settings, only bringing me into conversations whenever he felt his words ought to be witnessed by a larger audience.

He was telling Katarina about his work for the seminar. 'I was up all night,' he said, picking the crust from the corners of his eyes, 'just getting really fucking mad at those people on the forums.'

'Those people': homophobes with selfies as profile pictures, bearded and staring down the camera; sexists with 2480248 usernames; suburban racists with images of their families on their Facebook pages, all white and red and perspiring.

'I tried to stop, at like three a.m.,' Lars said. 'But the discourse.' He whipped his hair back, as though there were several live cameras in front of him, all eager to capture his latest musings. 'It's so important for them to hear the other side.'

'You're right,' Katarina said.

'It's such a big responsibility, being online, and talking to those dicks. You know?'

'I do.' Katarina tilted her head to one side, and looked at me, briefly, before turning back to Lars, who was now sitting on his stool in a commanding manner, chest out and upright. It was incredibly difficult to tell if she was being genuine. 'It's a very good thing you do.'

Lars touched Katarina's shoulder, and let his hand hang there. The entire interaction was extraordinary; she looked as if an eel had lodged itself into her upper body, burrowing into the skin where Lars's touch had been. Lars sighed a short, puttering breath into Katarina's face.

'They were awful. I talked to a few in a private chat afterwards. I'm probably on one of their whatever-the-fuck 4chan databases now.'

'Impressive.'

'I printed the conversations out.' He brought a slim black bag out from beneath his chair, and pulled out a plastic envelope. There were several pieces of paper inside, containing all of the internet threads, angry emojis and slurs, in black ink. 'It's performance art, like –' Here, Lars paused for effect, and then said, heavily accented, 'Ambrey-meeveych – and Hancock.'

Katarina squinted as Lars lifted his project up, close to her face. 'Abramović,' she said.

'Sorry?'

'Oh, it's nothing, really.' Katarina smiled. 'But that's how you say it.'

When it was my turn to present, Lars made his disinterest clear to everyone, his head angled downwards, his hands running through his hair. I didn't really care. The project wasn't groundbreaking – even I was bored by it. I carried the painting over to the centre of the room and faced the group. I had finished it in under an hour, sitting in the dark, under the blue light of my phone. On the left-hand side, there were splashes of water and turmeric, mixed together, and on the other side, there was yellow acrylic paint, burnt ochre and flaxen, applied without skill.

'This,' I said to the group, one hand behind my back, 'is *Outer Man*.'

Our theme for the week was 'rot'. Lars had taken the metaphorical route – 'Brain rot,' he had said. 'Those people have worms up there.' I had gone with the biblical route, by which I mean that I had googled 'Bible passages on rot', and had plucked a verse at random from resoundinghislove.com: 'Though our outer man is decaying, our inner man is being renewed'. The institute seemed to like this kind of thing. There was a direct link between my more 'successful' paintings and my religious titles.

'That's just fantastic,' one student said. 'I see that you've captured the idea of redemption here,' he flicked his hand in the air, to mirror the movement of paint on the canvas, 'through the upwards turn of the brush.'

There wasn't a hint of irony in the speaker's voice. I looked at the other students, to gauge their reception. They weren't offended; a few were even writing things down and nodding. It was beautiful, thrilling. I could have said anything, and I would have been rewarded for it.

'Thank you.' I smiled with faux humility. 'I'm glad you see that. It's exactly what I wanted.'

'We have to really ask, though,' Jules, one of Katarina's friends, began, 'whether, in some cases, the whole idea of redemption might just be bullshit? Like, just another construction?'

Several more minutes were dedicated to that discussion, by the end of which we had discussed the alienation of art from its source, the memeification of oppression and our generation's sense of apathy. All I had to do was hold the painting up, and receive their words, like heavenly gifts, and smile.

'But, back to *Outer Man* – I really enjoyed the sense of emotion and movement there.'

I started to pay attention when I heard Katarina, barely recognizing that *Outer Man* was mine, and not some strange manifestation of the group's latest topic.

'Oh,' I said, 'I didn't know it had any emotion.'

'The colours.' She blinked, as though it were painstakingly obvious. 'You used the same ones from Rothko. The colours of *Untitled, 1969*. It's terrifyingly sad.'

I wasn't sure what she wanted from me – an assertion that yes, I was a deeply haunted person, or that I had studied the works of her 'Rothko' in detail. It was unsettling. 'I guess,' I said.

Perhaps she was thinking about my father, trapped in his early grave. The painting seemed to mean more to her because of it. She saw suffering in the twist of acrylic, a feigned desperation in the curling, nonsensical turmeric.

After we had finished, and the other students had fled from the room, pulling out their phones, I looked at Katarina. She seemed to be waiting for something. There was some kind of expression there, in her face. It might have been pity, but I did not know.

4

When I first arrived in America, three years earlier, I had done all sorts of things for the hell of it, or the 'fun' of it – though, in hindsight, nobody was enjoying anything I did, least of all me. I stayed at the institute for the entirety of first year, which was, as I told my father, because I had no money for the plane journey back home. I met Matthew then, in spring, when the other students had retreated back to their warm homes and tick-filled holidays in the Hamptons.

Matthew was 'traditionally American' in that he looked like an Abercrombie model, all smiles and abs, nothing pliant or yielding in his body at all. This gave me a general impression of his impenetrability, a certain kind of stability in him, and I wanted his robustness to rub off on me. Standing over six foot tall (as he proudly told me on our second meeting, over vodka and cheap lemonade), his head bowed, like he was always involved in a covert operation, Matthew was the son of a board member at the institute, and I would frequently see him leaving his father's office for the smoking area. He had a tense disengagement with the world, a way of looking without really seeing, which appealed to me. Katarina later called this 'creepy', though, at the time, I had only been aware of low-level whisperings about his ex-girlfriends, and his family, which, of course, just encouraged my interest in him.

I met him when I was waiting to speak to his father, sitting in an uncomfortable chair outside the office. Matthew was in the chair opposite mine, and looked up in my direction before returning to his phone. He seemed tired, and had one of those washed-out, lined faces, contrasting with his body (which I was to discover to its full extent a week later). Over the next few months, I would learn that Matthew was a very sad man – a boy, really – and that he didn't know what to do with anything. He had been very kind, very willing, and his hands would fumble around my body nervously, as if it was both very dangerous and very fragile.

I told him that we should stop sleeping together just before we moved into second year. 'Oh,' he said, his face shining, red. 'Okay.'

I looked up at him. We were in his room – his room, because it gave me the chance to leave swiftly if anything turned ugly. I imagined, even fantasized, about being held against the wall, though I knew that Matthew was an unlikely candidate for such things.

He blinked heavily at my words, eyelids falling and pressing upwards in quick succession. 'I thought you liked me,' he said, bringing his arms up to his chest, crossing them over like one of those warning signs on the back of an aeroplane seat: Brace for impact.

'I did.'

This did little to help Matthew. 'I was – I was going to ask you to move in with me, today. I had a whole thing ready.'

While his hands remained fixed, I thought about what

I had just missed out on: rates for a one-bed flat, and part payment from Matthew's father.

'I'm sorry,' I said. And I found that I was.

Now, almost three years later, I thought about Matthew with occasional twinges of regret, the way someone might think about the loss of a baby tooth, or a gift voucher. I rarely saw him around campus, though his presence was required by his father at the institute's 'showings', where he would stand, back against the wall, saying very little. Everett held these showings each month, and, once a semester, the best pieces would be featured in a 'final showcase'. This allowed members of the institute to boast their influence in the art world ('exhibited in The Everett Institute, March 2017') on their CVs, or on Instagram posts (more common). It also gave those majoring in curation – 'the exhibitionists', as Katarina called them – the opportunity to explore their 'craft' of arranging paintings on a wall.

It was late September, and the area was lukewarm, adding to the general numbness of the local weather. I had thought of America as a place of extremes – snowy peaks, the hot Californian sun – and the tepid air of that final year had an odd effect on my psyche. As I stepped out of my apartment building that afternoon, I felt as if I had been inserted into a simulation. The greys of home and the rain-soaked, oily scent of the streets which had accompanied most of my childhood had been recreated there, on different soil. I felt then, as I sometimes still feel now, that there was something unreal about moving away, something wrong. I knew that my parents would have been pleased with this thought, and so I tried to focus on something else.

Katarina and I had planned to meet at the exhibition. She asked if we could arrive together, 'to make it less stressful'. It was an odd thing for her to say; I could not imagine her, in any context, out of depth. I waited several hours before replying to her. Silly things, like courtship rules from romcoms in the early 2000s – 'Never text first,' a nasally voice told me – popped into my head. I did not know why this happened, and chalked it up to uneasiness at having a potential (albeit unlikely) friend.

'That sounds good,' I texted her eventually, 'see you soon.'

By the time I arrived, a crowd had gathered at the centre of the exhibition hall. Most of the people there were students, wearing long coats, hats of varying eccentricities, neon greens, and torn fabric at their waists. They were all determined to stand out, talking loudly in front of paintings as they held on to the person next to them. I could not find Katarina.

I walked over to the 'mixed media' section, where five works lay, splayed out against the white walls. *Change*, the first placard read. Across the space, there were layers of expired film reel, placed in a diagonal format. The reel was faded, brown and twisted at its edges, and was held up by some form of Blu Tack.

'Wonderful,' one of the students said, in a ripped shirt which revealed their collarbones. 'That's really something, isn't it?'

I laughed, then coughed, and settled for a noise somewhere in between the two before turning away, to reach

Katarina. She was talking to a blond man with dreadlocks. There was an umbrella at her side, and she swung it in front of her as she spoke. As Katarina moved it back and forth, the people around her moved, too, from one section to another, until their motions came together, coalescing, and she was at the centre, creating the rise and fall of the place.

'You look nice,' I told her. She had done her hair differently, pinned back so that it revealed more of her face, tightening the skin around her cheekbones. Katarina waved the comment away. As I thought about what I was going to say next, I felt something behind me, breathing, on the back of my neck. A tap, on the edge of my shoulder, and I turned around to meet it, and there was Matthew, thinner now, looking at me as if I were devastating, and cruel. All the trimmings of fear.

'It's been a while,' he said. Matthew appeared reduced: he was shorter, as if he had been made aware of his height, and was afraid of it.

'How are you?' I asked.

'Fine. Better than last time.'

'That's good.' I looked around. Katarina and the blond man were attempting to make an exit, Katarina shoving the man away from us. 'This,' I reached out to take her hand, 'is Katarina.'

'Nice to meet you.' Matthew nodded his head in her direction.

'You too. I think we met outside the textiles classroom, last year.'

'Did we?' His expression was so vacant, and his question so removed of any interest, that the space between them flitted out and died.

'I think so,' she said.

'Ah.'

Even Katarina looked nervous: she rolled her hands over her skirt, catching bits of tulle in her fists. She was skilled, she moved through most groups and rooms seamlessly, without thought, but here she looked bereft. She was sweating, the light making her forehead, and the raised bumps around her temple, shine. Had I liked her more, it would have been endearing.

'I think I'm going to show Jacob over here,' she hit the man beside her on the back, like a frat boy, 'some of the new stuff.' She started to walk through the other people, making faces, stopping briefly to greet them. Matthew and I stood on the same side, just watching them both leave, like morose twins from a funereal catalogue.

Shortly after our 'break-up', which I thought of as a natural parting (we never had a relationship, not really), Matthew had tried to kill himself. I told myself that the two things – the conclusion of our activities and Matthew's body, hunched over and pliable on the hospital bed – were entirely unrelated. It was an unfortunate, dramatic coincidence, like any natural disaster, the flood impervious to any kind of human interaction.

In the white gallery space, Matthew stood, warm skin, warm flesh, by my side. I could see his hand, the tips of his fingers: three seconds of movement away. I wanted to touch him. Not in a sexual way – I just wanted to brush over the fingers which had used such resolve, such morbid desperation, and had tried. Just to see if there was something I had missed.

'It's a good turnout,' Matthew said. 'My dad will be pleased. He's getting remarried soon, too.' His pattern of speech, and the way he expressed the words, like dropping small stones into a hopeless river, was so much like the shipping forecast my father would listen to at home that I wanted to shake him.

'What is it?' Matthew tapped the side of my arm: movement, affection, the living.

'Nothing.'

'Really?'

'Well.' I picked at my skin.

'Go on.'

'Are you happy?' I looked up at Matthew. He was staring at the wall. 'About the wedding, I mean.'

'I think so. It'll be good for him to have someone else.'

I understood the implication of these words, and chose ignorance; that he was speaking generally, in a 'more-the-merrier' kind of way: good to have a new addition to the family, the 'else' omitted. Love, I knew, involved a wilful ignorance, a cherry-picking of words and interpretations. Seeing a person in their entirety was too much.

Other students moved around, on to new works, while we were stuck there, the two of us, in a part of the exhibition which was completely blank. I searched for a tiny plaque with a name, hidden at the bottom of the wall, which could make a vague postmodernist point about the essential nothingness of everything. But it wasn't there: it was just a wall.

Matthew waved at the students as they walked past; it was a tentative gesture, as if he was anticipating rejection before he received it. Some of them smiled, then immediately turned away, as if they had been hit. Others didn't respond at all.

'That's rude,' I said, after one pretty obvious case (Matthew had said, 'Hello,' and was met with silence, the back of a head).

'They think I'm catching.'

'What?'

'They think I'm contagious,' he said, as if that made his point clear. '*This* –' He lifted one hand – thin, delicate wrists, crusted over like bark – and pointed to himself.

I told him that I had no idea what he was talking about.

'You do,' Matthew said.

'I don't.'

'Yes, you do. Honestly.'

I smiled, enjoying our little pantomime, while Matthew's face remained a terrifying neutral. It seemed to me that part of his condition involved the absence of humour and fun. I had a vision of the two of us as if from the outside, looking down at us. The whiteness of the wall reflected onto our faces. Emptiness. Terror. Matthew touched his shirt – light blue, clean, freshly ironed – with his hand, and pinched it.

Matthew's father, simply known to us as Mr Bayard, was a rich man; that had been made obvious before I even met him. Rich, moneyed, well-off, upper-class. However anybody wanted to call it. Mr Bayard had no hair, and gave the impression of never having possessed any in the first place. His son's hairline was set to follow suit: there was a shadow of the next movement on his scalp, back, back. Matthew placed one fingertip to his brow, before wiping at his forehead. He looked at me and smiled, almost apologetically, before taking my hand.

Matthew led me to another project, near the water fountain.

'Look at that,' I said, my back to him. 'It's actually something.' The part of the fountain containing the water had been painted green. 'WHAT WILL HAPPEN IF WE CEASE TO HAPPEN' had been printed, all uppercase, at the bottom. I started laughing, but Matthew stood, silent, a metre away from me, in front of something else.

'It's wonderful,' he said.

'What – the fountain?'

'Sorry?' He turned his head to look at the project. 'Oh, you're kidding me.' He covered his mouth with a hand, and bent towards the floor, winded.

'Are you all right?'

I almost knelt for him (how familiar, the indent of the floor on my legs, and his breathing above me), until I realized that he was letting out short, joyful exhales: laughter. It was disturbing, this display, and so I stood closer to him, to shield him from the students. 'Christ,' I said, 'what is it with you?'

'Lots of things.' His smiles only increased between breaths. 'So much.'

I did not feel personally responsible for Matthew, even after the attempt, though he would often feature in my dreams. He would call out to me, as if a small child, then hold his hands up in the air, veins wriggling and bluish before being cut, right in the middle, a scientific inaccuracy.

At the exhibition, Matthew asked me if I would like

to get a meal with him. 'I'll pay,' he said. (He usually did, before, and I would let him.)

'Maybe not.' I smiled, and tried to shake my head as gently as possible.

'Okay.' He stepped away from me, and nodded. 'That's okay.'

'It was nice, today, though. Seeing you.' I looked at him, and he was silent, staring at the painting with an intensity. 'Not that – not that I don't *want* to go somewhere afterwards,' I continued. 'I just don't think it would be good, you see? And you've only just –'

'Hey, it's fine,' he said, his body inching towards the exit with every movement. 'Don't worry about it.'

Matthew had a tiny crease above his forehead which I hadn't noticed before. Let him have more, I thought, as he walked away, his shoulders hunched, morphing into an older man. Back twisted. Greying hair. A cane, even, and a wife. Grandchildren. I wanted him to grow old so much – so much – that the space around started to shrink, as if by the force of the wish, accommodating it, tiny white walls becoming smaller, tiny paintings, small people, and myself, too, unable to act on anything, unable to make reality, to bend it to my will, for him, however desperate I became.

Matthew had gone. I stood opposite the painting he had wanted me to look at. In the image, a child stood by a pool, one foot touching the water. In the child's reflection, there were grey houses with flat roofs, each with four windows, families inside. Around the child, there was a brick wall, just blocking his view. I didn't know what any of it meant, though I was convinced that Matthew did. But he had left, taking the words with him, and there was no point.

5

Because I was an idiot, I believed that if I could cut goodness out – laughter, kindness, generosity – I might be protected from negativity, simply by becoming an emotionless eunuch. This was unsuccessful, obviously. I left the exhibition drained, and drew my blinds the minute I got back, keeping them closed for days. I kept seeing Matthew's bony frame everywhere, as if he had died already. I'd been so successful in pushing all of it down that I hadn't thought about him in months. After the break-up, I had shaken myself out, slept with a few other people, panicked, slick and pained, and had tried to draw a nice line under the whole thing. I felt like an unrelenting businessman: 'Well, you've had a tough run,' I might say, with a Wall Street twang, 'no need to dwell on it.' And it worked. It really did.

The attempt was a little more difficult to think away, which wasn't my fault, really. Mr Bayard had delivered the news himself, arriving in the studio in a suit and tie, which made his head – reddened, puffed up – look way too small, like a fish. Mr Bayard didn't knock: he walked inside, told me about his son, and what he had done. Perhaps it was difficult for Mr Bayard to keep any kind of accusation out of his voice, the falsely sweetened, heavy nature of it. But if it *was* difficult, he didn't try very hard to overcome it.

'He'll be fine, though,' Mr Bayard had said, only after describing at length his son's fatal expression, his resignation at being lifted into the ambulance, not looking anywhere but the sky; not grateful, but cursing. I imagined rain, though the day itself was perfectly clear. Mr Bayard's image made rain feel appropriate: the parting of the heavens, salt water, that sort of thing.

With images of Matthew in my head – Matthew at the exhibition, the others staring; Matthew being swiftly, coldly rejected by me; Matthew, white-faced – I scrolled through Tinder until each face became unrecognizable. Every profile told me their best things, their most exciting triumphs. 'Drinks', 'It'll be the best night of your life' and 'Bet you can't beat me in any games', followed by several winking emojis. Tell me your worst things, I thought. I began to type out this phrase – tell me your worst things – as a response to a sweet image of a man (Alex, 24, non-smoker) and his dachshund, but felt it was far too pathetic, even for me, and stopped. Seconds later, I was rescued from the indignity of agreeing to a disappointing date with Alex, by several messages. It was Katarina.

'i'm thinking of having a few friends over,' she had texted, 'it'll be on Monday night.'

'Oh, nice.'

'it starts at seven. you're invited, obviously, if you can make it.'

I waited – for what, I do not know – and opened the blinds. Across the road, people were leaving for work, their children trailing behind. My phone vibrated on the table, causing little shocks to ring through the plastic.

'i'd love it if you could come. we all would. but no problem if not!'

On the walk over to Katarina's, I thought about my father, and every little thing I had said about him. It was difficult to believe what I had done: some evenings, I almost forgot about the whole thing. And so it arrived in waves, the truth, making me sweat. It was like an appalling dream which started off peacefully – clouds, candyfloss – but morphed into something strange and uncontainable. Moving past shitting dogs, smokers on the street and wailing children, I thought about him struggling to drain pasta by the sink at our old house, and tried not to cry. (I didn't, in the end. It would have left marks on my shirt.)

Katarina lived close by, a fifteen-minute walk away, in another apartment building much like my own. The night before, at four a.m. – a bleak time for workers struggling to wake and morose teenagers struggling to live – I had searched her location, and mapped out the journey. On the Street View, there had been a girl in pigtails walking a ginger cat, her features blurred, captured the moment before she stepped off the pavement. And then, in the day, the same road, now empty. The images had been taken years ago. That cat was probably dead.

I smiled and crossed at the same place where the girl had been. My blouse crumpled in the wind; I tucked it into my skirt and looked into the windows of a stationary car, parked outside Katarina's block. I was rearranging my hair, pulling it up, then letting it fall, using the window to see my reflection.

The hair was still bunched in my hands as the window

rolled down, removing my makeshift mirror, and a man with a pointed chin and dark hair was revealed, middle-aged and grinning. The man took his own hands, which were large and beefy, and mimicked the gestures I had made with a crude expression on his face. It was awful. As I walked away from him, placing a middle finger into the air (briefly, as I didn't want to be murdered), I told myself that it was good to get the humiliation out of the way early, before I'd spoken to her.

Katarina did not answer the door when I texted. A man with curly hair got to it first, looked me up and down, and stared at my face, without any kind of shame.

'You're friends with Matthew,' he said, without smiling, as if he was listing the first of my sins.

'Yes?' More of a question, than anything, from me. I thought it was only a matter of time before the man replied with: 'Your father died; his body can be found at Trent Valley Road.' He was that unsettling.

I stepped into the apartment hallway. The man didn't move, and I was forced into a shameful kind of shuffle around him. I smiled. He didn't.

When I reached the main room, vintage lampshades adorned the space, and the room was filled with books, arranged haphazardly, on the verge of being picked up again. The sofas had been pushed against the walls, leaving the guests to sit on a patterned rug. Katarina was at the centre. Everyone sat cross-legged around her, like a prayer circle. If I had liked her less, I would have said that she looked like a stand-up, or – even worse – a spoken-word poet, deriding her desire to be at the centre at all times. A joker, pre-empting the laughter of others by making herself the object of it. But, as I watched her speak, I found her more difficult to dislike. Even elements of her face, which would never work on anyone else – weak chin, pitted scars, almost distended eyes – were perfect on her. I took a seat on the floor, accepted some wine, and embraced the feeling of joining a flock, or a religious sect – this time, without the bigotry.

The man – the one who knew Matthew – sat down next to me. Katarina and I had an awkward hug. The rest of the guests, all carrying drinks and wearing different pastel eyeliners, were talking about their families.

'It's just so hard,' Tamsyn was saying, 'especially as they don't even try to understand me.'

A few of them made sympathetic noises, and the group moved as one, nodding heads, like a group therapy session. There was a certain charge in Tamsyn's movements, a birdlike quality to them, as if, at any moment, she might attempt to attack, or escape. 'I am aware,' she said, this time looking at me, as if I had been offering some silent reproach, 'that it goes both ways. But I try so hard. And they don't give anything back.'

I stood up, said nothing, and walked over to the sink, where Katarina had lined up bottles of wine and vodka, with a separate section for mixers. I poured out the liquid, my back turned as the party-goers offered support, Katarina's voice discernible over the general tones of sympathy, all low and sweet. Every generation believed themselves to be eternally misunderstood by the one which came before. We relied on them, we loved them, we despised them, and were surprised when it turned out that they did the same. When

Tamsyn spoke about her parents, I imagined bowling alleys, '70s haircuts, and the thick scent of discos. I poured more wine into the glass, while the group talked about attachment styles, complexes, laughing at their little buzzwords. And Katarina, dancing away, oblivious.

Perhaps she looked stupid, ugly. But I was trying not to think those sorts of things (definitely bad for my skin, supposedly bad for my immortal soul), and so I focused on how free it was: her torso, the arms above her head, sweating face, as if dipped in oil.

Then it was after midnight, and we'd all been in that space for far too long, the air taking on a sweetened scent, tinged with metal. Everyone seemed so happy. Someone had put on music, and so Katarina's movements became beautiful, floating in the yellow light. I watched her for a while, content and breezy – perhaps for the first time in months, years. The lamps in Katarina's apartment glowed. I took another sip of my drink, and was surprised that the acidic taste had faded to nothing, neutral and clean. I didn't care what I looked like, on the outside of things; doing nothing was more natural to me than anything else. My personality could be characterized by a distinct lack – of almost everything. Lying was one of the only things I did for myself, the only time I felt active, a real person, and I was good at it. But it was just another absence, this inability to be honest.

I stayed by the edge of the table and drank, beery and separate, and continued to watch Katarina, who was still dancing, only pausing occasionally, to wipe her forehead. She smiled at me. Everything around her appeared glossy and bright, like a Christmas carol. This thought brought me to Jesus, and I imagined Katarina playing all of the parts in the nativity.

'What are you smiling at?' Katarina asked me, leaning forward, damp clinging, one of the straps on her dress falling down. She adjusted it, and then looked back, in a brief moment of shame. The others spoke around us, tired, branching off.

I had more of the makeshift cocktail in my glass, handing it over to Katarina the moment I swallowed. Though the liquid was lukewarm, the glass had been cool, and she pressed the edge of it to her lips, still smiling. I thought about Genesis, a half-forgotten phrase about beginnings in my mouth, as she placed the glass down on the table, and leaned in closer. I felt white wine, orange juice, an old hall, and Sunday school on her lips, on her tongue. Between kisses, Katarina kept smiling, her mouth widening slightly as she pulled away for a moment, before moving back again. We were there together. She said my name.

Katarina insisted on walking me back to the apartment, despite the rain which had begun, ever so gently, in the hours after I came to hers.

'It's nothing,' she said, putting on a jacket. It was hanging up, at the entrance, alongside other things of hers: patterned jumpers; an oversized blazer I had seen her wear, once; home-made scarves, unfurling themselves on the peg. A proper place for everything. 'I'm too hot here, anyway.'

It was just us, the lights and Katarina's things everywhere, suddenly too much to bear. I felt ashamed, and started playing with a desk drawer, opening and shutting it to a rhythm.

I watched Katarina as she went to wash her face, the coat restricting her arms as she placed her hands under the tap. The door was open, and I stood outside, looking in at something private, the way her hands twisted over the sink, skin against the ceramic. I was dazed, there. Katarina scrubbed at her face aggressively, making large circles, as if she was trying to extract something deeper from it. I hoped that this was unrelated to what we had just done. But I couldn't be sure.

'I really don't mind going back by myself,' I told her.
'Don't be silly.'
'I'm not. It's, like, ten minutes away.'
'Ten more minutes with you, then.'
'Sounds like a nightmare.'
She laughed at that, and grabbed her keys.
In the rain, we walked through the same streets, each step blurred and impressionistic. The journey went by quickly, and, as I stood by my door, I tried to see myself from her perspective: my hair was damp, I knew that; it dripped onto my shoulders, the shirt now a film, almost beneath my real skin. She touched my arm, and I thought about becoming a store mannequin, separate and dripping under the store lights. Katarina put one hand just above my head. I looked around for other people, but nobody was there, only a few parked cars. Not for the first time, as she kissed me again, or I kissed her, I thought about how unashamed she was, how free, and smiled. I wanted to consume it all, taking it, taking it, as my own, all teeth.

6

I ignored Katarina's texts the next day. My phone buzzed constantly around the time she usually woke up – ten o'clock, entering the day with an unalienable, detestable optimism. The texts eventually stopped, and I started chopping up bits of paper, pages from old notebooks which had been preserved from my first year, fragments of poorly drawn faces, triangles for noses and square heads. When my phone's ringtone went off, I lay down on the floor, hair covered by the paper, my own funeral lilies, and looked at it. It was 'Dad'. I picked it up.

'Hello?'

The other line was surrounded by static, hands slamming tables, and male voices joining each other. 'Oh, hi. I'm just in the middle of – I'm just at the pub, actually. Big day today. Irish James – do you remember Irish James?' (He did not wait to hear if I did.) 'Well, he's just agreed to buy us all a round, later.'

It must've been about five in the afternoon; time to watch the game on the pub TV, permanently fixed on the football channel. Every day, the regulars gathered around the screen, which was close to the toilets, the scent of beer mingling with the garbage, their weak rose air-freshener and urine.

My father was still talking. 'Irish James just got a promotion, you see, up at the plant, so we're all out celebrating. And he said to us that morning, before he got it – he went: "A win for one is a win for all." Isn't that true?'

I told him that it was, and imagined them all – my father included – holding large, beery hands to each other's throats.

'Anyway,' he said, louder than before, over a cheer, 'what was it that you wanted to call about?'

'You called, Dad.'

'Did I?'

'You did.'

'Well, I'm glad we're speaking, anyway. It's nice to hear your voice.'

Seconds later, he had moved out of the earshot of the speaker, to talk to someone else. I got words and phrases, echoed across the space: yes, the score, America. The kid. Yes. A shame about – I know. 'And how are you doing? How is the painting, and all of that?'

'Good, thank you,' I said, pleased that we were getting onto comfortable ground. 'I was in last month's showcase.' (Another lie: Tamsyn had got it instead.)

'Brilliant. That's really brilliant,' he said. 'I'm so proud.'

'Thank you.'

'Any – issues, up there?'

I felt the top of the carpet, pulled some hair out of it, like my very own growth, and looked around the apartment. 'None at all,' I said. 'It's all great.'

'Good for money?'

'Perfect.'

'That's grand, then –' There was a pause in his speech, to

make room for a cheer, and the sound of the phone being placed on a hard surface. 'That's grand.' After I had been silent for a while, and someone laughed, he said, 'I'm sure you've got lots to be getting on with, so I won't keep you.'

'Sure.'

'Have a good day – is it still day, over there? – but have a fab time anyway, and, well, make sure you're eating right. I've heard bad things about the stuff over there. Articles, and things, about preservatives. So. Look after yourself.' He hung up, and his Nokia, which he affectionately called 'the brick', gave an old-fashioned click.

I put my phone, the offending object, by my side on the floor. The movement created a head rush as I tilted upwards, to make sure that he'd really ended the call. 'Look after yourself,' alongside that titbit about the fast-food industry – declarations of love, made in my mother's format. I was sure that, had I been from another family, the words would have meant something entirely different. But he wasn't a different person, and neither was I, however much I wanted to be.

I felt so sickened by myself that I considered praying, asking for some kind of forgiveness. The apartment was quiet, just the low mechanical hum of the fridge, the occasional flushing toilet from downstairs, travelling up the pipes. No thick incense, burning resin or hardwood floors – but good conditions, all the same. I pressed my hands together, closed my eyes. But it felt silly, self-conscious, and I could still hear the men in the pub, laughing at me.

It was old-fashioned, believing in God, but my parents did it anyway. Not only that, but they attended every church service possible, as if everything was at stake, to which they would have replied that it was. My father sometimes told me that he had met my mother there, in the pews, making it sound as if she had been summoned by the Lord himself. Even as a child, I had been sceptical of this story, and, when I asked, my mother told me that they had met through a friend (Jane, a hoarder, box-dyed hair). My suspicion of my father's tale, and the confirmation of its falsehood, came to represent something more fundamental about faith. I had not believed him, and I had been right.

By the time I was twelve, I had become so sure of my disbelief that I made no attempt at hiding my expressions when in church. I still went, of course, dropping my mother's hand as soon as I entered the building. (People were watching. There were appearances to keep up.) My mother typically wore a black hat with a feather at the top; it looked like an exotic bird, trapped in the dust of English life. As for my father: a suit, which might have been black once, turned grey, like slate, from the times it had been forced into our faulty washing machine, then pulled out, and slapped onto the drying rack.

In church, their accents became posher. Around other people, they were like cartoons of themselves, each flaw emphasized for the stage, every eccentricity (that hat, that voice, that opinion on Mrs Dougherty next door) made larger as we walked through the foyer. They moved as one during services, like a couple from a sitcom. They shook hands with everyone on their way to their usual pew (third row from the front) while I followed behind, an ill-fitting part of their show. If anyone else saw this change, and spotted our fabrication of middle-class English life, they never said. But I knew that they could tell. There was something in the way they smiled.

*

Our holy routine was simple. First, Sunday school, where, after handing out biscuits and lukewarm orange juice from little cartons, we would be taught the basics: what happened on what day (the days seemed very important), and why it was Good. In my chair, I would shred the plastic straws in my hands, tearing off strips one by one, making a pile at my feet, or, if I felt more bold, on the table.

At some point, I graduated out of the kids' area, leaving behind the soft toys of Noah's ark for the wooden benches beside the altar. There, we were spoken to in a different manner, in hushed tones, filled with references to 'beginnings', and there, we learned desire, bodies all close to one another as we listened to them talk about the beauty of marriage, and the kind of sins we should hide from. They never really told us, specifically, what they were, and so we were all left to our imaginings, all kinds of shadowy, warm things.

Father Stuart, the priest at St Mary's, was 'a good man', according to my mother, who had been raised in a rural town in Ireland for the first five years of her life. She said this phrase – 'good man' – with a slight lilt, one which reminded me, through her, of cool wind, eye-watering, plastic hairspray, all those things she had talked about in a slightly distant voice.

He was a big fan of chastity and wafers, our priest. But he loved *Mario Kart*, too: on Sundays, after the trusting parents dropped off their children, he would play the game loudly, in one of the rooms just behind the second altar. 'All right, children,' he always said, 'I'm off to do some reading.'

Then the power-up sound, quiet, but recognizable, followed by the quick, agonized sounds of the *Mario* theme, bass notes followed by the clicking of a remote control, and then, finally, the occasional exclamation of, 'Jesus Christ.'

7

Katarina appeared as I was leaving my studio, a few days after the party. She was dressed in black – sweater vest and skirt – like an avenging angel, stark and defiant. She looked severe, and stood there in silent condemnation for a few minutes, just enough time for me to prepare a monologue on how I owed her nothing; that nobody required an explanation, or justification, for their existence. I had even prepared a pseudo-therapy phrase about 'providing mental space', when I looked back at her, and immediately apologized. 'I'm sorry,' I said, hoping the phrase would cover several damages. I looked around at the room, the circle of light around her, the open door. 'Sorry. I'm actually on my way out.'

She looked at me. 'Are you?'

'Yes. I think I need – I need to get some materials, some extras.'

'And you're not avoiding me?'

I thought about telling her that I had lost (or broken) my phone, and decided against it. There were too many lies to keep track of. In the hall, Katarina bounced on her heels, waiting for an answer.

At some point, her expression turned, and I saw a rustle of hurt there. It softened her cheeks for a few seconds. 'If you are, that's fine, whatever.'

'I'm not avoiding you,' I started to say. 'Well, I might be, just a little. But it's nothing to do with you, or anything we did.'

Though I was familiar with some kinds of shame, this one was new, unplanned, and entirely justified. Once, I had been given a plastic monkey, a wind-up toy, and it had broken down, in a slow process which made its movements infrequent and erratic. Opposite Katarina, I thought of that monkey as I moved my arms, and tried to think of what to say, exhausted by the most basic levels of apology.

'What I mean is,' I looked at her, 'is that I got a bit stressed out – all me, I promise – and I thought I'd take a little retreat.'

'A retreat?'

'Kind of.'

'As in, you went somewhere? Like Bali, or wherever the fuck?'

'Well, no.' I closed my eyes. 'A retreat from technology.'

'Ah, I see. So the retreat was you not responding.'

I nodded. 'It was surprisingly inexpensive.'

'But,' Katarina threw her hair back, as if she were the star of a telenovela, 'what did it cost?'

We laughed, and she moved to touch my arm. She stopped herself, seemingly halfway, and started to pick bits off the wall instead. Pieces fell, in flakes, at our feet, like confetti. 'It's all right,' Katarina said. 'We don't have to talk about it.' She waved a hand in the air, as if to reinforce her point: it's nothing at all. 'Also, like, my wider group of friends make out all the time. It's all very incestuous.'

I raised an eyebrow. 'Really? Which ones?'

We moved away from the building, heads bowed, as she told me about which friends had been together, however briefly, and we laughed about the most awkward ones before turning away from the studio entirely, to maintain our tense romantic disengagement from each other.

In a surprise move, one of the artists scheduled for the showcase dropped out at the very last minute, citing a sick bug. By some act of God, I had been placed on the institute's exhibition waitlist, leaving me, and *Trying, Air, Resistance* (the latest splashes on canvas), to take the fallen artist's place.

I dressed up for the event, wearing a mid-length black dress which I had previously worn for a funeral (my first mistake), a stomach which protruded after having eaten an entire loaf of sourdough (my second), and a small cut at the corner of my eyebrow, having accidentally taken the skin off while trying out a new thing called 'dermaplaning', which involved shaving off all the hairs on my face (my third). Katarina said the cut made me look 'rugged' when we met up over coffee, where I apologized, again, for ignoring her. She could not attend the exhibition that evening, though she had hand-crafted a card, with a massive, smiling 'CONGRATULATIONS' on its front. I kept it in my jacket pocket, and the card dug into my side as I entered the exhibition.

This showcase was filled with portraits of various public figures, inserted into new contexts: celebrities thrust into landfills or industrial factories and hoisted onto operating tables. Trisha Paytas on a marble throne, a Burger King crown on her head (oil on canvas, 20" x 24"). Frank Sinatra in Walmart, 2018 (oil, 16" x 12").

I was about to leave, when I saw a man, his back hunched, sitting at the edge of the room. He was in uniform, a grey button-up with the institute's cleaning company logo stitched on his chest. His eyelids bulged, the whites were revealed, like a patient with Graves' disease, or Courbet's self-portrait, the eyes wide and watering. And he was crying. I did not know what to do. It was so rare, to be confronted with such strong emotion – and from a stranger, too. I was almost jealous. That he had experienced these things here, in the gallery, and not in the privacy of his own room; that he was capable of intense sorrow, when I could scarcely feel anything at all. In the evenings, I tried to summon things by watching documentaries on people my father hated: Andy Warhol – 'It's just a bunch of cans, isn't it?' – runway models – 'Pick up a book, girls' – and Margaret Thatcher (obviously). I played Blur songs on repeat (too posh), and sang Cher in the shower (too gay). But there was nothing, not even a brief kick of rebellion.

All this jealousy, summoned by the man's crying face, soon gave way to pride, the moment I walked towards him, and saw the painting. Sweeping brushes of 'Sap Green' acrylic, accompanied by droplets of cobalt, as if fallen from a great height, or produced by a particularly nasty nosebleed – the painting was unbelievable, nonsensical, and it was all mine.

I cleared my throat, in the hope that he might turn around. No luck: the man was engrossed, despite the state of the room, which was littered with abandoned bagel bites and wholegrain crackers. He made no attempt to clean any of it up – not even a faint twitch of movement from his position on the bench. I wondered what Katarina would do, standing there instead of me. As he touched his face, and stared at his fingers, wet from the tears, I decided to pick up the rubbish around the room, feeling the sweet benevolence of Katarina working against all my true instincts.

I had moved on to the wine glasses by the time the man saw me, and started to get up. 'Thanks,' he said.

'It's really no problem.' I picked up a used napkin. 'You sit down and enjoy.'

The man smiled, revealing a row of yellowed teeth, and said, 'You're an angel.'

This is it, I thought, buoyed by the man's praise. This is what great art can do – extending a hand, provoking feeling, beauty, dredging up salt water. My self-congratulation was so extreme that I did not see his eyes, which had moved away from the painting towards the floor in the same time it took to award myself a Turner Prize.

'Do you like the work?' I asked.

'The what?'

'The work.' Two glasses chimed together. 'I thought you were moved by it.'

The man sniffed. A part of me enjoyed his pain, its relationship to the painting, and its subsequent relationship to me. This was real power. 'I painted it.' I smiled. 'It's one of mine. I actually did it in about thirty minutes.'

The man looked at the ceiling, his forehead glistening under the overhead lights. He had a scar on his forehead, and it stretched open, skin migrating, as he started to laugh. 'Oh no. Oh no,' he said. 'You think I'm getting emotional,' he raised one flabby hand, pointing at the canvas, 'at that.' He laughed again. 'Definitely not.'

I watched as he pawed at his cheeks, wiping away the

tears – the same tears which, moments before, I had been convinced were a product of my Michelangelo-like talent. The man turned around to look at me, entirely still. After a moment, I felt as though he were seeing through me, and some strange switch were taking place, in which he knew more than I did, staring at my rotten core. 'You're a fun one,' he eventually said.

'Oh no.' I smiled, repeating his words. I ought to have been humiliated beyond belief, beyond words – and I was embarrassed, it's true – but his smile, and his soft expression, allowed us both a strange honesty.

'I might as well tell you, now, seeing as you mentioned it first,' he said. 'I can see how you might think that this,' he gestured to his face, which was less tear-stained now, 'might have been a result of that.'

We both looked at *Trying, Air, Resistance*. The movements of blue and green, isolated. 'It's actually the anniversary of the day I proposed to my wife.' He looked at the spot on the wall. 'My wife,' he repeated, before taking another large breath, and adjusting his uniform.

'She was wonderful,' he continued, looking at the painting. 'She liked looking at art. That's why I'm here, by the way. Saw I would be working here tonight and thought of her.'

I nodded, and thought about what to do with my hands, my face. Picking up the glasses had previously provided me with something to do, and so I returned to the task while the man paused, returning to his speech.

'I suppose I'm a bit lonely, too.' He swung his legs back and forth once on the bench. 'It gets like that after a while. It's been six years.'

Six years. It could have been six years since anything – a

divorce, their move to the suburbs, since she had taken their used Camry and left – anything at all. But, of course, his wife was dead. It was in the way he spoke about her: it was with a sense of disbelief, as if he were half expecting her to walk around the corner, taking a seat beside him, telling him to quit whatever it was that he thought he was doing.

'That must be difficult.' I was behind him now, making my way around the room. People had left their glasses near the bins in an almost organized fashion, as if their mere proximity to each other would absolve them of the fact that other people would have to clean it all up.

'It is.' He looked at me. 'Where are you from, anyway?'

'Lichfield. It's in England.'

'Thought you sounded fancy.'

'That's funny. It's really not, I promise. There's hardly anything there. My dad actually lost his mind a few years ago, when they built the KFC. He drove up to watch them set up, and everything.'

This went ignored – the man had no interest in a conversational detour; he was thinking of dinners, softness and perfume, all of those things attached to his married life. 'My wife used to put on a British accent,' he said. 'For years, even, she would slip into it, whilst doing the dishes. "Woold you pass me the plate."' The man laughed at his own imitation. 'It was hilarious, because she's from Boston.'

'She sounds lovely.'

'She was.' The automatic light, which had been on for the first few minutes of the conversation, turned off. 'I wasn't trying to be mean about that thing,' he said. 'I'm sure it's very good. I just don't have an eye for it. But I'm sure my wife would have loved it.'

'That means a lot,' I said, finding it to be true.

Just before I left the building, I turned back to wave at the man, though he did not respond, his eyes fixed on the image in front of him, even in the dark.

8

My behaviour with Katarina, appalling as it was, did not go unpunished – in fact, I sought it out myself, in the form of a meeting with Lars. It was self-loathing, in the end, that made me agree to see him, after he had sent a message detailing his condolences, his 'deep, deep regret' for my loss. Opposite the man, however, I thought that no crime could be worth this: listening to his fifth question on the exact circumstances of my father's fabled death.

'And then what did you do? Did you shake him, or something?'

'I just waited for the ambulance,' I said. 'I might have got my phone out, and asked them if they could get there any quicker.'

'That's awful.' Lars frowned, and then smiled. His teeth were an impossible colour. I had seen several paints like those in the studio, batches of the freshest ultra-white, loaded up, a thousand-dollar palate selection. All false, wholly American.

I looked at the floor. 'It's actually a bit foggy. But I do remember being woken up by him. The rest is quite faint.'

I thought I might have overdone it. I felt my eyes widening, and my face twisting into all sorts of things, in drag. But Lars was loving it. His head bobbed forward with excitement. 'That must've been so difficult.' He shook his head. 'Do you get flashbacks, or anything like that?'

'Not really.'

Lars was devastated by this news. His face sagged, and, as he asked more questions, I tried to remember details from medical dramas, the elderly pensioners drooling over themselves. Tragic athletes falling in the red sand, bone-snapping pain. If he had pulled out a notebook from his jacket and started taking notes, I would not have been surprised. Last spring, he drove out to Cooperstown, for the sole purpose of visiting the site of a recent school shooting. His 'findings', sketches of young, traumatized figures and empty chairs, had been plastered everywhere, linked in his Instagram, and presented to his seminar group the next week with distinct pride.

'I don't know if you can tell,' he continued, 'but I'm really interested in death. I'm thinking about that theme for my next project. So all of this is good to know.' He smiled. 'I really fucking like talking to you, by the way.'

Lars told me he had something 'which might be of interest', and pulled out his iPad, where he played a ten-minute video of a caterpillar being stamped on, over and over. I felt quite nauseous by the end of it.

'What do you think?' he asked.

'It's excellent.'

The caterpillar film was not the end of it: he was still on the device, holding it out in the space between us, threatening me with more 'documentary-style' films from his Vimeo account. When my pocket buzzed, I stood up, looked down at Lars, who was attempting to sign into the account, and answered my phone as quickly as possible.

'Hello?'

'It's me, it's me.' I looked down again, sweating, in order to check that it was really him, my father, and waved to Lars seconds later, mouthing 'sorry', as I walked towards the sign labelled 'restrooms'. Down the line, there was the muffled sound of my father's breathing, pressed against his cheek, and mine.

'How was your day?' I asked, by default, and then, remembering: 'Isn't it late over there? Is everything okay?'

'Yes, love.'

I looked at the mirror, placing a hand on the silvery surface.

'I've been thinking, quite a bit,' he began.

'Never good.'

'Don't be cheeky.' He gave a short sound, like a tyre flattening. 'Do you remember that time, out by St Annes? After your mother's promotion?'

Slight, faded dungarees; an attempt at a crisp sandwich, my mother laughing when my father swore at a cyclist. 'Sort of.'

'She wasn't too pleased with me. I don't remember why. I'd probably forgotten to pack something.'

I tapped the metallic sheen of the mirror; here, the image of my finger, being touched by the real one.

'And then next day,' he said, 'the cat, it was just gone, out the door. And you were so sad.'

He was drunk, he was carried away, but there was an addictive quality to it. I'd once seen our old priest scribbling his notes on a receipt, right before his sermon: 'talk about the ark, talk about PARTNERSHIP and the HOLY PLAN'. My father's words were like that, a drawing back of the curtain. 'You were so sad,' he said again, 'you had a sad little face. I went out to find her, in the dark, but she wasn't there. And we both waited for her – do you remember us waiting? At the table?'

I told him I didn't, but I could imagine it, the blue kitchen tiles, passing midnight, waiting for tiny footfalls.

'At some point,' he was slurring his words now, 'I went up to bed. Your mother was there next to me, of course, already under the covers.'

Someone was talking, high, girlish, from outside the toilet door. 'I might need to go soon, Dad. Are you home yet? Or are you outside the pub?'

'And I tapped her on the shoulder, she was always sleeping first, and instead of saying sorry for whatever that bad thing was, the jacket left upstairs, or something, I looked at her, my wife.'

'I know, Dad.'

'My wife. And I asked her if she had done it.'

In the bathroom, I turned the tap on to lukewarm, and let it run over my free hand.

'The cat,' he said, 'did she do it? Did she let it go? I think she looked at me for a bit. And then went back to sleep.'

'Okay.'

'She bought that animal for you, and went to Tesco every week for its food. She got the bowl, and the bed, too. Stuff like that doesn't arrive from nowhere.'

'I know, Dad.'

'So much of every day is getting all of it. Packing groceries, cooking them, and it never goes anywhere. Have you noticed that it doesn't go anywhere? We just shove it in, and it's gone.'

My father's approach to my mother was both traditional

and contradictory; he felt as though he loved her so much, it didn't need to be expressed. My mother cleaned his bedside table, scraped the dust from the drawers, folded his work shirts and left them in a pile on his bed. She watched the shows he recommended, listened to the two-hour compilation YouTube videos he loved ('top ten best guitar solos'), and had a stack of his favourite CDs in the car. And my father, in turn, rejoiced at the impossibility of having a wife who shared his interests so completely.

'Your mother saw your little face wanting an animal, like the people in your class had — Oh God,' he said. 'Oh God. And I really thought –'

'It's okay,' I whispered into the speaker. Hand still under the tap, I thought about the comfort of absolution, how neat it was: three Hail Marys and you're done, off you pop.

My parents had gone to mass together for decades, but I had always suspected my father as a fake. For an entire year, I would pester him in the back seat of our car, asking if he believed in God: 'You don't, do you? I won't tell Mum, ever, come on. Just say it. I technically already know, so if you say, it's no new information. Come on.' He would tell me that he did, of course he did, and that I should focus on applying this energy to my history work (a sharp decline in my results came in with spring). On days where I managed, through coaxing, to get a more fruitful answer, he told me, as we passed the half-closed shops and teenagers in tracksuits, that he might have his doubts, but he didn't want to influence my decision. Such was the weight of his word; I would take his verdict, and make it mine.

In the toilet, I stood, hoping that the stalls would remain

empty. He was still on the other end. 'Charlotte,' he said, 'I don't know what to do. I just don't know.'

I had not blamed my mother for the cat. We hadn't made a very nice home for her, in the end. She had been riddled with fleas, scabs and eye sores, green crusted over in the corners of her eyes. Nobody was kind to her. She had never been house-trained, or outdoors-trained, and so she leaked ammonia everywhere, turning her white bed yellow. I tried to hold her, and might have loved her, my sticky, outstretched hands reaching for her matted fur. But nobody cleaned her; they didn't have the time or the energy to. It wasn't my mother's fault that she had left; I saw that. But my father hadn't, and he had even asked her, his wife, if she had killed her. The cat had been a soft thing, kind and welcoming. I kept forgetting to feed her.

'Do you remember her?'

I told him I didn't. Only seven, not enough time – months, really.

He breathed out. 'I wasn't bad to her,' he said. 'I'm not bad.'

When I came back, Lars was waiting for me, iPad still fixed to his hand. I might have been crying – red-rimmed, a raw, bloated face – but it was hard to tell. I could have been fine.

Lars asked if I was okay. He bent down to hear my answer, and, as I spoke, I found that his video was still playing. 'This one's due on Wednesday,' he said, a hand on my back. 'I'm trying to get it perfect, before then.'

On screen, a half-naked man jumped into the water, arms first, in a dive. A woman in a ruffled top laughed, as behind her, in the waves, the man struggled, hands thrashing in the sun. The camera remained on him for a few seconds, before turning back to the woman, a flash of her cleavage. And behind her, in the background, the man, moving through the waves.

'This is very different,' I told Lars.

'I know,' he said, proud. 'It's actually good.'

We watched as the man was dragged up, into the boat, while the figure – poised, dainty, and self-conscious in front of the camera – sipped her drink, unaware of the waterlogged body behind her, and the rapid movements of the man's chest. I looked at Lars's pert smile, garishly pleased by his work. 'It's not very subtle,' I said.

'It's a documentary.' He shrugged. 'It doesn't have to be.' Lars paused the screen. The man's gasping face was at the centre, frozen, and Lars's full name had appeared in the credits beneath him.

9

That evening I walked back alone, and stood in the doorway to my apartment, imagining for a moment that I was returning to someone. They would be dark-haired, their head resting on the sofa, standing up to meet me as they saw me enter. The strength of this image was so inescapable that I swayed a little, and squinted. Perhaps there was someone there. I stepped closer, and looked at the apartment properly, all of the furniture just waiting to be used; little indents on the counter; the mark at the window where I had smoked the week before, stubbing the end on the sill. I opened the fridge, which was, inevitably, empty. I often believed myself to be immune to hunger, which I mostly was – until I felt it, coming in sharp waves at the most inappropriate times. I'd scarfed down a tuna sandwich at a funeral once. It had raw onions and mayo. The relatives had swerved away from my face when we hugged.

I looked out of my window, where the other residents of the building were returning from work, lifting prams and carrier bags up the stairs. I watched one neighbour, who always seemed to wear a suit, cross the street while the tap dripped. The flat's plumbing was faulty: showering was only possible between ten and eleven p.m., and the toilet needed to be flushed three times before anything went down. I believed that telling the landlord about these issues would remind him of my existence in the flat, which would lead to an investigation about the rent, and his realization of how cheap it was, and how I was staying there – in all essence – for free. A fixed toilet, a fixed shower, and three hundred dollars more per month.

I leaned back on the sofa. It had started to emit a slightly sweet, damp smell, like trousers worn far too long. I looked at a few cooking videos on my phone, scrolling down seconds before they finished, so that it became one long, senseless movie. Katarina texted either ten minutes or three hours after the first video – I couldn't tell. I might have spent my whole life just there, eyes watering.

Katarina had sent,

how was your thing??? :) :) :)

> My thing?

the thing with Lars. you did go??!?

> Yes! It was okay!

just okay???

> Lars was a bit mean actually

mean mean or like normal Lars?

> Normal Lars.

can't do much to save that man.
i went to a sushi place with him last year
and he kept talking about how he would've

been institutionalized in the 18th century.

> Wtf?!

it was very intense. i was like please,
i just want to have a salmon roll, stop
talking about your hypothetical suffering

> HAH.

i thought you'd be able to handle him
though. given your aloof self.

> I think Lars is out of my league, intimidation-wise. He asked me twenty questions about how my dad died, with a huge fucking smile on his face.

i'm going to get him a book on
psychopathy. and full disclosure, i'm
trying to impress you with my word choices.
i just googled the word aloof like five minutes ago.

> Really?

yep.

> What did you type in to get it?

Katarina spent a while responding to that, and I smiled down at the phone, oil sizzling in the background.

word for cold English woman.
and then your name :)))
what are you doing now?

> Literally nothing.

> want to come over?

>> Just put some food on. Mine, instead?

I was of the belief that the fewer words I used, the less excited I seemed, and thus the more likely she would be to agree. She replied four minutes later, telling me that it sounded wonderful, and that she would arrive in thirty minutes.

> i'll bring bread! became friends with this gma
> who works at the bakery with me,
> and we made focaccia together.

>> Focaccia. Of course.

> don't be homophobic.
> i can sense it from over there.

She sent several more emojis.

> i'm super looking forward to seeing your place!

I started to clean frantically, wiping the surfaces: the sofa; the tiny TV, which skipped channels at random; the table, breadcrumbs from weeks ago still at the edges. I sprayed the couch with a bottle with a floral label, hoping that its aggressive femininity would help. I threw T-shirts into cupboards, and decided that the side table should be moved opposite the door. I walked through the room, and imagined Katarina doing the same. The space was bare, like a serial killer's home: 'This is where he lived,' the television reporter would say, in a grave voice, 'before the incident.' I ripped out a few pages from a 'coffee-table book' (I would have murdered a small child if my work ended up in one of those), and placed the pages onto my walls with Blu Tack, in a random arrangement, then stood back. The whole space looked unhinged. It was impeccable.

Katarina texted that she was waiting for me outside, though it was still a surprise when I opened the door and found her on the other side of it. She told me that she had thought about smoking outside, but that she didn't want 'to waste time'. 'Your cooking, and everything,' she said, smiling. 'Thanks for feeding me, by the way.'

'You haven't tried it yet. I should be featured on one of those kitchen nightmare shows, it's that bad.'

We were still outside; I wanted people to see us together, as a way of confirming everything.

'Come in,' I said, as if I had just realized where we were. She stepped through, and looked around the flat. Moments before, I had been running around the same space, with that cheap floral spray, dancing about like a maniac, half-clothed and sweating. Katarina stood at the centre of the room. She looked like a buyer, and I was the estate agent, trying to convince her that this vacant, peeling property was worth it.

'It's so nice here.' Katarina sat down. She reached into her bag and pulled out the bread, placing it on the plastic table in front of her. 'When did you move in?'

'Second year. I saw it online, and there was this sweet old man standing in this room alone. So I booked a viewing.'

The landlord had been bumbling, and remarkably lonely, shuffling up to meet me in faded brown slippers. 'This was my son's,' he told me when he opened the door. He did not say another word, and scraped his feet through the four rooms in the flat, gesturing at any remarkable features in the rooms (the bed, the table, the empty frame on the wall).

On the sofa, Katarina complained about her rent, and Tamsyn and Damien, who cooked elaborate meals for the whole apartment, and then abandoned their dishes to go putrid in plain sight.

'Will you stay here next year, then, after college?' I asked her.

'Oh God. Maybe. The alternative is going back home, and, while I love my parents, that idea terrifies me.' Katarina scrunched her nose, in demonstration of that brand of awfulness.

I moved into the kitchen, and stirred the sauce. It was so dreadful that I had to keep going, the investment too much, now, to go back. 'I just want to make it clear, okay, that this,' I waved the spatula around, getting a splash of the sauce on the counter, 'is going to be so bad.'

Katarina stuck her head in front of the pot. 'I'm sure it'll be fine,' she said, though I could tell she was trying not to breathe in too deeply.

We both sat down at the table beside the wall, so that our legs touched. Katarina started eating first, no caution in her movements at all, and I joined her. It tasted like the ashes of a dog, and curdled milk, left out to form a film in the sun. Opposite me, Katarina's eyes watered slightly, and she barely turned a cough into a swallow.

'I have ice cream in the freezer,' I said.

She pushed her bowl away. 'Perfect.' She placed one

foot on top of mine, under the table where we sat, bowls propped up.

'What are you doing?'

Katarina smiled. 'Nothing.'

'I'm suspicious,' I said, keeping my leg so still beneath hers that it made slight movements up and down, tremors which bounced. We were too far apart for anything, I reminded myself, thinking frantically of the things around me: the radiator on the wall, used the week before; ceiling fans, American builds; the red stain on the edge of the counter. If we hadn't thrown the sauce out – 'As soon as possible,' Katarina had said, 'or it'll really stink the place up' – I could have thought about the liquid rotting there, pulling it inwards, in through the veins, getting thick with the blood. But instead, there was just her, and her arm, which lifted from the table to touch mine. Katarina looked so stupidly good, her hand so warm, that I breathed in, quickly. She asked if I was okay. I nodded, and stood up.

Katarina pulled at the bottom of her shirt, as if reaffirming that it was still there. 'We won't be drunk this time,' she said.

'I do have drinks, though.' I gestured to a drawer, and pulled it open. There was a bottle inside, the red cap still screwed on, untouched. It wasn't for an event, or anything special; I just had it there, as insurance. 'If you want, we could open this.'

'I'm okay.' Katarina placed her fingers into the loops of my belt, jolting me forward. I laughed.

'Do you have a speaker?' she asked. 'I promise I won't dance again.'

'I quite liked your performance last week.'

'Quite liked.' Katarina scrunched her face, and slipped into an appalling British voice.

'That was so bad,' I said. 'Please God, never do that again.'

In every action that occurred next, those little mysteries – one hand here, tight and bare; another on my jaw, near my cheek – all I could feel was a sense of being taken further out, to somewhere I did not know, nor could attempt to know. I was used to looking away from female nakedness, and having sex with women wasn't always transcendent. They were watching themselves, and I was watching myself, and we were both consumed, however briefly, in pretending that this wasn't the case. The idea that the act itself was revolutionary, and that I had to be engaging in its 'higher' nature, took another mental toll. Having sex with the men I did was a magnificent relief. They were entirely uninterested in my pleasure, which, in turn, meant that there was no pretending. Yes, I would do that. Of course. No problem.

Katarina stubbed her toe on the edge of my bed, and swore, her face reddening, hand moving down, with the rest of her, to press her fingers to her foot. 'Fuck,' she said, and then, seeing my face, on the edge of laughter, she shook her head. When she moved closer, I could see the little hairs on her face, and her stomach. I was terrified of making her part of the wider collection of people who had fucked me, or I had fucked, but her hands were at my sides, soft, painful, and I couldn't think about it too much. I wanted her to keep pressing until she reached the edges, raw and hurt. My head twisted away from hers, though my body still jerked, and flicked upwards, to her touch. Katarina asked if there was something wrong. There was a wrapper at the corner of the room, curled up on itself. I had forgotten to pick it up earlier. It rolled over, slightly, as if in response to Katarina's breathing, all warm.

Katarina stopped. 'Are you sure that everything's okay? You're not giving me much, here.' Her hands surrendered, returning to their sides.

I wondered what it would be like to be the person who asked these kinds of questions, instead of them being asked of me; if she was the one who was separate, undeserving, and I had asked: 'Are you fine, really?'

I sat up. 'It's all good,' I told her.

Katarina placed one knee between mine, and sat up properly on the bed. 'I'm not sure I believe you.'

The window opposite us was closed, and the room became filled with a soft chill, working its way from the corners into the centre.

Everything became easy, if I just focused on her, Katarina's movements beneath me, her stomach going up and down in my peripheral vision, where I lifted my head up, reaching, and she gasped. I reminded myself that this was a different kind of sex as I tasted the same, what had been tasted before, and tried to get back to the person beneath it. It was difficult, to reconcile Katarina and the thing I was providing her with. I shook my head, and commanded all of the limbs in my possession to work properly.

Katarina's face was sweating, and her eyes were squeezed tightly shut. When she lifted her head to see me, I asked her if it was good.

'Of course.' She rolled her eyes. 'You just stopped.'

I looked down; we were on the outside of some sort of ecstasy, swollen and wet. It was unbelievable, as she jerked upwards, again, that this was the same room I had cried in, the same room I had filled with everyday dullness – food, my sleeping form – and yet this too, was possible. 'Oh God,' I said. Oh God, Oh God.

Katarina's version of what others called 'pillow talk' involved the exposing of her soul, ever so slowly, so that, by the time she lifted her head to get up for a glass of water, she had stripped away all the elements of her life story. It reminded me of the minutes before a reality TV star sang, the interview conducted with the screen in the back: So how old were you when your parents divorced, and your sister tragically committed suicide?

Katarina told me about the first time she ever 'did anything', her nose inches away from mine, her entire face relaxed. 'I thought it would be a lot better than it actually was,' she said. 'But it was so bad that I actually cried afterwards, and I thought, This? I did all of that, for this?' She laughed. 'We never spoke about it afterwards, which I'm insanely glad about, otherwise I probably would have done something stupid, like apologize.'

'How old were you?' I asked.

'It was in high school, so around seventeen.'

Katarina was still looking at me. I had no idea what time it was, and felt sectioned off from everything in that room, simply blinking up at her, trying to make the link between my body and my head work.

'She was my best friend at the time.' Katarina smiled. 'Classic.'

I could see how much Katarina enjoyed honesty. Each word was expressed in such a measured way that there was no ambiguity in anything. It was wondrous, and baffling.

'I checked her Instagram last week,' she continued. 'She's with this tall guy. He does cars, works on them, and she helps him out with the phone calls, or something.' She touched a hand to her forehead, and said, 'I don't blame myself for that one, though,' and smiled. 'My thing, anyway, is that it's not always good, the way people make it out to be.' She felt for my hand; I let her.

'Is this a pointed remark?'

'Oh no, honestly. I was about to get on to my next bit –'

'Were you?'

'About how this was very different,' she rolled her eyes, 'but you jumped in there.'

'I tend to do that.'

'Always the pessimist.'

'I'm trying not to be,' I said, and kissed her. If anything could pull me out of sickness, she would have been the one to do it, and, as my lips touched hers, I became afraid that I was contaminating her, moving the disease from one exhale to another.

'I was trying to say something important here,' she said, as I kissed the rest of her, 'about the way we are treated, and lifted up,' I moved one of her legs onto my shoulder, smiling at myself, 'made more beautiful, and above things like fucking.'

When we were done, we laid back in the bed, as if it were natural, a married couple returning to rest. There wasn't enough space on the mattress, and I held on to the edge of the bedpost, pressing my cheek into the very end of my pillow. Katarina told me that I looked like an escapee, or a statue.

I tried to make each limb shift away, becoming heavier, as I heard her breaths turn into snores. I had seen her, every twist in her, and felt as if I knew her as much as anyone could. When she kicked me, turning in her sleep, I had to reconcile myself to the possibility that she knew me now, too.

10

We had very little in common. Katarina had brothers, and her parents had met at a board games convention in Milwaukee – which meant that they 'got really serious about Clue'. Her family seemed to prioritize this sense of silliness, and fun, over everything else. Like Katarina, they could be characterized by a series of impulses, and their only metric when it came to decision-making was as follows: if it felt good, they did it.

Our differences didn't end here. Katarina's dreams, which were absurd, featured animated Labradors and cashiers breaking into song, wind-chimes and rainforests. She added sugar to everything – cereal, oatmeal, pasta sauce – and scraped her tongue, 'to stop the cavities'. She fought with her mother often, over small issues – whether it was fine to eat right before bed ('Yes,' Katarina argued, 'absolutely yes') – and sent photos of her day to the family group chat, affectionately named 'The Brookes'. She had a sprawling array of friends, with a rotating cast which varied from charming to irritating, and she wanted me to meet them all.

The following week, Katarina invited me to see these 'key players' at a bar. It was a tiny, dim place at the edge of campus, and I was already tired and drunk. Katarina leaned into my side whenever she stopped talking, which had a comical effect in the bar setting, her body bobbing up and down between her tirades about Colombian coffee and twentieth-century patchwork designs. The group included Katarina's roommates – Damien and Tamsyn – and Tom, Damien's boyfriend. A gallery had booked the couple for an exhibition: *Bodies and Fucking and Timespace*. I looked at Katarina and blinked every time they mentioned it, and she would smile back, in our own little ritual. Tamsyn asked me if I had an eye problem ten minutes after we arrived; Tom and Damien talked about it that much.

On the walk to the bar, Katarina had tried to summarize each of her friends – what they liked and what we could talk about if there was a sudden lull or she had to leave the table to order a beer. She had given a brief report on Tom: he was a postgraduate, and tall, studying something related to theatre. 'It's like visual media, or maybe directing,' she had said. 'But we don't hear about it too often. Either he wants it to remain a secret,' she raised an eyebrow, 'or he is failing, and doesn't want us to ask. So we don't.'

Other things I could not mention in his presence: exes, relationships and love generally. 'This thing with Damien is fairly unstable – it got super messy a few months ago, lots of tears. We think he might have cheated.'

'Who – Tom or Damien?'

'We don't actually know,' Katarina said.

Across the table, Tom was kissing Damien with the ferocity of someone who had recently been unfaithful. Damien's eyes were wide, and turned to look at Katarina mid-snog, giving him the expression of a meerkat.

Tamsyn leaned back in her chair and moved a pale hand

through her hair, which had been gelled back, like a helmet. She was wearing a black lace top and dark trousers, which made Katarina, and her blue dress, stand out in contrast.

'Are you done?' Tamsyn asked, looking at the happy couple. She often said things with a smile, as if everything were one great joke, though they were mostly insults.

Tom just smiled at her over his drink, and did a half-nod, like a bow, and said, 'Almost', before kissing Damien's neck. 'Now I am,' he said.

I looked at Damien, who was silent, his mouth twitching. A candle had been placed in the middle of the table by one of the waitresses, an attempt by the bar's management to transform the sticky tables into a semblance of a Michelin restaurant. Damien was directly above the flame; the light went across his face, revealing his eyes, which were watering. He took a drink from the glass, and told me that it was soda, when I asked. I had very little to say to that; I was tethered to Katarina, and her good graces, and our ill-defined relationship. One slip on my part, and all of the members of the table would have me tossed out, in the rain. Under the table, Katarina put a hand on my leg.

'You paint, don't you?' Tamsyn asked, leaning on her hand in mock-interest.

'Not very well.' I smiled, and Katarina just stared, her eyes slightly wide.

'I like your stuff,' she said, turning to look at me. 'I always have. It's fun.'

'That's nice,' Tamsyn said. 'Though it's always amazing when people study a course which they have little interest in, like – all of your money is going towards this. Be serious.'

'Talent is not the same as interest,' Tom said, and

nodded, as though he had the final, holy word. He had other words of wisdom to dispense. Tom, on politics: 'Let's just remember that we're people at the end of the day.' Art vs the artist: 'My uncle Tim is a monster, and I really can't imagine any good shit coming out of him.' And, finally, the meaning of life: 'FUN! It is to have FUN!' He had the delightful ability of reducing everything, engaging no one, and saying nothing, and he managed it all, while looking extraordinarily pleased with himself.

Despite Tom's best efforts, the group quickly fell into a healthy and impenetrable rhythm: what did we think about Caryl? And did we hear about Lin's girlfriend?

Damien sneezed into his hand, and pretended to read the menu.

'Are you thinking of ordering anything?' I asked. 'Apparently there's some deal for the students. The cocktails look good, anyway.'

Damien smiled. 'Maybe.' He flexed his hands as Tamsyn turned her head to look in our direction, now interested.

'Damien doesn't drink,' she said. 'At all.'

'Oh, shit, sorry,' I said.

Tamsyn was smiling, though Damien was becoming increasingly uncomfortable, flipping the laminated sheet over in his hands, cartoon glasses decorating the menu's margins. 'It's not a problem.'

'Any more,' Tamsyn said.

'Any more. Yes.'

Damien's boyfriend leaned forward, and downed his soda in one, tapping his empty glass with a fingernail. 'We all have our things,' he said, smiling up at Damien, who was decidedly looking at the waitress walking past our table.

'So true, honestly,' Katarina joined in. 'I've diagnosed myself with almost everything.'

'Really?' I looked at Katarina. She was the best person I knew – not only that, but I thought of her as the pinnacle of functionality and general wellness. Whenever we saw pharmaceutical ads pop up – 'With Zalanaphorax, you, too, can be this happy' – I'd point to the woman on screen, blissfully smiling, and say: 'That's you.'

'I'm not kidding,' Katarina said. 'Just this morning I convinced myself that I had five disorders. I had a stomach ache, in the end.'

'That's like mental Munchausen, or something,' Tamsyn said. 'Which is probably an illness in itself.'

Tom was staring at Damien's lips. 'I wish we were doing a useful degree, like research or medicine.' He drew his words out, swirling them in his mouth between sips. 'Then we could actually do something.'

Tom was a slow drunk, a pseudo-philosopher drunk. The more alcohol Tamsyn had, however, the more energized she became. At Tom's words, every movement became amplified, and her hands went to his shoulders, to shake him into sense. 'Don't say that.' Her hands, still there, were pale pink, and clutching him. 'Don't.'

Accusations of futility – that what we were all doing was essentially pointless, an exercise like any other, to be held beneath window cleaning or office meetings – were the worst, and most true, of the accusations held against those in the institute. Students like Tamsyn held charity galas, exhibitions with the theme of 'refuge' or 'panic', in order to stave off these claims. All students had to be constantly looking over their shoulder, mid-paint, anticipating the crime of self-indulgence as they worked. I was relieved, in a way, that I did not care enough about anything I made: nobody could accuse me of believing in it too much.

Tom twisted his fingers into Damien's. 'I just worry,' he said, 'that the things I make won't matter.'

'Enough of that, now.' Katarina jumped up. 'Let's dance, please.'

Dragging Tom by his hand, she moved towards the centre of the bar, where couples were leaning into each other, the lights reminiscent of an eleven-year-olds' disco, orange juices and slow dances. The DJ had rigged the lights so that there was a concentrated patch of red at the centre. Katarina and Tom fell in line with the light. The pair had met in first year, and bonded over their love for mooncakes. This was enough, this shared love, to form a tentative foundation in freshers' week, and their friendship had only strengthened. I stared at them both, and thought about how mysterious, how like romance, their friendship seemed. Perhaps it did not have the same intensity, that heady rush of attraction, but there was still something, a pull of some kind, which drew these people together, in mutual safety. They even looked good together – better than if I had been up there with her. Katarina tripped over the edge of her boots, and looked up at me, smiling from afar, as if to say: Did you see that?

I started to mouth something at her, but she had already turned away. Tamsyn nudged my side with an elbow. 'How long have you two been together?'

'Oh, I don't really know.'

Katarina was still swaying, her boots weighing each jump

up and down, in slow motion. 'It hasn't been long,' I said. 'Not that – I don't even know if we are together, honestly.'

I was deeply afraid of asking her anything about it: having it confirmed or rejected was far too concrete.

Tamsyn laughed. 'Have you guys talked about it?'

'Not really.' I looked back at the dance floor; Katarina was gone, and was now at the side of the bar, leaning against the table to get another drink.

Tamsyn stared at me. 'She mentioned that you two had fucked, though, the other day.'

'She said that?'

'Yeah.' Tamsyn drank her brown-coloured liquid, and threw her head back. 'It's no big deal, though,' she said. 'She does that with lots of people. Especially those who are new to it.'

'New?'

Tamsyn kept going, bolstered by the drink, and Katarina's distance from us. 'New, like kind of straight girls. You all have this kind of,' she leaned forward, 'fresh look.'

'I've literally no idea what you are talking about.' It was as if Tamsyn had been discussing slabs of meat, or the extraction of eggs: two days old. Fresh. Just removed.

She shrugged. 'Okay.'

I imagined Tamsyn's skin peeling back, very slowly, and shook my head to get rid of the image, the rawness of the thin layers, chicken skin ripped off too soon.

'Don't worry,' Tamsyn put a hand on my arm, 'it might not be that. Katarina loves a tragic story, so. It could be that, too.'

'Jesus Christ.'

*

When Katarina got back, I pulled her over to the toilets, locked the door from the inside, and kissed her, almost aggressively. There was nobody there, though we could hear the low thrum from outside, bass notes and the occasional shout.

I touched her cheek, first, and then wrapped my hands around her body. She removed her underwear haphazardly, snatching it from the floor with one hand as it caught around her leg.

'Are you okay with this?' I asked her.

'Yes, of course,' she said. Katarina looked jubilant, and I felt some vindication at having put that expression there. She was already laughing by the time I felt inside her, and she sat on top of the sink, all warm and shining. She just said, 'Wow', as I continued, in and out. She placed her lips on my forehead once she finished, suddenly very soft. In the mirror, I could see my front, and the back of her dress, the thin fabric of it.

'What was that about?' she asked, when we were done.

I did not answer her, and washed my hands. I steered her out of the room after I'd unlocked the door, one arm around her. The thrill of knowing her body, in that moment, without her knowing mine, was astounding. That I could guess what she was thinking and feeling, and at what pace she wanted it, without her having a clue as to my own pleasure, made me feel superior, and harsh, like a robot.

Katarina looked at me in confusion when we sat down at the table again, and I took her hand, opened it up on the fake granite table, and watched as Tamsyn raised her eyebrows. I had bastardized our earlier gesture, and

Katarina's sweet touch of the thigh, but it felt worth it. Katarina's fingers itched beneath mine, but I held on, waiting for Tamsyn to say something, but she never did.

When we got back to the flat, Katarina wanted to discuss Tom and Damien's relationship. 'He deserves better,' she said.

'Who?'

'Tom – who else?'

She told me that my question had been disloyal; Tom was one of her best friends. 'And he's attractive.'

'Is he?'

'He is. Objectively speaking, I can appreciate a man's face.'

'That's news to me.'

'They're like paintings. Pretty.' Katarina's head was on a pillow, her eyes closing as she spoke.

Tom and Damien had left us half an hour before. 'We're a little tired,' Tom had said, leaning into Damien as they walked, folding into each other on the streets. Katarina kissed them both on their cheeks, asked them to text when they arrived back home, and took my hand, watching them leave.

'And what do you think about my face?' I asked Katarina, smiling down at her on the sofa.

'Not very painting-like. More real, obviously.'

'I don't know if I should be offended,' I said, as she took my hand, and, pulling on it, made me stumble over to her.

'Don't be. Painting is shit anyway.' She lifted her chin, adopting an air of gravitas. 'Unless it's yours.'

I laughed. Her face was close to mine, her hands cold

and her expression peaceful. Being with her, alone, felt incredibly closed off; the idea that anything could be happening outside of that space was unbelievable. I could say anything, and do anything with my body, and it would somehow be safe. As a child, I'd have a random, yet persuasive, desire to scream, a sudden weight: Do it. With Katarina in my flat, I had a similar feeling, excavated somehow, reconstructed into a smile, or the pressing desire to kiss her. We were still in our clothes from the bar, and she was reading a leaflet on internships, left at my apartment the week before. Other things of hers were around us, of course, and I had gone out to the shops to buy her a cheap plastic toothbrush, leaving it, still in its package, on the side of the bed she liked to sleep on.

Across from me, Katarina was only half reading the text, and half staring at me.

The sex that night was very intense – that was the word I used to describe it, right afterwards: 'God, Katarina, that was intense.'

I cried, which might have been intensely embarrassing, had I not turned my head immediately away from her, and she'd pretended not to see. We watched a film, one which was neutral and forgettable, while she lay next to me, our arms touching and one of her legs over mine. At certain points in the movie, which seemed to involve a cartoon girl getting lost in a magical realm, Katarina would move away from me, and I'd grab on to her side, pulling her back in.

11

Before Katarina, my days had a general formlessness, each morning marked by the taking of tablets, an assortment of vitamins and chalky pills in little blue tubs. When she stayed over, I would do the same thing in the morning, twisting the child-locked cap, but I would do it with a certain elation: Yes, I am alive, I would think, and these help me. Swallowing the pills was decisive, and I thought it would represent the rest of my life, a transition from lukewarm resignation into cold, pulsing, water. I believed a lot of myself, and of her, back then. Images of John the Baptist, dunking the body of Jesus in a river, seemed appropriate, though I couldn't work out which one of us took which role.

After three weeks, Katarina knew where everything in my apartment was, every plate. She pulled out two from the cupboards, and I just watched her, fully domesticated. She had made two slices of French toast, and was still in the T-shirt she wore to sleep, a navy tee, found in the goodwill bins the year before.

Katarina was prone to saying lovely things between the hours of nine and eleven in the morning, and told me that I looked good. As she flipped a piece of toast over, transferring it from the pan onto a plate, I thought about the sudden luxuriousness of it all, and understood, alarmingly, the narcissism of the couples I had seen out on the street, taking up extra space on the sidewalks, moving as if they had an unlimited amount of time available to them. I could see how everything else could stop existing – death and damnation (the double Ds) – and there could only be this, the way she jostled around, touching the warm handle of the pan.

It was a Sunday, and neither of us had anything to do.

'Is there anywhere you want to go?'

'I really, really do not mind.'

She turned the tap off, blocking the window, and I almost saw the room as it used to be, terrifying, until she moved back again. 'You're absolutely hopeless,' she said.

We finished eating, and Katarina packed several of her home-made bags, crafted together from different materials. We got into her car, a small, navy Volvo. 'I wanted a green one,' she told me, 'but it was too expensive.' She handed me the keys, and laughed as I asked what to do with them. I couldn't drive; it seemed mysterious, a whole other language. Katarina unlocked the doors, and we got in, myself in the passenger seat. The whole scene was terribly adult, and Katarina leaned on the wheel decisively.

Around us, there were pieces of shredded yarn, dispersed on the dashboard and the cracks in our seats. 'Sorry about the mess,' she said, more out of politeness than any real concern. Katarina looked down. 'I might've got carried away with the materials.'

On the way there, we listened to songs I had never heard before, and, as she played each one, vibrating through the speakers at the front, Katarina moved her head, ever so slightly, to look at my expression. She asked if I liked them, and I told her that I did, every time.

'I don't believe you,' she said, after a particularly loud track, with some screaming at the end, a little encore of suffering. She was wearing a long shirt with flared sleeves, jeans and no bra. I found myself dressing more like her the more time we spent together, as if I had picked up her personality by proxy, looking into my closet in surprise when I found that its belongings could have been in hers. When choosing my outfits, I looked into the mirror, and tried to find myself more attractive, as if the energy could be transferred from her onto me.

Katarina turned the music off, and the car made a clicking sound before she got out. She took the bags, and then said hello, as if we were meeting for the first time. She kissed me before we walked inside the store, quickly, and shook my hand off when I tried to take it.

We got one basket, and passed it between us at random. As we moved about the aisles, and I followed behind, I would feel an intense and pervasive need to touch her. A woman with a short bob, and children, looked at us, then nudged her children closer towards her, one hand on their shoulders, as if they had been contaminated.

Katarina paid for everything at the checkout, though I tried to argue about it. 'Let me get this,' I said, 'come on.'

She shook her head, and turned to face the machine with her card.

I pulled her back. 'We can halve it, then.'

Katarina ignored me and pressed her card against the till. It made a small, high sound. I stared at her face, which was resolute, and a little flushed. She started shoving all of the items, the things we had been seduced by (dark chocolate, nice cheese), and none of the things we actually needed, into the bags. The supermarket, and those store lights, became very beautiful, and I saw in every face around me the potential for their own loves: men with greying beards with false soccer-enthusiast wives; the young woman behind us thinking of her girlfriend, out of state, waiting for a call when she got home.

I pretended to be annoyed with Katarina, and her bout of generosity, on the journey back to the flat. The more I pretended, the more it felt real. But even this frustration became a treat, and, leaning back in the grey seat, I thought about how fortunate we were, and how indulgent it was, to have someone to be frustrated by.

Over dinner that night, the side of her mouth shining with grease, Katarina said that she'd never been this comfortable – 'like, in any relationship'. 'You don't seem to be bothered by anything,' she said, her spit mixing with the oil.

'That's because I'm not.'

'I weirdly believe you.' Katarina wiped her face with her palm.

Of course, there were plenty of things to be bothered by. She spat out her toothpaste in the shower, and blew her nose as soon as the hot water ran, in a little stream of congestion. I would hear it, even if I was in the kitchen, or listening to music in my bedroom – the strained sound of her waste. She picked at her forehead, too, flecks of white getting beneath her fingertips, and smeared them moments later into our pillows, the duvet. But I never said anything. I fought all my instinctive feelings of disgust, and tied them down to some inaccessible part of me. Most of the time, this involved doing, or saying, the exact opposite of what I thought, or committing an action so random so as to get out of myself entirely. The week before, after jumping onto my living-room table after a particularly heinous thought about her, I told Katarina that I was training for some obscure aerobics from a YouTube video. (My worst work. She did not believe me.)

And sometimes, I wondered if I was doing enough, if I failed to hide these impulses on such a catastrophic level that they infected her, too. She often asked if I thought she looked okay, or if what she called her 'ugly time' ('It arrives once a month, I swear to God') had hit her at last.

'Maybe I should join you in your aerobics,' she said, once we cleaned up the dishes.

I shook my head. 'Please don't.'

I also told her – and I really did say this – that she looked perfect. Despite everything, this was true. Despite my gripes, projections, those minor peculiarities – I always found her beautiful. The damp, and the traffic, ran out from the window. I put my hands around her. I suppose I loved her, in a way. The only way I could.

12

It didn't take long for the lying to become a state of being, more than anything else. I still did it, even when she started to come over more often. I did try not to say anything explicitly untrue, though, when I did, it was intoxicating. Katarina would ask about home, about whether we had pets (no), whether I had witnessed any fights (no), or had any aggressively inappropriate make-out sessions, or even crushes (also no).

'God, you never did anything, did you?' Katarina once said, by which time I *had* to invent, just to keep a modicum of excitement between us.

I told her that my early life had been turbulent; the family uprooted me often and consistently, packing me off to different schools. (I had only ever attended one primary school, moving to the secondary on the other side of the street, by the landfill.) My uncle was an unemployed addict, who stopped by the house for food (Maths teacher). My mother had wanted me to enter the glamorous world of tormented theatre-kids, in order to fulfil her own faded dreams. ('You're like me,' she had said, after she overheard a makeshift-karaoke session, 'there's not a tune in your body.') But whatever the tale, Katarina always believed it. Her belief in those words felt proof that she thought kindly of me, that she saw me as a better person than I actually was.

Her mother called that evening, after we had gone shopping. Katarina was the youngest of three; her eldest brother stayed at home, and the other had a wife and lived out in Maine. She presented me with a portrait of simple family devotion, and overwhelming sweetness. They all seemed like good people. They called every other day, sometimes when I was in the kitchen, and I would slow my breathing, in an attempt to be as silent as possible.

Katarina felt as if it was time to introduce me to them, and held her phone out, revealing her lock screen, which was a photo of herself in her mother's arms. They looked like catalogue people, entirely unreal. I had always consoled myself with the idea that people were never as happy as they appeared in those glossy pages, but it appeared that, in this case, they were.

'Do you want to talk to them?' she asked.

I forced a smile. 'Let's do it.'

She accepted the call, and sat down next to me on the sofa, our thighs touching. They spoke loudly from their car, compensating for the traffic, and the nine hundred miles between us, by shouting at the phone. They asked her about her day. She replied, and there was a sweet, low-stakes quality to her response.

'That's really great,' her mother said.

I leaned back on the sofa, blinking quickly. I was very far away from them all. Katarina was smiling, relaxed, as if there could be nothing wrong with any of it – not me, or her family unit. She picked up my hand, and started moving it with her fingers, a marionette operator. 'They're asking after you,' she said, as if aware that I was unable to register anything.

'Oh. Hi, guys. It's so great to meet you.' Was I meeting them? Did this two-minute call (even less, if I stood up, and walked out, which I could do, I told myself, I could do it) count as a proper introduction?

Katarina's mother said something standard: You too. A pleasure. Always good. She was closest to the speaker. Around her, we heard traffic, and someone in the back seat. 'We've heard so much about you from Katarina,' the mother said.

'Thank you.'

There were several balls of yarn, resting against the wall, from where Katarina had left them. I stared at them. I had nothing to say to anyone, and Katarina, seeing this, picked up her phone, took it off speaker mode, and left for my bedroom. I heard her walking outside my door, and the twist of the handle, as she continued to chat about one of her brothers, who had been accepted into an amateur softball league. 'Well done,' I heard her say, on the other side of the wall. 'You should be so pleased.'

In bed, later, Katarina seemed entirely uninterested in doing anything, and my whole body had begun to shake. I had relied on it to draw her in, regardless of what I had said, or what she'd said, and all the ways both could go wrong. Friends of Katarina's, like Tamsyn or Damien, would have called us a casual relationship – or, that dreaded term, 'situationship'. But because I didn't have many friends, I couldn't ask anyone else what they thought, relaying my version of us out, on the table, to be analysed. Matthew sent me strange memes every few days, grainy cartoons of communist Russia, or 'your mom' jokes, somehow related to the public ownership of property. There would be no text attached, just the meme itself. I was always relieved when I got them – it meant that he was alive – though I could hardly ask a question about emotional vulnerability beneath a dancing Karl Marx.

Katarina was the one I texted if I took offence at the way someone in a shop spoke to me, or if I bought a new type of candy for the first time. I found myself sending her things like, 'saw a cute rottweiler and i'm convinced it was your brother in dog form', or, 'i'm scared of poly people does this make me bad', when, less than a year ago, I would have said that these were the texts of a clinically insane woman or, even worse, a needy boyfriend.

The beginning and end of my days were marked by her, so that each moment had a cyclical quality to them, a captivating loop. I watched all of her favourite films – Wes Anderson, Studio Ghibli, anything featuring vampires – alone, so that we might talk about them later. I saw a kind of melancholy, and loneliness, in her tastes, and tried to match up these preferences to the Katarina I knew. She did not present like a sad person, though I knew that a part of her emotional life would always be closed off to me, and I didn't want her to tell me about it.

While she sat, unusually silent, against the wall, I asked if there was something wrong.

'Tired, I think. I'll just go to sleep,' she said.

In the morning, she was already dressed, and said good morning brusquely, as if she was only honouring a tradition.

Her hair was frizzy near her hairline, and her face had an intense, alive quality to it.

'You were strange with me yesterday,' she said, after asking how I slept.

I sat up, propping my pillow against the wall. 'In what way?'

'Just generally odd. Even more than usual.' Katarina started picking out a loose shirt from my wardrobe, and laid it out, on the duvet, in front of me.

'Not true. If anything, that was you.'

Katarina waved a hand in the air, in dismissal. 'That was just a result of earlier.'

'Earlier?'

'When I was, like, "my family are here", and you maybe said three fucking words.' She smoothed out the wrinkles in the top sheet, and folded the arms of the shirt. I wondered if it was too early to go out and smoke, though I hadn't had a cigarette in months.

'I just can't help feeling like I don't know you very well,' she said. 'I sit next to you, and we talk sometimes, and sleep together, or whatever, but if I were to describe you to someone, I quite literally would not know what to say.'

'Okay.'

'I don't know, honestly, why I keep coming back here. You make me feel as if I have to beg for the smallest – the absolute smallest – thing from you.'

Was it possible that, while I was thinking about the things she left around the apartment – paperbacks, her cracked lip balm – looking at them with some form of worship, that she was sitting there, stewing in her resentment? I had oriented this new life around her. It felt ugly, my helplessness.

I looked at her, and started putting on the top she had put out for me. It was long-sleeved, and green. 'What do you want to know?'

'Anything,' she said.

I was a terribly ugly child, so ugly that I felt marked out for something. My chin was rounded, and the flesh underneath it poked out. My stomach, too, was convex, like the rest of me, stubby legs protruding to where my knees met, the joints only noticeable in those mounds of flesh through tiny indents, lines between the upper and lower parts of the legs. I did not fit into regular clothing. I dreaded clothes shopping so much that I was content to wear my mother's things, dressed tightly in floral T-shirts and ruffled blouses, like a pilgrim grappling with the wrong century. Pre-puberty, I would wear items from the teenage section of the supermarket. These consisted of cropped tops and neon shirts, terrifying and incomprehensible: NY. 1978. C'EST LA VIE. I did not know why anyone would want to see more of me, and spent most of my childhood pulling at these polyester and elastane blends, dragging tops and dresses down towards the lowest points, stretching the waistbands. Adults used the phrase 'growing girl' around me at dinner tables, smiling away. The idea that I might simply keep growing was so alarming that I considered the possibility of plastic surgery for years, with a fervour.

My mother had a stack of magazines under the bed, for when she was sick. In the evenings, dinner already sloshing around my intestines, I would walk upstairs and feel the smooth edges of each copy, that sheen, staring at the models' jaws, the delicious curve of their bodies – not too much, the right kind of delicate. A controversy about one of the models would, inevitably, be mentioned somewhere between pages ten and fifteen. 'It's unfair, perhaps even unethical, that Chrissa should make so much, given her recent surgeries.' Words like 'unethical' or 'immoral' (they never went more specific than that) meant nothing to me; I was never tempted to look them up in dictionaries.

Holding the magazines up, beside my head, I would imagine that I was there, standing with the tiny woman in the image, my eyes blurred.

Katarina was sitting towards the end of the bed. She was waiting, facing the door, as if someone might walk through and tell her all that she needed to know about me, leading her by the hand. It's over, the saviour would say. You know everything now. It felt as though we had been married for years (rainy day, no presence from my family, sandwiches after the ceremony), and it had been revealed that I had murdered her grandfather. That kind of accusation was thick there, in our cold, soon-to-be-divorced bed.

'Tell me quite literally anything,' she said, again.

'I'm not sure I even know what "anything" is.' I picked at the floral, aggressively feminine bedsheets (her choice, of course), and tried to be honest. 'My parents were a bit shit, and we lived in a two-up two-down together, and we couldn't afford to move.'

'I thought you said you changed schools all the time.'

'I did.' I breathed in, cursing the brief moment of honesty, my own stupidity. 'I mean, they shut the first one down, so I had to transfer into the next catchment area. But anyway,' I made a (real) expression of embarrassment, 'nothing ever happened. It was pretty dull.'

'What do you mean, "nothing"? I want to know about these things.' She ran a hand through her hair. 'And what the hell is a "two-up two-down"?'

I answered, relieved to have something else to give her: a concrete fact; the four-roomed houses littering our street.

Katarina stood up, and sat back down again. 'I don't think I'm asking for much. Just a little less distance.'

I felt as if we were having two very separate conversations simultaneously, a game of Chinese whispers which had no start or end. There was a single fleck of black above her eyelid; it became smudged when she closed her eyes. 'I care about you, obviously.'

I couldn't help but smile. My body was constantly betraying me; our relationship was founded on it.

'But,' she continued, 'I feel,' she waved her arms, 'disconnected. And it's affecting things.'

'Is it?'

'Yes. Come on.'

Sometimes, when Katarina was lying back, I would see this purity across her face, eyelids fluttering. Her mouth would form a soft shape, and I knew exactly what she wanted, and where. When she pulled her body upwards, I could tell that everything had become heightened, swollen, and when our bodies were together, all slippery, we felt like one animal, shivering and rippling. It was sacred, and warm, and when I saw her properly, outside of the sex, washing dishes or folding a towel, there would be a slight sense of disbelief at what we had done. The idea that she was disconnected in that moment, and in others, too, made everything I had done feel cheap. All of the words I had said to her in the evenings came back to me, like an actor suddenly remembering his lines: 'We're not in Kansas any more!'

'Maybe we should forget about it,' Katarina said. She was paler than usual. One of her sweaters fell onto the floor. She picked it up, pulled it over her head, and hid her arms, before she reached out, as though a ghost. I laughed, grateful that the conversation had already broken.

'Thank you,' I said.

The following month, Katarina had an art showing on campus. It was due to rain. This seemed important to her at the time, and she rushed around my flat, opening wardrobe doors and cabinet shelves. 'I'll have to think about a coat,' she said, very seriously, looking at my jackets, scrunched and wrinkled on the floor. 'Are umbrellas unprofessional?'

'I don't think they'll punish you for not being waterproof.'

'I know, but,' she hit the wardrobe door, 'looking drowned adds to the whole thing. They're not going to buy things from me, or value the work, if they think I'm sleeping outside.'

She was right: desperation, or even the hint of *needing* an opportunity, was the enemy of getting it. We had been told, in a seminar, that there were five career moves, five showings, which could make our career: paths into the Guggenheim, the Met, the Gagosian. High school had been like that, too: the desire to have friends rarely led to the making of them. People thought loneliness and desperation were catching.

I left Katarina in the bedroom, to throw around more of our things, which seemed to help.

The 'showing' was really a stall, a market-style operation propped up outside the canteen. Students Katarina knew dropped by the side of the road for a few minutes, taking photos for their Instagram stories, or 'underground, undervalued, but totally vital' Substacks.

'Thanks so much,' Katarina told them, after they stood by the work, humouring her with pleasant, but uninterested, expressions on their faces.

Katarina's project, which had taken her several months, was a half-sculptural, half-textile-based coral reef. She had taken used bottle lids, plastic bags and old yarn, and, though these textures danced in separate directions, together, there was a distinct cogency to it all, a beautiful, and almost tender, tapestry. I couldn't help but think about her when I saw it, all of those hours spent, back cowed and eyes focused, on the piece. It was the perfect evidence of her dedication.

Watching the students' slow disengagement opposite her work was terrifying. They were all bored as hell. I asked her if she wanted me to leave. 'You know, if it makes the whole thing easier, I can go to the library for a bit.'

'And read what?'

'I don't know. Might do some actual research for once. You've inspired me.'

Across from us, a couple were eating hotdogs, their greasy hands damp in the rain. One of their napkins flew over to Katarina's exhibit, and the man ran over, not looking up at the stand while he picked it up.

'At least I've made an impact on someone, then,' Katarina said.

We both watched as the man with the hotdog caught the white tissue, standing close together.

'You have. I'm a changed woman.'

To distract herself from the showing, which was a 'complete failure, honestly', by her standards, Katarina booked a meeting with her favourite instructor, a woman she spoke of with the same reverence my family used to talk about underfloor heating, or Paul the Apostle. The session was meant to be dedicated to Katarina's career. I had seen the instructor on campus: she was in her late fifties, and was all eccentricity. She was notorious for her pet raccoon, which she carried across courtyards and departments, and her costume chainmail, which she wore to every lesson. Katarina wanted to know more about academia, and this woman, she decided, was her mentor.

She saw this instructor's involvement in academia as noble, her career path the ideal model for her own. Whenever Katarina spoke about art, and 'the duty it has, we all have, to real life', I saw the instructor's eyes, blinking down at me through the little metal holes in her helmet. Katarina believed in 'collapsing art boundaries', that there was no separation between 'high' and 'low' forms – terms which were, in themselves, frustrating. She kept talking about 'The Frankfurt School' when we brushed our teeth. One particularly grating moment (of many) saw Katarina creating a comparison between public executions and the show *Married at First Sight*.

'It's the same impulse,' she said, as the bride was left, red-faced, at the altar. 'You know – the spectacle of it all.'

'I'm just trying to watch the hot people cry,' I said, after a moment of silence.

'Exactly.'

When Katarina returned from the meeting with her 'guru', she went straight to the bathroom. Once she emerged, glistening, I asked her how the session had gone.

'I learned absolutely nothing,' she said. 'Nothing. The woman went on about her pension for hours. And the weak coffee in the faculty.'

'Not good.'

'Eventually I had to say: "I just want to know what my next steps are." And the woman actually laughed. And then talked about the packets of sweetener in the cafeteria.' I had seen Katarina this angry only once before, after Lars went incognito on a dating app specifically designed for lesbians – it was a sight to behold.

'The only remotely interesting thing,' Katarina continued, 'was when the woman got around to why she started in academia in the first place. She said she was from Bay City – it's in the South,' Katarina waved her hand in the air, as if this was some great Americanism I could not possibly understand, 'and I said a little about my hometown, the jobs there, that sort of thing. So she got back to talking about the city: the museum-turned-Ren-Faire by the fishing park.'

I had no idea what Katarina was talking about, and,

not wishing to prove her assumptions about the ignorant English to be correct, I settled for nodding occasionally, while pushing an expired cupcake further in her direction.

'But what started this, her career, was this hot day, in the doctor's office. The instructor said it was cramped, and she had an ear infection – and there was this man, normal-looking, and everything, standing by the entrance. He said nothing, sat down. And, after a few people were called in, a guy walked through, shouted a name, and punched the man so hard, he fell to the ground.' Katarina pushed her cupcake away. 'And obviously, I'm sitting in her office, like: What does any of this have to do with your career? Or mine?

'But she keeps going on – the blood, she kept saying, all on the floor, on the smooth chequered floor. There was a little on the tip of her shoe. And when she looked down, she saw a splash, all over the patent. And then, the instructor thought: If I can get as far away from this, from the bleeding man, and this goddamn smell, I will.' Katarina blinked. 'Isn't that awful?'

'Poor guy,' I said.

She ignored me. 'I thought one thing – that I could do some good.' Katarina pressed her index finger into the table, creating a rush of red at its tip. 'But it turns out she's just a coward.'

'You should write that down,' I said. 'Notes for your next project.'

'Fuck off,' she said.

This phrase characterized much of her behaviour for the next few hours.

Katarina's crisis of confidence, disguised as a greater loss of faith in the artistic culture as a whole, lasted three days, in which she was sexually frustrated, unhappy with the temperature in all rooms, and complained about a litany of people: New Yorkers, Californians, straight people, academics over the age of fifty and the English – 'Why the hell do you put beans in tomato sauce anyway?' The crisis was solved on day four, following a good meal, a John Berger documentary and the arrival of her pay cheque from Panera. I rather enjoyed the whole thing. She was so busy being annoyed, she forgot to ask me questions.

By day five, the malaise was back, and Katarina started to throw herself into preparations for a vacation. She told me that she was thinking about 'somewhere warm', and would express this often around the flat, folding her clothes and putting her art books down to conjure different places in the air.

'Come on,' she said, only thirty minutes after our last discussion about whether Italy might work, or Greece. 'Warm. Sun. It's got to be somewhere in Europe, anyway.' (For Americans, 'Europe' always meant Rome or London – never Manchester or Great Yarmouth.) 'Can you think of anywhere?'

'I don't know.' I smiled mildly, like an extraordinarily non-committal husband upon hearing of his son's fights at school. 'We could always go to the park, have a picnic.'

This offering of poorly made sandwiches and the threat of even worse weather did very little to persuade her. A restlessness had settled, and I found her looking out of my apartment windows almost wistfully, like a trapped servant.

In truth, I could not afford to go anywhere: Katarina was significantly better off. For much of college, I had been relying on a small pot of money from my mother. I struggled with my rent frequently, despite my landlord's amnesia (or generosity), and would email the institute at the beginning of term, threatening to drop out due to a lack of funds. In second year, one of my artworks – *Evanescence* – won a prize, resulting in two thousand dollars. But I was approaching my final semester, and these funds – cherry-picked, random acts of God – had dried up. It was March, and I was, quite significantly, in debt.

Katarina sat at our table, eating an expired sandwich from work. 'I'm thinking of April, for the vacation,' she said. 'We could get out of the cold, get a tan. There's a semester break on the eleventh, which gives us over a month to plan.'

I pretended to tidy up after her, as though I might make up for my lack of speech by assuming the role of her personal cleaner.

'If you don't say anything, I can just book it for myself, and you can wait.' She looked out of the window again, her lack of holiday, of sun-screened shoulders, staring back. 'Actually, if you don't want to go, that's fine. I suppose it's a kind of commitment.'

'Obviously, I'd love to.' I sat beside her. 'I actually just have no money. I can barely make next semester's tuition, on top of rent, so it's sort of out of the question for me.'

'Oh.' She turned back to me. 'I literally had no idea. Jesus, I thought it was because you couldn't see us together for that long.'

'Please, God no.'

13

We went back to that little dance of ours: Katarina came over most days, at six o'clock; she'd stay over until nine in the morning, when she would return to the studio, or the Panera on Monroe Avenue. Weekends were her own, or the company's, and she spent them with Damien and Tamsyn. They went to bars and pubs, from which I would often receive texts, sitting on my bed, telling me to come and see her – that she had to see me.

The first weekend after the showing, Katarina asked me to join her on the night out. 'call me,' she'd texted. 'i miss you.' The message was accompanied by several missed calls.

'Oh, here you are,' she said, when I phoned her back.

'All okay?'

'Yes.' Katarina elongated the 's' sound, creating a hissing at the end of the line. 'Yes, I'm so good. Very good. It's strange over here, though.'

'How?'

She paused, thickly, and I could almost hear her thinking in her drunken state, everything slowed down, made more important. 'The others are weird with me,' she said. 'Not like usual. They don't like you. Apparently.'

'That's okay.' I had suspected as much – Tamsyn had launched a strange, almost 'what are your intentions with my daughter' investigation the previous week. It consisted of several glares and passive-aggressive comments, punctuated between questions on *Mulholland Drive*.

'No, it's not okay,' Katarina said.

There was a kind of heat in her words. I wished that I might be able to record it, so that, when she returned to her normal state, we could laugh about it, and I'd tell her it was sweet. An opportunity to prove my warmth.

'I miss you. It's silly you're not here. Why are you not here?'

'You're at Forest, right?'

'Yes.'

'Okay. If you want, I can be there soon.'

'Thank you thank you thank you,' she said.

'I'll be twenty minutes. Don't go anywhere else, or I won't be able to catch up.'

'Hey, hey. I literally couldn't, even if I wanted to.'

From the entrance of the bar, I could already see her, as if I were a homing pigeon. Katarina was the furthest away from the entrance, and was alone, one elbow lounging on the surface of the table. She was surrounded by empty glasses, marking the space where her friends had been sitting. Several men from the other tables were staring at her. Katarina looked around, almost wildly, noticing, and then smiled. 'Thank fuck you're here,' she said.

'Where did the others go?'

Katarina hugged me tightly, pulling us both towards the floor.

'I don't know.' Her arm was around my waist. 'I think they went to smoke at some point. Tom's place is five minutes away, anyway, so they've probably gone.' She looked up at me, and seemed small. 'It's okay,' she said. 'I told them you would get me.'

I rolled my eyes. 'Your friends are lovely. So considerate.'

She held on to me, and we began to walk towards the door. I could sense that Katarina had been a kind of spectacle there, and, by extension, I had become one too. She was warm, and there was sweat at the edge of her hairline. Her trainers made squeaking noises as she moved, letting go of my arm as she teetered towards the bar. 'I have money to give you,' she said to the bartender, waving dollar notes over her head, like a flag. Katarina always had money on her, from the Panera tips, doled out from tiny glass jars at the end of shifts.

I looked at her. 'Do you think, alcohol-wise, another drink makes sense?'

'No, no.' She shook her head. 'I have extra for him. For the time I was sitting there.'

The bartender, an exhausted man in a navy polo shirt, looked perplexed.

'Here,' Katarina said, sliding the money across the table: thirty dollars. 'Sorry for tonight.'

When we got outside, people were already scattered about the street, men leaning into each other in a way they would never do in the daylight. A soccer game had ended hours before. One group, a sea of red shirts, shouted at us as we stood waiting for the Uber. They called from the other side, and the sound became warped as the cars passed, one long jeer. Katarina pulled me closer, and I was unsure who the closeness was for.

'It's cold,' she said. Her legs were covered in a thin, filmy pair of tights. They had a split near the knee, and, as the car moved towards us, I realized that she had been cut, a line of blood making its way down from the top of her thigh.

'Katarina.' I tapped her shoulder. 'You're bleeding.'

She shrugged, and didn't even look down to where there was a steady, sticky stream of red.

In the Uber, we moved past brownstone buildings, the yellow drive-through signs, soccer fans and workers in uniforms. Katarina leaned her head against the window, still drunk, and closed her eyes.

'We'll sort something out when we get back home,' I said.

'What?'

'The cut. We'll fix it. I think I've got some plasters in the cupboard.'

'*Plasters*,' she said, in a terrible imitation.

'I don't sound like that.'

'You do to me.'

The driver had a photo of a dark-haired child on the dashboard, and a jelly-bean air-freshener at his head. He looked at Katarina in the mirror. 'I'll charge extra if she pukes,' he said.

'It won't happen.'

'Just saying. It's an extra thirty dollars if she does.'

'She won't.'

We stopped at the lights, and Katarina's face became orange. She looked sculpted, dazed. I thought about the impossibility of knowing what she was thinking, just as I noticed that her eyes were watering. 'They said that you were cold,' she said. 'My friends.'

We were five minutes from my street. The driver looked

between us in the mirror as I put a hand on Katarina's unhurt knee. 'I really don't mind any of that.'

'You should.'

'Well, obviously, they're your friends, so it matters. But they were never going to like me.'

'They have before,' she said, twisting her head further away, to get a new spot of the window on her face.

'Have they? With who?'

'My ex, last year.'

We said nothing, and the driver returned to staring at the road, and the picture of the child. The car's interior felt falsely sweetened, a coconut beach-scent doused around us. Katarina still managed, in her toppling, uneasy state, to tip the man on our way out of the vehicle. She stood behind me as I unlocked the front door, and I felt as if I could have been the drunk one, my key missing the lock over and over again as Katarina waited, unmoving, on the street.

As we walked inside, Katarina started to move with a kind of electricity. A strand had made its way out of the rest of her hair, dampened and curling at the edge, and her pupils were wide. There was a rabid quality about her. I got her a drink of water from the kitchen and handed it to her, making sure that we only touched for a few seconds, her sweaty palms pressed against me.

In the bedroom, she was almost swaying, the water in her hand held out, like a relic. I started undressing, back into my pyjamas.

'I still feel weird,' she said. She touched her stomach, and then her face.

I made a sympathetic noise, and went into the bathroom

briefly, to find her a plaster. I gestured that she should sit down on the bed, and she did, mercifully. Her cut had dried over, poking garishly through the black material of her tights, and I knelt and started wiping at it with a cloth.

'What are you doing?' Katarina asked.

I told her that I was helping as she continued to stare down at the mark in her skin. I was as gentle as possible; though when I returned to stand, I found that she was crying. 'Oh shit, Katarina,' I said. 'I'm sorry.'

She shook herself, and the sleeves of her dress went with her, bird-like. 'I'm just being stupid. Nobody's ever done that for me before.'

We were on tentative ground, and I could sense that we were swaying into something new, and previously untested. It was easier to think of her as someone happy, floating above it all, and this softened the worst moments of my guilt, the idea of her resilient, smiling face rising in spite of all the bad I could do. I shouldn't have been with her at all – I knew this – but, strangely, I couldn't deny myself.

'There are things you don't know, either,' Katarina said. 'Tom was saying all this stuff, about how his closeness with Damien was about them opening up, emotionally.'

'Didn't one of them cheat? Not that long ago, either.'

'That's not the point. They're happy, and it works.'

'I'm just saying, they're hardly the world's most stable couple.'

'And you know so much,' her lips moved rapidly, 'about what's healthy, and what isn't.'

'It's fine. We can talk about it in the morning.' I watched for her reaction in the half-dark. There was a stack of her clothing at the bottom of the bed, all folded up, for the next day.

Katarina shook her head. 'I have things to say now.'

I pulled the covers over my body, already lying back, and tapped the duvet, for her to join me. She lay on her side, a sheen over her neck, her face and the top of her arms. We were beyond physical closeness, then. I felt as if I could slip inside her skin, her brain, and stay there.

14

The woman had no children, a husband who worked in Chicago, and a perma-tan. She was her mother's friend. Katarina found this perplexing; no two women could be more different. She could not imagine, in any world, where the woman would ever be friends with the mother Katarina knew: long dresses in summer; no make-up; thick trousers in winter.

The first time the woman arrived to give her a lift, Katarina was outside the gymnasium. The woman pulled over in her Volvo, and wound down the window. During the drive, she complained about the cars in Illinois – 'There are no decent ones, out here' – and offered Katarina a can of soda, pointing to the glove compartment. 'Open it,' the woman told her. Inside, the can rolled around, warm and compressed. 'You can drink it, if you want,' she said.

Katarina watched her in the mirror, pink lips moving in the glass. 'That's nice, but I'm okay.'

'Go on.'

It wasn't that Katarina had no other options. Once, after gym class, she had kissed one of her classmates, the pair of them waiting for the other girls to file out the changing rooms. Neither of them told anyone, which was fine. Instead, Katarina looked at the back of the girl's head, the soft hair at the back of her neck, and made several promises: that she would become so beautiful that the girl couldn't help but stare, and be a little insulted, a little begrudged; that she would buy a house in Putnam County, with two storeys and a raised porch, and she would have a wife. The journey towards these objectives seemed less important than the knowledge that she *would* do it, that it would be done. She felt her body moving around her whenever she thought about it too much, running away.

Still, Katarina thought, sitting in the front seat of the woman's car several weeks later, she had something going for her.

The woman was humming to herself, and smiled when she caught herself in the rear-view mirror. 'Do you want to put something on?' she asked. 'We've got twenty minutes left, so we might as well.'

'Sounds good.' And then, afraid that the silence she fell into would be interpreted as a kind of ungratefulness, Katarina thanked her. The woman rolled her eyes, and pressed the button for the music.

'But I mean it, thank you,' Katarina said. 'You're saving me the bus. So, yeah.'

The woman shrugged and looked at the road. 'It's on my way back, anyway. And your mother,' she twisted the steering wheel, moving into another lane, 'helped me out when I was in a tight spot.'

The woman's red nails blurred as they went past gas stations and Evangelical church signs, the 'Jesus Saves' becoming a smear on the side of the road. 'Strange people,' the woman – who now insisted that she should be called 'proply', by 'Lacey' – said. They passed a billboard advertising television worship, a glitzy, soap-opera version of

Christ plastered to the front, all fake tan and white teeth. Lacey shook her head again. 'They're real strange. One of my neighbours – this stuffy woman with kids – goes to the mission there. Says there's a lot of dancing.'

Katarina moved around in her seat. She had just finished gym class and her old clothes were in a small bag by her feet. She was sure that she smelled bad, stale, and she made subtle attempts to prise the windows down, her fingers on the button.

Lacey looked at her again. 'You're a quiet kid. I used to be like that.' The woman made that humming sound again, off-kilter and to no perceptible tune.

In class, Katarina would think about Lacey, and the mood the woman would be in when she picked her up. She had the energy of what Katarina could only describe as belonging to an addict, women with long hair and wasted faces. There was an untrammelled rawness there which scared her. She saw it in those women, and in Lacey, too, and perhaps in herself: all shades of wrong.

They were ten minutes away from her house. Reaching the end of the street (Lacey never went inside; she did not want to bother Katarina's mother), the woman placed a hand on Katarina's back. As the car drove away, Katarina kept her upper body very still, very smooth.

Approaching her graduation, Katarina could count the times she would be with Lacey on one hand. Lacey, in the driver's seat, was tapping her fingers to an '80s hit. 'I used to dance to this on weeknights, in the centre on Sterling,' she said. 'Closed now, of course.' Closed, like the glass factory which had made the centre possible, the same factory which had employed Katarina's grandfather, and Lacey's father, too – now a little plaque under a billboard.

They drove past the high school building, past the other students and their tiny backpacks, bobbing in the distance, getting smaller. Katarina's friends all seemed much younger now. She had very little to say to them. The more fascinating Lacey became, with her odd, unfulfilling marriage, her addiction to Diet Pepsi, and her great, curving lash extensions, the more Katarina found herself dull by comparison, bored by her own voice.

'Did anything interesting happen today?' the woman asked.

Lacey typically wanted the highlights: cheating scandals; catfights out in the yard; teenage pregnancies. Katarina enjoyed the woman's shallowness; she wouldn't pretend, like other adults might, to be interested. She had to be on her game, embodying the stand-up, or the government official, wooing Lacey over. 'Mr Barratt got fired,' she said.

'What was he done for?'

'We don't know.'

Katarina looked over at the woman, who was facing right ahead, at the stretch of road. They passed uniform houses and beige fronts, all in neat rows. 'But,' Katarina continued, 'Daisy from the basketball team is saying that it's because he was with one of the girls in tenth grade.'

Across from her, Lacey reached a thinning, yellowed finger out to turn down the music. 'And was he?'

'I'm not sure. Maybe. Probably, actually. He had a funny look about him.'

'A "funny look"?'

'Yes.'

The drive went by quicker than usual, and Katarina felt untouchable, rising above it all. She did not thank Lacey when she got out of the car, and simply smiled at her as the woman stopped at the lights, gesturing at her to get out.

Katarina had a match, just before the summer, and there was nobody to collect her. Katarina's mother had taken to running a club for children whose parents worked late, leaving her own child (and she was still one, she had to admit, in her room, very late), somewhat dejected. Seeing the note about the game on the fridge, Katarina's mother knocked on the door. 'We could ask Lacey,' she said.

Katarina agreed, and pretended to look appropriately eager. It was difficult.

When the match ended, Katarina took out a spray – cheap vanilla, sweet – and placed it on her wrists and her neck, as she had seen people in shows do. She put the wrapper in the bin, and walked outside, where Lacey's car was already parked. Katarina looked at the woman's frame in the rolled-down window, the lit cigarette poised outside. The woman was just staring out, at the empty pitch, the end blowing hot-red. Katarina felt terribly lonely, looking at her. She made her way over in a half-skip, half-jog, to put another expression on Lacey's face.

'Hey, you,' the woman said, opening the door for her. 'How did it go? Did you get the fuckers?'

Lacey appeared like an Italian mobster, and Katarina laughed. 'No, we actually lost, five–two.'

'Ah.' Lacey stubbed the cigarette on the exterior of the car. Katarina watched her do it.

'Won't that make a mark?'

'Probably,' the woman said. 'It's Nathan's pride and joy, so I don't really care.' The grey ash stuck to the car's ceramic coating. It made a little blackened circle. Lacey looked over at Katarina before starting the car. 'Do you want to stop somewhere?' she asked.

'Where?'

'I can show you where I went to school. The building is gone now, but the whole space is still there.' Lacey shrugged her shoulders. 'Or I could drop you back. It's up to you.'

'God, no. Let's see it. I'd like to see it.'

The woman looked pleased; there were red patches on her cheeks. Katarina tried to see herself in the wing mirror, and did not mind the unsmiling outline of the woman who stared back.

Lacey tapped her fingers on the steering wheel. 'I could teach you how to smoke, if you're interested.' The woman was often saying things in this way, hedged by insecurities: if you want; maybe; whatever; if you're interested. Katarina found it touching.

'I'd like that,' she said.

'It's only because I used to spend so long, especially at your age, breathin' out. I'd take it to my lips, look around, like I was real brave, or something. What a waste.'

Katarina did not know where this old, almost Southern, intonation had emerged from, but it was exciting to hear such a difference, as if the woman had been changed just by the act of remembering.

They stopped the car in the retail store parking lot, where the woman's high school had once been. There was a grassy bank, the surface of the bank dehydrated and yellow from the sun. Lacey got out. Her heels made tiny, high-pitched sounds on the tarmac. She tottered over, like a doll. Across from them, there was a fast-food chain. Katarina watched the grey workers move around as Lacey sat beside her, as close as possible.

The woman pulled out a pack of cigarettes, unwrapped them, and threw the plastic behind her. 'Here you go,' she said, lighting one for her.

Katarina scrambled around in the grass for the wrapper, and shoved it in her pocket before accepting.

'You breathe in, like this,' Lacey was saying.

She looked at Lacey: frayed hair, red heels, skinny jeans bunched up at her waist. 'Why do you do this?' Katarina asked.

'What?'

'Like, all of this.'

'Do I need a reason? Can't I just be fucking nice?'

'Okay,' Katarina said. 'Thank you, then.'

'I can be nice. I am nice.' Lacey blew smoke into Katarina's eyes. 'It's like a muscle. You can forget, so I'm giving it some exercise. Do you see what I mean?'

She nodded, and Lacey reached her arm around Katarina. It was so sad, Katarina thought, that Lacey had to get affection in this way: not begging, but the opposite, so sure in Katarina's surrender that there was nothing to it, no risk. Lacey dusted the ash from Katarina's shirt, just below her collarbone. Then the woman kissed her, and it was sloppy, half saliva and half drugstore lipstick. Katarina did not move away, and kept her eyes on the blurry McDonald's sign, the cashier through the window.

She thought about what the cashier saw, the dirtied dollar notes under his fingers. She smelled it there, on the bank. She really did.

When they returned to the car an hour later, the woman was in high spirits, asking all sorts of questions about Katarina's plans for next year. She told the woman that this journey would be their last.

Lacey turned to the mirror. 'Thought so,' she said.

'I've only got one week left, and Mom's picking me up. She says it'll be good. Thank you, though, for everything so far. It was super nice of you to even do it.'

'That's sweet.'

Lacey lifted one hand off the wheel, inching towards her trouser pocket, searching for something. The car – red Volvo, ruined front – pulled up, right outside the house, where Katarina's mother stood at the window of her room, looking out. Katarina turned to Lacey. The woman had wrinkles at the corners of her eyes, little ridges in her face. 'Best get out,' she said.

'Of course.'

Katarina shut the car door. And even as she moved inside the house, towards her room, she imagined that Lacey was still outside, in the driver's seat, one corpse-like hand stuck out the window, letting the smoke out.

When Katarina finished talking, she looked young again, like a child. She held her knees to her chest and blinked quickly. The last of the sunlight cut through the carpet, creating a line through her body, yellow and pale. She looked unreal and almost ghostly. I did not want to touch her. I did not want to talk to her, either. The coldest, easiest option – Ignore her, my body pulsed, leave – stretched out. She looked so vulnerable, it was frightening. This dynamic – she the consoled, me the consoler – was too much. I had not been taught the language. I considered staying inches away from her on the carpet, then leaving, onto the street, the cool air whipping about me. But what kind of person would I be (and later, I wished I'd asked this question more) if this happened? What would that make me then?

I moved closer, as my body itched for the door. The fan, which had churned out sound throughout her tale, stopped whirring. 'It's okay,' I said.

Katarina nodded, and tried to smile. 'I just thought you should know, in the event I leave you for someone in an old folks' home.'

There wasn't enough humour in it to go around the room; the air was close, stale, and at our throats. I held the top of her head. 'I don't think it works like that.'

Katarina had more – she had not finished her unloading. Mystery is sometimes okay, I wanted to tell her, as her mouth opened again, it can be good. Yet she kept going. She told me that, at first, it was all some great joke, rolled out and performed for her friends over drinks – the two a.m. show, breathed out with bitter vodka breath. 'The whole thing was like, look who I could bag: a milf, and so on.' She smiled. 'It gave me credit with Tamsyn, in particular. And even back then, I felt flattered. She was good at making me feel flattered.'

I nodded.

'But whenever I go home,' she said, 'I'm so ashamed. And it gets less funny at the dinner table, or when I see the high school kids get out of class, and they're so young, I can't imagine – genuinely, cannot imagine – feeling anything but irritation when looking at them.' Katarina's head was bowed. The hairs on the back of her head and her neck moved under my breath.

'I don't know why I went along with any of it,' she said. 'I guess I just thought I was ugly. And that I should take the attention whenever I could get it.'

I felt her need to be weighed down, my head slotting neatly onto her shoulder. I could sense each movement of hers, how alive, and beautiful, it all was. The window was closed. Underneath me, Katarina made a silent request, which was really my request, too, a kind of begging: please be nice to me. Just be fucking nice.

15

In the lecture hall, the usual suspects sat in the front row – Katarina, myself, Lars and Jules. A shrew-like boy talked about his viral video with Lars, his voice just audible over the removal of laptops and the opening of cellophane packets. The week before, the boy had convinced a construction worker to sell his Carhartt jacket to him for thirty dollars. It caused a minor sensation on campus – some were appalled by the politics of the thing, the sheer spectacle of the older man, removing the brown canvas material off his back, to be handed the stale cash.

'It was the perfect amount of distressed,' the student told us, as we waited for the lecturer to arrive. 'I had to ask – and I couldn't believe it, when he actually took the money.' The boy's new jacket, his relic, poked over his open bag, while he described, with a great smile, the man's walk back to the scaffolding, his T-shirt damp in the rain. 'For just thirty dollars,' he said again.

Our regular adviser, a grey-haired, corduroy-blazer-wearing cliché of a man, was ill. His replacement, we had been informed by email, had arrived from the city to discuss 'art' across 'cultures and histories'. Our replacement arrived late, after the 'Carhartt-stealer' (as affectionately named by the institute's Communist Society) had repeated his tale twice.

The hall was poorly attended, though the students who did arrive were always on death's door. The space quickly became a soundtrack of coughs and sniffles, and the lecturer, who was without a satchel, or notes of any kind, said a quiet 'Bless you' as he walked through the door. He wore avocado socks, neon and jarring alongside his brown suit and brogues. He raised a hand to us, said, 'Hi, I'm Jo,' and clicked on the projector screen.

'I'm going to put an image up here, now' – Jo did so, with a dramatic flourish – 'and I'd like you all to take a guess at the figure.'

A woman with a white, rounded face looked down at us from the institute's projector. Her eyes were large. There were no cheekbones of any kind: it was as if she had been formed from dough, rolled out onto the painting's surface. The woman was all paleness and no uniqueness. She could have been anyone.

Jo gestured towards our row. 'Any takers?'

A few hands, a few guesses: Mother Teresa; Lady Gaga; Mona Lisa's ugly cousin (a few laughs).

'Perhaps this will help.' Jo clicked through other paintings, other women, of no uniform shape or skin colour. With each slide, it was as if we were being presented with a new, entire woman, paintings moving from oils to watercolours, imitations of the greats, the Manets and Picassos and Rembrandts.

'Does this clarify anything?' Another image, a dark-skinned woman in royal blue.

Jo shook his head at our silence. 'It's funny,' he said, 'when

I visited NYU, they had no idea, just like you all.' There was a hint of a y'all, there, aborted early, in self-consciousness. 'But Brigham, Utah, got it from the first slide.

'The purpose of my specialism, you might be interested to know, is tracking both minor and significant "cultural shifts" through painting. Which is, I admit, super vague – what even is a "cultural shift", anyway? It's like the word "zeitgeist" (which should be banned).' He smiled. 'But I believe that one of the easiest ways of monitoring turns in centuries – what Marx calls "epochs" – is through a single figure. By following that figure, we can interpret a great deal about its culture.'

The room sat a little more upright. A student moved her open bag of Cheez-Its under a chair.

'The great philosopher *Grimes* once said,' Jo revealed an image of the musician, posing for paparazzi with *The Communist Manifesto* in hand, 'that art is not made in a vacuum. That artists bring every work to it, in both the process and the finished product. Derrida, too, says something similar about language: when we say *anything*, x means y, we bring with it everything x does *not* mean. And so everything contains the ghost of all words and phrases, all artworks before us.'

Jo took another look at the manifesto-reading millionaire, smiled, and changed the presentation back to the painting. 'I'm getting away from today's topic: these women.' The next slide contained a cross-section of portraits, varying races, most cloaked, their hands tucked into their sides, or reaching out to the viewer, in surrender.

'And, now I'll spoil it for you.' He moved on to a final slide, one haloed woman and her son.

'It is, of course, the Virgin Mary. No woman – in the Western world, at least – has been painted more. From Banksy's *Toxic Mary*, feeding her child the waste we produce, to Chris Ofili's work, crafted from pornographic magazines, we have painted her.'

Jo turned to an image of a young girl, the front of her face shining, the rest of her hidden beneath blue cloth. Her eyelids were purplish, dark, the tips of her lips red. Everything – every potential beauty – was heightened, face inhuman in the darkness.

'*The Blue Madonna*,' Jo said, 'Carlo Dolci. Mid seventeenth century.' He stepped away from the podium and joined us. Throughout the room, the students started to type furiously, the buttons sounding like rainfall in the old hall. 'Just,' Jo began, and pointed at the painting, 'give this your full attention. I know several of you – the lucky art historians in the room – are graded, and your notes might function as a form of revision. I understand. But, for just one moment, put it aside, and look.'

Katarina leaned closer to me, and put her mouth to my ear. 'I like him,' she said. Onscreen, the woman looked down at us, her expression unchanged.

'There is so much we can already interpret,' Jo said, 'in our *Madonna*. Perhaps, in her face, you see innocence or a softness.' He pointed at Lars. 'Or you might see nothing interesting at all, just another woman, the light in her face not godly, no – but a product of the light from the candle, which we can assume is held outside the frame.'

Lars moved closer to the screen, and cleared his throat, as if he were about to dispute the interpretation. But Jo waved a hand, and changed the image. 'We can hold space for both interpretations, of course. And I consider getting you all just to stop, and look – you, the camera-ready, Kardashian-watching generation – a victory in itself.

'You'll notice that, as we move into the late Middle Ages and beyond, the images become less centred on the Madonna alone, and more about her relationship with her son.'

A child's finger, looping round a slightly larger one. A curved nose, looking down at a strange flesh-mass of a baby, with adult features. Jo was right: even the woman's gaze had shifted; where the paintings used to stare at us, or at an indiscernible spot in the distance, she now looked at the child in her hands. 'Here, the people,' he pointed at us, 'do not wish to see her as remote, instead emphasizing her human qualities.' As Jo moved through the next slides, the woman's face started to stretch out, her cloak expanded, in a stop-motion video of enlargement.

'The reason I started this strange project,' he said, 'is that it offers me the chance to study the Madonna as some kind of vessel. She is a historical record, of sorts, which time carves itself into.' The students all started to type again. 'And looking at this – Murillo's *Immaculate Conception*, or Lippi's *Madonna and Child* – you would assume that these portrayals are natural: that's just what she looks like.

'When Carlo Dolci was crouched in his studio, with the sawdust, and the oil, blue arrived onto his canvas – not because it was *natural*, or in-built in him to do so – but because it was part of the Medici family's history, that lapis lazuli be associated with riches, and "higher" qualities, like heaven.

'And the whole series of portraits, *Madonna and Child*, *Virgin and Son*, etc., emerged following Tyndale's translation of the Bible, personalizing the text, which had started to reveal Jesus as human, Jesus as *like us*. It follows, then, that his mother would be as of our "fleshy substance" as possible.' Jo flicked his own skin with his hand. 'Which leads us, finally, to the idea of the female body.

'We can see from these paintings that we start to move away from depicting Mary as stick-thin, to larger, more plump versions. This, too, follows a historic – or, rather, economic – pattern, which prizes fat as the most beautiful female form.

'You see,' Jo continued, 'everything we think we know to be inherent – thin as model, thin as the standard – is yet another product. And if something can be made, it can be unmade. The stasis of history' – Lars rummaged for his notebook in a wild panic, his pen hovering – 'is constructed to give us the illusion that things have been this way, have always been this way. And the study of our figure, the Madonna, reveals that.'

Jo turned off the projector. Its startling blackness showed our faces, laptops cutting off our limbs. 'Any questions?'

After a coffee, and an argument between Lars and Katarina (was Jo an intellectual poser, a 'pseud' or an available genius?), Katarina and I walked back to her flat. We looped around artificial grass, tennis players with rippling muscles and a quiet environmental protest. Their bubble-lettered signs pulsed in the air. An image of our campus, consumed by flames, lifted in the wind. Katarina ran over to catch it, and stopped to talk – good day, yes, good luck with the boycott – while she handed over the poster. It was remarkable, the lengths she went for strangers; the complete urgency with which she moved, sweating for the students' sake. When she returned, breathing heavily from her jog, I asked if her obvious moral superiority bothered or flattered her.

I felt proud of the question.

'What are you even talking about?' she said, laughing. 'No one else says stuff like that in real life.'

'It has to bother you, though.'

She started walking faster, towards the main street. 'I don't care about that,' she said. 'A relationship isn't, like, a moral exam.'

She was lying; she did care. Katarina often described people's 'kindnesses' first, opening her description with some great tale of their good character. When describing the artists she admired, she would begin with, 'They're a fascinating person, honestly,' and would complete her opinion with a wondrous event: Wisconsin water park, late August, 1997, where he ditched his pastel paints and dived in to save hordes of sticky, screaming children. She took 'stuff like that', then, very seriously.

Even Katarina's dedication to lesbianism had a moral quality to it: for her, being a lesbian involved a political feeling, a commitment not just to fucking, or six-hour-long dates, but to a wider ethical movement, in which she imagined herself, and myself, holding hands with Ruth and Cece and Chloe and Olivia and Lily. She was constantly telling me to 'expand': to 'expand' my idea of goodness, to 'expand' my definition of 'the important things'. Plenty of things were Our Business, according to Katarina. Katy, moving out of the two-storey apartment block on South Street: Our Business. The closure of Wisconsin's only community centre: Our Business. It was like her church, her congregation: her seeing eye, with fingers in Livingston County and Pendleton and Leavenworth. She was the most religious person I knew.

Katarina did not appreciate this comparison.

'It's not the same, at all,' she said, as we walked into her apartment block. 'Don't get me mixed up with them.'

Then it was probing time for Katarina, the return of the dangerous hour. She sat on the bed, smile lines deep, and said nothing, her typical questions abandoned. I looked at her. It was as if she were waiting for a confession.

'You're stressing me out,' I said.

Katarina held on to my left hand, and started tapping my knuckles. 'What did you really mean,' left hand, third knuckle, 'earlier, on the walk back? About me being better?'

'I don't know.'

She said nothing.

'Okay,' I kissed her cheek, where her skin was raised, rough under my lips, 'I just think you're kind.'

'So are you.' Katarina started to laugh as I made a face. 'My God, that makes you so uncomfortable, doesn't it? I have discovered,' she said, 'a complex.'

'No complexes.'

'Liar.'

When I left for the bathroom, attempting a quick exit – 'Sorry, I'll be back in a second, just need to pee' – I looked back, and saw that she was following me.

'I've really hit something here,' she said.

'I'm just not like you.' I looked at the tiles. 'I'm not going to save a pug from the wheels of a car, or anything like that.'

'That's not right at all,' she laughed. 'You have such a strange way of seeing things.' And then, eager to correct me, she said, 'I used to move my mom's things around the house.'

'Unforgivable.'

'No, no,' she flushed, 'for months and months, I'd take her lipstick – black cherry, her favourite – and would hide it under the sink, or I'd roll it under the table.'

'Come on, Katarina,' I poked her side as she flicked the bathroom light on, then off, in a slow blink, 'that's nothing.'

'You don't understand. It was crazy. I even got my brothers in on it, and we'd say things like, "Didn't you leave it there yesterday?" And she'd be so tired, she'd nod, and we'd sit around laughing at her while we could hear her searching downstairs for the next thing we'd hidden – her mascara, or watch, or something.'

'All kids play games.'

'Oh man,' she leaned back, 'we'd even laugh at her accent. After a while, with all of us doing it together, she started to change it, until everything sounded rehearsed. Which only made us get at her more.' Katarina looked at the floor. 'I don't think I ever saw her as properly human, until I left home. It's so embarrassing to admit, but it's true.'

Katarina touched my waist, and said, as if the two were connected across the Atlantic, her remorse and mine, 'I'm sorry about your dad.' She held on to me as I tried to move away from her, and the conversational whiplash. 'I know I've said it before,' she continued.

'You have.'

'But I want to say it again.'

I closed my eyes. It must have been convincing: I was so ashamed, it almost felt like grief. Yet when I looked at her, in all her innocence, blue dress and splotched shoulders, I knew the lies were worth it.

'Thank you,' I said.

I slept for the rest of the day in her bed. It was already dark by the time I woke up. Katarina was gone, her things – pearly strings, half-finished projects – lined up on the shelves. When she walked in, she had changed into a low-cut top. Some form of butter, or cream, made the skin around her collarbones – her prized physical feature, she once confessed – shine. I reached one groggy hand for her to take, while she fumbled around with necklaces on her bedside table.

'Up,' she said, her hand warm. 'We've got to meet the gang.'

'The gang.' I groaned. 'Tamsyn included?'

'Sadly.' She sat on top of me, kissing me before I could move away, dirtied by sleep.

'I can never tell how much you actually like them.'

'Who?'

'Your friends – Tamsyn especially. She's a deeply confusing person.'

'I don't like her all the time, of course.' She shrugged. 'I mean, she called my *Oranges* project' – a canvas littered with orange peelings – 'derivative. That was the word she actually used.'

'Does she get any nicer?'

'When it's just us, and the others are gone, yes.'

I thought I understood. Because Katarina did not like Tamsyn very much – objectively, as a person – she did not have to perform for her. It was a space where she could be cruel, laugh along, with very little judgement. There were no stakes. 'Anyway,' Katarina said, 'Tamsyn's Tamsyn.'

And indeed she was: when we reached the bar, Tamsyn was leaning over a drink, her wooden crucifix dangling into the black liquid. She wore it for 'aesthetic reasons', she was quick to say. 'I'm into Catholic-grunge-core right now.'

The others nodded.

It was, to my horror, open mic night, where the usual 'nostalgic' '90s hits had been replaced by trust-fund babies discussing their acts of poverty-tourism or their dog's final expression in the arms of New York State's best veterinarian.

'Next,' Tamsyn said, 'she's going to discuss how she's a moth, and how her father never loved her.' She laughed as the student opened her mouth again, swaying side to side in time with her line breaks: 'brown wings/ hit me/ like on that/ day'. The poet looked over at our table as Tamsyn continued a performance of her own: those large, almost fantastical, cackles. She was like my perverse twin, but with more expensive clothing.

The poet continued. 'Batted/ black eyes/ of no comfort,' she recited, feedback ringing. It made me viscerally, frightfully embarrassed. A shout of 'Don't give up the day job' would have been uttered minutes, if not seconds, into a recital of this kind in Lichfield.

Once the poet had finished, there was a round of polite applause, and Tamsyn clapped her hands together in an exaggerated movement. 'I wonder what it takes,' she said, looping an arm around Jules, 'to deliver stuff like that.'

Katarina moved around in her seat. 'Confidence,' she said, at the same time as Tamsyn's 'delusion'.

I tried to think better of Tamsyn. It helped to imagine her young, and ashamed. From a deeply conservative family, pastor father, Bible-study-fanatic mother, crying to the *But I'm A Cheerleader* VCR once the parents had gone to bed. But this could only take me so far. Each time I looked at her, I forgot my resolution to be kind, and the image of the child vanished. Jesus was wrong: you couldn't love everybody; at least, you couldn't love Tamsyn Saunders, even if you were trying to be good.

Onstage, we witnessed a tale of sexual subjugation, a trip to a Congolese river and a discontinued line of Pop-Tarts – 'A red/too artificial for/ you, America'. The poet gave a little nod, and left the stage, before another student walked over to the microphone. She was frighteningly young, and described hands twisting around a beer bottle. The room fizzed, and descended into quiet. It was good, her poem. The kind that drew several members out of conversation, and then more, dragging the students along. Even I could see that she had somehow lifted herself from mediocrity.

It infuriated Tamsyn, this artistic trick. She looked personally aggrieved by the poet's success. 'I'm going to get another drink.' She stared at me. 'You want one?'

'I'm okay, thank you.'

When Tamsyn returned, there was an alarming energy to her movements. I watched each gesture of hers – the extending of her fingers, the way she threw her head back before laughing. If I could study her, if I could take down each moment, I might be able to prevent a potential explosion. Tamsyn handed me a glass and slammed her own down. 'I got one for you,' she said.

'You didn't have to do that.'

'I wanted to.' She smiled, and even that was infused with an infernal wickedness. I thought about poking her in the eye with her crucifix. How it might have bulged in its socket, the eye, yellowish pus ruining her face. Tamsyn pushed the drink closer towards me. 'You need it, anyway. I hear you've been going through a rough time.'

That 'rough time' allusion: my father, alive as could be, watching *Pointless* in the living room with a Guinness in hand.

'Come on,' Katarina said. 'Let's not.'

Tamsyn looked at me. 'I'm just saying, we're all here for you.'

'That's kind.'

There was an ache in the roof of my mouth. I pressed my tongue flat against the bridge. I knew, by the cadence of Tamsyn's voice, and her thrumming fingers against the table, that she had not finished.

'Though it is weird,' she continued (because, of course she did), 'how quickly you two,' Tamsyn pointed at Katarina, 'got together. Like, scarily quick. And you seem so damn pleased with yourself.'

'I don't know what you're talking about. Last year, you literally moved in with Katie after five days. Five days,' Katarina said.

'It's just strange is all. How you don't seem that sad. I mean, if my dad –'

Katarina said something – her voice was quiet, and it had no weight, competing against the microphone, the glasses and Tamsyn's restlessness. The three of us could only look on, as the discomfort settled at the table.

'If my dad were gone,' Tamsyn said again, placing

emphasis on that final word, dead as a stone, 'I'd feel insane. Totally scooped out. I wouldn't be able to chill, or smile, or fuck, or anything.' She jabbed a finger my way, one pointed index. 'I know grief. I do. And this is not it.'

'What the fuck, Tamsyn?' Katarina said.

I decided to be generous. I had no leg to stand on. I might have congratulated Tamsyn on her remarkable detective skills, had she not been as abhorrent as congealed blood. 'It's okay,' I told Katarina. 'Don't worry about it.'

Tamsyn continued her tirade, louder now, doubling-down: she's disrespectful; totally inserting herself in the group; talentless, anyway. I'd never seen the woman so upset. She looked moments away from crying. People were always frustrated, whenever their vision of suffering – eyes permanently stinging; a constant, and mournful, discussion of the dead – was contradicted by another's. There were moments when we were all taken over by Victorian ideas of propriety: there was a right and a wrong way to go about things, even grief.

Sitting at the table, charges levied, I thought that I would quite like to go back home. I had to fight this thought at the strangest of times: empty apartment, standing by the window. Yes, I'd like to go home. And it was easier to imagine the place when away from it, my mother, laundry in hand, walking upstairs. When I looked up again, I became startled by the surroundings: dim light, empty glasses, the word 'tepid' repeating from the stage.

Jules smiled politely – it was just us, the others had gone. I did not know anything about her, beyond the 'big three': her course name (History of Art 3A); her hometown (somewhere in Northern Vermont); her friendship group (us). She touched her neck, then reached across the table for my hand. 'Sorry about that,' she said. 'Tamsyn just got rejected for a showing, so.'

'I get it.'

Another nervous neck touch. 'And there's something going on at home, with money, and I think it's getting to her.'

'Sure.'

'I heard her on the phone, and she was genuinely upset about it. But she keeps spending anyway. You know how she is. Her eBay habit.' She spoke as if we had all been friends for decades – age-old friends, unconditional forgiveness. 'Anyway, she's not like that normally.'

I lifted Jules's sweaty palm, which had been resting on mine. I inspected the short nails, short fingers, and dropped it back onto the table. She leaned back in surprise. 'Jules,' I said, 'don't bullshit me. I know exactly what she's like.'

A fucking cunt, I might have added, and I imagined, not for the first time, gathering all the saliva in my mouth, and expelling it, projectile-style, into her open eyes. Doing the same in her hair. My mouth watered, my tongue rolled, and I almost did it. Instead, I folded my hands in front of me, like I was in the front row at church. And, if there is a divine balance to be checked, and upheld, I would like Him to refer to that moment of restraint, and the others which were to follow: my smiles upon Tamsyn's return, not a disparaging word from either of us.

We walked back together, wet grass getting into our shoes. Katarina was remarkably silent. I tried to loop my arm around hers. She smelled like cherries, and damp. Her free hand shook, and her shirt lifted up in the wind. She looked like the ghost of Christmas Future, forcing me to change: repent, and you will be forgiven.

'I'm not proud of myself,' she said. 'I sat there, saying nothing, while she went on and on and on.' Katarina was so uncomfortable, viscerally so, the kind of upset only those used to being good could feel. She looked flushed with the effort of her self-flagellation.

'It wouldn't have done anything. Tamsyn's never liked me, anyway.'

Katarina looked unconvinced.

'Genuinely. Did I ever tell you about that time she said I was "experimenting" with you?'

'No.'

'It was really funny,' I said. 'She basically accused me of faking this whole thing.' I touched her waist. 'Like a fucked-up performance.'

Katarina smiled, and leaned in closer. 'Super convincing, if so.'

'Thank you.'

She shook her head, and pulled us onto her street. A man stood at the edge of the pavement, holding a can. He shouted at us – a few incoherent words, a punching movement with his hand – and Katarina moved even faster towards her front door. She looked skittish, thrown off-balance by one stream of discomfort after another.

'Tamsyn is right, in a way,' she said, now inside, pulling her shirt over her head. 'Not what you think. It's not bad, I mean,' Katarina quickly added. 'Just that things don't seem to affect you.'

'Now that's definitely not true.'

'I mean, the guy outside. You didn't even bat an eye.' Her hair fell over her face. I tucked it back. 'I think it's strange,' she said, 'how, if you're like us, you have to have some baseline of confidence to even date.'

We were in New York State, site of American progressiveness, beyond both our ancestors' dreams, and so on. Yet I understood her completely.

'What if I was a coward?' Katarina said.

'You're not.'

'What if I was? It doesn't make sense, that for the rest of our lives, we have to actively be unafraid.' Katarina wrestled into her pyjama top. She looked jittery, restless, though she had not drunk enough. Her drunkenness typically followed a pattern: humming, at random; flirtatiousness; then, finally, melancholy. We had bypassed several steps.

I felt drained; her thinking was infectious. I didn't know if I had it in me, all the effort required to be together, to be myself, the daily relentlessness of it. I turned off the main light, as Katarina's shadow shifted into bed. We lay under the covers, arms touching. She pressed her fingers into mine, whispered 'Goodnight', and apologized again.

I watched her mouth move, the dark wetness of it. I squeezed her hand.

'I've been thinking,' I said. Time for honesty, an 'I've lied to you, I'm so sorry' – or, at least, a brief reference to a potential separation. But the mere idea of being alone, without her, made the back of my neck damp. I moved closer.

'I've been thinking about your holiday idea,' I said.

'And?'

'Let's do it.'

16

It was easy, in the end – our first (and last) holiday together. Katarina was in charge of the flights, and the accommodation, which she found through an app. You could stay anywhere in the world, in exchange for a little work: some upkeep around the garden, farming, cleaning, dog-sitting. Katarina found a house in Villalago, a town in the province of Abruzzo, Italy. She said she wanted to see where Palizzi painted. I tried not to laugh at this, and hid my face in my hands. We were to stay in Abruzzo for three weeks, returning in time for the summer term in May.

'We're 46C and B,' she said, as we reached the airport tunnel. 'Ready to go?'

She was, of course, adept at flying, as she was most things. She even made conversation with the woman opposite us on the aisle: insurance worker, cancer survivor, two grandchildren in college. The pair talked for several hours, while Damien and Tom kicked the back of our seats. We could hear Tom's low, exuberant chatter, and Damien's silence. Flying over Boston, Tom made several unsuccessful attempts to engage us in conversation, his nauseating cheese-and-onion Pringles making their way towards our seats.

I suppose we were all evenly matched, then. Katarina and Tom, the energized pair. Damien and myself: quiet, weighed down by our lacklustre personalities, in comparison to our partners. It was impossible to think about the other couple's merits without thinking about our own shortcomings. Katarina and I were too unusual, too intense. I thought that other people just knew how to do things, how to go about intimacy and create relationships, as if everyone had a rulebook I didn't have access to.

It was a long flight. Four hours in, Katarina waved to a baby; a short, exclamation-filled exchange followed, and Katarina was handed the wriggling, red-faced bundle from the air. The child went back to its mother between Dublin and Paris, leaving Katarina to fall asleep on my shoulder for the rest of the journey. The weight of her head was comforting. I looked back at her often, to remind myself that she was there.

We arrived in Rome, in the heavy warmth of Fiumicino airport. Katarina and I went to the duty-free stores, while Tom and Damien sweated and searched for their bags: a black rucksack and a zippable tote bag, which was, as we had been told by Tom, 'really in'.

When we returned, the couple were at opposite ends of the conveyor belt, separated in their suffering, their hands always reaching for an item in just the wrong shade. After picking up another wrong item, Tom started to shout, over several children in baseball tees, that it was 'insane' and 'typical as hell' for Damien to have packed 'the most basic bag there is'. Around us, children squeaked in white trainers, their parents arriving running, bags in hand, from the smoking area, to drag their progeny by their shirts.

Tom and Damien, having found their items, weighed up

the benefits of going for a drink before we left – remotely, as if they were preparing for a debate.

'Cons: drunk?'

'Pros: also drunk?'

Katarina stood to one side, on her phone, tapping furiously. She took my hand, and Tom's. 'We're headed this way, out the exit over there.'

'Of course, Mother,' Tom said.

The four of us walked towards the bus terminal. A series of vibrant orange vehicles were lined up ahead, and we boarded, Katarina handing out water bottles from her bag. We moved past the airport, the power-plant glass building and the thin roads became a rush of green hills, the bus jolting to accompany the turns, changing from English-translated signs into pure Italy: *Viale Italia*, *Via del Rio*, *Fion le Mura*.

The bus stopped outside a train station, where we got off, Katarina looking more perplexed the closer we got to the station's brownstone entrance. 'I'm not sure about this,' she said. 'The map said it's here, but,' she held up her phone screen, her evidence, 'it doesn't look the same at all.'

Damien stared at the phone, then at us, the waves of green foliage and decaying signs. 'The thing is telling us it's twenty minutes, right?'

Katarina nodded. There were no cars on the road; we were blissfully, and inconsolably, separate from it all.

Tom kicked his sandals into the gravel. 'We'll sort it out. We should just start walking in one direction, and ask.' Everyone accepted this: he had a breeziness, an unfazeability, which was addictive.

Walking at the edge of the road, on a stretch of faded grass, like a biblical image, we practised our Italian from the white light of Damien's phone.

'Toilet?'

'*Bagno*,' we chorused.

'Thank you?'

'*Grazie*.'

Damien's language-learning prompts became increasingly inventive. 'So, I'm at a market stall,' he said. 'You've handed your change over. What do I say next?'

'Have a *buona giornata*,' I got in, just as Katarina started to say something. The botched, Americanized Italian drove the birds away.

It was significantly longer than twenty minutes, the walk to find the first person in Villalago. When the gravel became smooth road, the pine trees gave way to a small shop, a patio at the front. An older man in a white shirt was smoking, staring at us. He waved one wrinkled palm in our direction, as Damien, the most proficient in Italian, sweated, and attempted to ask for directions.

Damien returned to us a little shinier, a little more stressed, than he had been before. 'Dude says it's further this way. And then he might've said something about turning left, and left again.'

Tom smiled. 'Okay. We can work with that.'

'But then,' Damien continued, 'he said something about eggplant, and my mom. So,' he lifted his hands, 'I don't know.'

'Maybe it's the accent,' Katarina offered. 'And your mother is fine, so he could have sensed that, just by looking at you.' (Katarina was an enormous fan of the 'your mother' school of joke. The second time we had met, she had said unspeakable things about what she would do to my own mother, and I hadn't the heart to tell her, in all her feverishness, that she was gone.)

Tom was staring at Damien with an exaggerated expression of hopelessness. 'I can't believe we're relying on you this whole trip,' he said. 'What grade did you get last semester?'

'A low B.'

Tom fell to his knees in the dirt path, as Katarina started to laugh.

Standing next to them, I felt as if I had been introduced to another mode of living. I was able to watch it all, with a peacefulness. I wasn't interested in the low-level panic surrounding our whereabouts: the unnamed, unmappable area of the Abruzzo province. Katarina handed me her backpack, walked over to the smoking man, and thanked him with a perfunctory '*grazie*', before pointing to her phone. She showed him a photograph of the villa, and typed out the street name on her Notes app.

'I know it,' the man said. '*È lì che prendo i miei pomodori.*' He looked at us. 'Tomatoes,' he said again, this time in English.

'This guy is far too into vegetables,' Tom said.

A left, and several roads, our shoes chalky from the paths: the farm. Katarina broke away from our group first, moving towards the gate in a little half-jog. 'This has got to be it,' she shouted.

'Thank fuck.' Tom jumped onto Damien's back, and they teetered over.

*

The first thing I noticed – and what I will always notice, thinking back on that little spot in Villalago – was the cicadas, the slight, off-tune beating of those insects. It was an immediate symptom of the space's difference from its surroundings, the empty roads giving way to sound, energy. We all filed through the gate like animals, and looked up. The villa had been painted yellow, the tiling newest at the front, greyish towards the back. I stood beside Katarina, her arm outstretched to knock on the door. I kissed her temple, her cheek, and told her she had done a good job. 'With finding it, and booking, and getting us here. Thank you.'

She kissed me back, even though her friends were there, even though there was someone inside the house, and we could hear them approaching through the ground-floor windows.

The door opened, and our host emerged – late sixties, dark hair gone to grey, a loose, black dress falling to the very edge of her feet. She smiled as Damien and Katarina stepped forward. 'Come in, come in,' she said. She hugged us in turn, warm, like a beloved schoolteacher. Her words were accented, almost musical. 'I hope you had no problem getting here. Our last guests left two days ago. They had issues.'

The woman's name was Giulia, and we were to call her that. 'None of the Mrs, or I will go insane.' She placed her hands on Katarina's shoulders, forcing her to sit. Giulia poured us coffee, and we received it like an offering. The whole thing was mystical – the house, her. The space was lived-in, despite the décor, and had been dusted with ancient Roman mock-ups, vases with wrestlers caught in arms, well-used sofas either side of us. We were given a short history of the land: bought by her father in 1916, built in the 1860s, just as the unification began. Pointing out the low, open windows, Giulia reminded us all of the scheme: we were to work in the garden for at least three hours each morning, returning to have our lunch, which would be prepared by herself. 'Rest day on Sunday,' she told us. 'There's a piazza twenty minutes from here. And a church on Via Vincenzo.'

Tom was leaning back on the sofa, his eyes shut. 'That's amazing,' he said. 'Amazing. I personally love God,' he said. His boyfriend kicked him, as our schoolmaster, Giulia, watched us drink birdishly, eyes focused on our lips meeting the cup, our turns in expression, bitterness to pleasure.

'Do you like it?' she asked me.

'It's excellent.'

Giulia nodded. 'I will leave some outside your room tomorrow.' She smiled. 'But now, I will take you to your rooms.'

I liked her certainty, and the general strength it implied. It might have been a language barrier, the easily conjugatable words – 'you will' – but it was impossible to imagine our host as insecure, unsure of herself and her own expression.

She led us to a windowless hallway, cream walls and wooden doors. Giulia started opening each room, circling back to pick up our luggage and throwing it through the open doors. 'There you go,' she said.

Katarina looked at our allocations: a door each. 'I thought the website said there were only two rooms available?'

The woman looked at us, smiling. 'That was for my friends, if they were staying too. Or when I don't like the guests, shared rooms only.'

Here, Katarina called up all the sweetness in her face, that relentless chiding. 'Giulia,' she said, almost clasping the woman's hand, 'that's so nice. So nice. But we don't need the space.'

'*Piccolo è bello*,' Damien said.

I made a note to ask him what it meant after dinner.

Giulia just shook her head again. 'No. You'll stay there.' She pointed to the room closest to us, and then to Katarina. 'You, there,' Damien, and the room next to her.

'Part of the fun would be bunking up, like kids again, you know what I mean?' Tom said. The couple were standing close together, Tom's bare skin touching the outside of Damien's shirt. Perhaps Giulia knows, I thought. It was possible: her insistence was on the edge of both kindness and violence.

'You Americans,' she said.

It was a phrase which I was to hear many times that holiday: Giulia, smiling down at Katarina; in the face of our tastes, Damien's hatred for broccoli, and anything green. Any slight oddity she detected in us. You Americans. 'You can't accept the good,' Giulia said. 'Always looking for the bad, *intrigante*.'

I stepped away from Katarina. Though there was no natural light in the hallway, the rooms were wide and spacious, and the windows allowed for a syrupy kind of light to come through.

'Okay,' Giulia said, 'I'll leave you all now.'

17

We walked into Katarina's room first, the three of us watching her unpack. Tom had a hand in Damien's belt loop, unencumbered by the open door. Katarina took out her folded clothes: dark blue shirts, cut off at the sleeves; shorts; a linen dress I had bought her; wrap tops in varying shades of green. She stood back once she had sorted everything, proud of her work, outfits arranged into Giulia's furniture. 'I'm done,' she said.

Damien and Tom decided to leave, and 'practise their Italian'. Five minutes later, we heard moans from the next room. Katarina banged on the side of the door, and went for a shower, leaving me to lie back on the bed.

Her room was light, minimalist. There was a painting of a vineyard to the left of the window, which overlooked the farm. I picked up the Italian dictionary on the bedside table and chose words at random. Whole: *intero*. Own: *propio*. Chicken: *pollo*. Katarina walked back into her room, making the air thick, and smelling of pomegranate. A pale pink towel twisted around her body.

'Hey,' she said, and joined me on top of the sheets, her hair dripping water onto the pillow, my side of the bed.

'Everything is so good,' she said. 'It couldn't be more perfect.'

Giulia was preparing the dinner already; a sweetened, garlicky scent was making its way through the villa, towards us.

Katarina turned, so that we were facing each other, mirrors together, her face where my face was, her legs in line with mine. She put her hands around my stomach. There was something terrified, and lonely, in her face.

'What are you thinking about?'

'Nope,' she said. 'Nope.'

'Come on.' I patted the top of the bed, as if that action might convince her.

'It's probably stupid,' she said. 'I'm like a thousand per cent sure it is.'

'Might as well say it anyway.'

She rolled her eyes. 'It's so nice here,' she said.

'It is.'

'So nice it's, like – this is it. This is the best it'll be. And there's only worse things afterwards.' Katarina appeared tired from her shower. Her skin was warm.

I understood: every good thing had a nostalgic quality to it, an ending in it. I had infected Katarina with my brand of malaise, passed from my tongue to hers. I looked at her: too much heat; the French windows; no breeze, or relief. This is it, she had said.

'Do you just want me to go down on you?'

She laughed. 'Yes, please.'

Giulia rang a bell for dinner. Tom and Damien bundled down the stairs first, buttoning their shirts as they ran. Once we were all sitting down, Giulia handed around a plate of bruschetta; the bread was still warm. 'Everything,' she said, handing the plate over to Katarina, 'is from here. Signor B. made the tomatoes.'

We all complimented Giulia, and she seemed to relax. She touched Katarina's arm. 'None of you are vegetarian?'

'I am sometimes,' Katarina said. 'It saves us money. And, of course, there's the animals.' She wiped the side of her mouth.

Giulia brought out a large bowl, filled with unknowable meats. '*Pecora al cotturo*,' she said, pleased with her own ceremony. She requested a few minutes' silence; I looked around at the others. They were frowning.

'Prayer,' I mouthed.

Giulia took Katarina's hand first, and motioned that we ought to do the same. With the cicadas, and the faint breeze, we all bent our heads over that wooden table. Katarina started playing with the outside of my hand, tapping the knuckles one by one.

Giulia prayed for good health, generally, and then sang a few words of Italian as Tom tried to cover a laugh. (I had opened my eyes briefly, to see his shaking shoulders, and had to close them again.) The food made my face warm, and my eyes burned, and I thought of my mother's expression when I had done something wrong. Giulia clapped her hands together: she was done.

We ate the stew as our host asked us a series of questions about our families. Giulia seemed to be especially interested in our fathers, and the jobs they did. Katarina jumped in before she could ask about mine, to which Giulia replied: 'That's interesting.' Her personality left very little for subtlety.

'So, Damiano,' she said, after hearing about Damien's second house in Tuscany, 'your father is very rich?'

Her interrogatory subject choked on a piece of meat. Tom, practically gleeful, started hitting him on the back. 'Um,' Damien said, 'I guess. But he's divorced, and the settlement took quite a bit out of him, so.' Rich people were always looking for some clause to excuse or alleviate their status: but they're divorced; but the house is several decades old, and falling down; but we lost a great deal in the recession, you know.

Giulia decided to milk this knowledge about the divorce for everything it was worth, and started tutting, hacking into the stew as she went. I held on to the table, and dug my nails into its grooves, afraid, and yet thrilled, about what she might ask of me. But then the plates were cleared, and Giulia rushed ahead of Damien, who was intent on clearing his food away. She clicked her fingers. 'Don't,' she said. 'I will do that.'

The four of us sat, half uncomfortable, half pleased, as we listened to the tap running and Giulia's bustling, her shoes making contact with the floor. When she was done, she clasped a hand to her forehead, and insisted that we all follow her outside.

In the garden, there were several chicken pens, the scent of sweet hay mixing with urine and manure. We were, Giulia told us, to collect the eggs in the morning, and trim the vicinity, paring back the hedges. It was the best time of day; nine o'clock, just before dark. Katarina stood close to me, facing Giulia, so that we could afford to touch each other's backs.

'I'll leave you all, now, for you to go for a walk. A catch-up.' Giulia smiled, and I caught the sunspots on her arms, just below her neck. I was unsure if her suggestion was for our benefit or if she wanted time alone. But we accepted her words in good faith, and she reached up to kiss Damien on both cheeks. 'I'll give you until eleven,' she said. 'You might be back before then. But not later, please, or I will have to wait for you all.'

'Thank you, Giulia, for dinner, and everything else,' I said.

We walked away from her, closing the gate behind us. When I looked back, Giulia was still there, poised in the doorway. The woman gave a little wave, and the familiarity of the gesture was so sweet that I skipped ahead, grabbing Katarina by the shoulders.

Katarina had found a river on Google Maps, and we all sat by the water, backs to the last of the sun. Tom was breaking down Giulia's character and mannerisms, in what he called an 'investigation', or 'psychological analysis' – which, of course, meant bitching. 'Something's off,' he said.

Damien put his head on Tom's shoulder. 'Like what?'

'It's the vibe, firstly. Reminds me of my grandmother. Trapped in that big house.' The air had cooled, and the corner-shop sodas had been emptied hours before. 'That,' Tom shuddered, 'and the uber-religious thing, is really freaking me out.'

Katarina moved closer to the edge of the river. 'I did notice that,' she said.

'The church recommendation, firstly,' he began. 'And then the separate bedrooms.'

Damien started laughing, and stood up. 'Make-ah

sure-ah,' he said, in a thick Italian accent, 'you do none of that, what do you call it?' He hit Tom.

'I think – Oh, yes, I have heard of it. The gay-ah sex.'

'I like her,' I said. 'Giulia.'

This was not a popular statement. Tom loudly disagreed, and his boyfriend pulled a face. I could tell that Katarina disliked Giulia too, but she said nothing. The two of us never disagreed in public: we stored the complaint, and saved it for the walk home, or the sofa in my flat. It was one of the things we did well.

While Katarina and I sat on the bank, watching the others as though they were our children, we all started to forget our curfew. 'I don't know how they have so much energy,' Katarina said, as Tom and Damien pulled each other to the ground, making mock punches to their heads. Tom dipped his hand in the water, and flicked it at our faces.

'Oh God,' Katarina said.

Tom angled his body towards us, a racer taking his mark, his arm dripping. We both bounced up, at the same time, Katarina going for the head, myself for the lower body: a tackle. Damien headed for me first. Two minutes later, in various poses, we were all jumping into the river.

The water weighed me down, heavy and thick, until I broke the surface. Through stinging eyes, I found that I was at a distance from everyone. I waved at them, then slapped my hand down seconds later, back into the water. They did not see, and I watched their heads, bobbing, afloat, before Katarina turned, and swam towards me.

Once we returned to Giulia's, I went for a shower. I wondered if I was happy, in the way someone might consider menu options. I was in Italy, with Katarina. Money was, for the time I would be in Giulia's house, not a concern. I was well. We were all well. There was no disease, no cancer, and I even looked right, physically – no circles, no under- or over-eating, no UTIs, no immediate and emotional turmoil. I lay back on Giulia's fresh sheets. There was something bottomless about being content. I knew other emotions well, sought them out. I knew how to be in them, how to occupy them, and how to cover them up, so they looked like something else, all wrapped and packaged. Happiness felt disloyal, somehow, though I did not know who I was betraying. I closed my eyes, and asked if I could be good, just this once. I smiled, in the dark, at my own stupidity. I formed my hands together, like I had at dinner, and asked God, though I couldn't stay awake long enough to hear an answer.

18

The following day, the cicadas, birdsong: the first morning in Villalago. Twenty more left. Katarina opened the door, and moved onto my bed without a word. I pulled the sheet over her. 'Good morning.'

'I meant to come here last night,' she said, 'but I fell asleep before I could.' She lay on top of me, her chest on my stomach. We were both slathered in the aloe gel she had bought at the airport – its bitterness was there with us, too.

'Thank you,' she said.

'What for?'

She groaned, and said nothing more. I waited; it was only eight o'clock. We had hours before we were needed in the garden. 'You're welcome,' I said.

I opened the door thirty minutes later, finding a rectangular tray and coffee for one person. It was from Giulia; she had promised, at dinner, to give me some. The mug was cold, the liquid even more so, but I drank it all the same, wondering, with alarm, whether she knew, whether she had heard everything. I asked Katarina.

'Maybe she thinks we're really into acting, doing lines, or something,' she said. Katarina had a particularly gleeful expression, a sheen from the light and the cast of her suncream.

Tom walked out from his room first, and then Damien followed, a few seconds afterwards, as though they were making an attempt at coming out in stages, and had failed. Damien looked between us. 'All okay?'

'Perfect.'

When we traipsed downstairs, there was a note on the table, from Giulia: 'The food is for you. Bring back all the eggs. Instruments are for the shed.'

We spent five minutes trying to decode Giulia's 'instruments', before Damien, the ultimate translator, decided it must mean pruning equipment. Beside the note, she had left a plate of pastries, which we collected on our way out. In the garden, there were several unhappy birds, the distinct smell of shit and sweat-worthy temperatures. Katarina placed the pastries on the patio, and looked around. Cupid sculptures and old lamps were dispersed throughout the grass, seemingly at random. Giulia had hanging chairs overlooking the field, and their cushions were greenish, from previous rain. The grass had several summers' worth of growth.

Some personalities, I found, scraping the dirt away from Giulia's table, were better suited to work than others. Tom went to the gym regularly, and had an impressive physique, yet he sighed each time pruning was required of him, shaking his head. He would then produce a series of complaints: 'It's too damn hot,' and, 'I can't believe we're doing this,' or, alternatively, 'I'm not cut out for this shit, goddamn.' An hour into our work in the garden, by which time we had accumulated a large pile of debris, Tom started to blame Katarina. 'We could be,' he said, between shovels, 'in Lake Como right now.'

Damien, knee-deep into his efforts to scrub the patio, threw down a metal rod. It hit the tiles, and we all turned around to look at him. 'Tom, I swear, if you don't shut the hell up, I won't come into your room tonight. And you sure as hell can't come into mine.'

We spent the next few hours in silence, focused on uprooting dandelions and thick foliage which had started to emerge from all corners. We might have all remained there, Tom seething, sweating, Damien smug, if Giulia had not run out. 'You can come inside, now,' she said. 'No need to keep working. Save it for tomorrow.'

I loved her earnestness, her genuine concern. She smiled at us as we trooped back into her shed, and left, for a moment, returning with more pastries. 'Here.' She pressed a custard tart into my hand.

Then a late lunch – a salmon dish, with rice and salad – and we were ordered to take a walk around the piazza. It was fifteen minutes from the house. Katarina took Tom's arm once we were through the gate, leaving the more passive members of our group (Damien, myself) to walk together. We did not have much to say, beyond general comments about the weather and the niceness of the town, the buildings and fountains we passed. Damien asked about living in London, and I was confused, stuttering, before I remembered I had told them all I had moved from there.

Damien had visited the city once, following his parents' divorce, when his father felt the sudden, pressing need to 'be a good parent' (Damien's words) and 'make some memories'. They had visited the classics: Harrods, Little Venice, the Eye.

'But we went to one of the galleries – I think it was a pavilion, and had something to do with snakes?'

'Oh, yeah.' I couldn't have identified it with a gun to my head.

'Well, anyway, it was beautiful. And I actually felt something. Even at the time, I had been so angry – mostly at myself, in a very teenage way – but the paintings made me forget all that.'

I asked a few more questions about their trip: innocuous, really. Damien told me that the week before they left, his mother had 'gotten sick', and that his father had to navigate the divorce, his lingering affection for his wife and the increasing responsibility for his son. 'I don't think he knew how to do any of it,' Damien said. 'And the whole time, I was so stressed for my mom – I think we both were.'

I said that must have been impossible, as Damien soldiered on, determined to have the heart-to-heart. 'I didn't mean to bring the vibe down.' He tried to smile. 'I only mean – well, I can understand how you might feel about your dad, even if it's just a little. I am such a catastrophist that I was convinced my mom would be gone, which obviously wasn't a great feeling.'

'I know,' I said simply. It was true: I did.

Damien ran a hand through his hair, as if wiping away that unpleasantness. 'She got better, though,' he added. 'Sorry. I'm so bad at this.' He adjusted his sun visor towards the ground, hiding his expression, which must have been some form of wince. Before he could say anything more, I asked him, in a stilted, ultimately forced way, about how he and Tom had met, and he was happy to tell me, entering the easiness of their love story, rehearsed and fluid, as I thought about his dad, dragging the young Damien round Monets and Gaugins while his wife lay, pale and greenish, in the old marriage bed.

When we arrived, the locals walked on the other side of the street, as though we were diseased. Americans were famous in Villalago, Giulia had told us, for their brashness, their volume, their severe lack of tact. The Brits: their inability to leave Villalago's only cafe on time, and their old men, who she had been scandalized by, 'drinking alone on the street, even in the day'. At our backs, there was an abandoned water mill, yellowed by the sun, and the bitter wind, making its way from the Adriatic Sea. The town was on an incline, and the land was broken by greyish mountains, old brick and great lakes. Giulia had listed Villalago's beauty, across the seasons, with pride: orange trees in autumn, breaking away for spring; thick snow in the winter, mountains and streets turning white. And then, of course, summer, arriving earlier and earlier with each year.

The streets of Villalago were some of the narrowest 'in the world', Giulia had said, and we were to 'be careful'. (I was touched – Tom, insulted – by her warning.)

We walked in pairs now – Katarina and myself, the 'boyfriends' – taking the stone steps upwards, then downwards, to nowhere in particular. The four of us started a new game, and, as we moved onto unfamiliar vias, more French windows and bakeries, one of us would shout a direction in Italian – '*Sinistra!*' – and we would all turn left, accommodating it. Between our rapid directional changes, and the new alleyways, we would laugh at each other, and stop, to place a hand around our partner's waist, breathing heavily in the sun. I thought, then, falling behind, that this – my hand under her shirt, in late April – was the happiest I could ever be.

We stopped as Tom and Damien went inside a pharmacy, and Katarina tied her shoelaces. I felt as if my insides had been fused with hot oil, that something was falling out. The happiest I will ever be, I thought. And then the others emerged, and Katarina was still there, on the stone steps, and I anticipated a series of future happinesses – trips; an art showing; a cheque – all inconsequential, brief, when held up against this one. And then we left, another '*Sinistra!*', turning back onto the via for Giulia's farmhouse.

We spent the next week by the river, in 'gay paradise', as Damien liked to call it, our spot by the bank. 'Let's go to gay paradise tonight,' he would say to the group, looking at Tom for a moment, before smiling. In the mornings, we cleaned Giulia's garden, her patio, and ensured that none of her chickens became ill from the heat. Sunburn was as common as laughter. As were Tom's complaints, though they started to have a kindly, less malicious, feel. Katarina and I developed a morning ritual: wake up together; head down to the garden; return, before lunch, to shower together; back down again for a trip to gay paradise or the centre of Villalago. Evenings were softer, more vulnerable. Each day became the same, and I felt as if they were all slippery and untraceable: now fourteen days left, now ten. Our wardrobe became one long extension of the other's, and Damien liked to guess, across the week, which dress or shirt had once belonged to the other. The service in Villalago was so poor that we were constantly making games like this: inventing new ways to waste time, renaming cutlery and hiding behind doors, then jumping out to surprise each other. It was as if we had all been made clean from the world, without a history of any kind.

Nine days before we had to leave, we walked into the only cafe, for coffee and some rare Wi-Fi. Katarina tipped expensively in advance: 'We'll be here a while,' she said, 'so I thought I'd let them know.' She held up Google Translate at the middle-aged woman behind the counter. At the table, we discussed why the working staff in Villalago were a great deal older than we were used to, back in the city. Katarina's guess: migration into Rome. Mine: the laziness of the younger generation. And then we fell silent, Katarina opening her laptop to write a summary for her new series, photographs of the 'boyfriends' and myself. The plan was to paint over the film, or sew through it, in a filmic tapestry – she was not sure.

I connected to the internet, sent photos of Katarina and the villa to Matthew, who responded with a single thumbs-up. I looked at my emails, more out of obligation than anything else. Between adverts from companies, clothing stores with flashy discounts, there was something from my father.

'HOPE YOU ARE WELL,' the first one read, the content confined to the email title. He had attached a photograph of an abandoned water pistol on the wall just outside our house. The next one, sent a few days later, had no message, simply a photograph of my bedroom – a grey blanket, the books I couldn't throw away. There was a childhood drawing of four fat circles on the wall. 'Mum', 'Dad', 'Cat' and 'Me' had been scrawled at the bottom, the word 'HOME' added, in capital letters, at the top. The picture had not been there when I left. My father must have found it afterwards. That idea was bleak enough, without the knowledge that he had stood there, alone in the bedroom, and had taken his phone out to email me the photo. I breathed in, very quickly, and pushed the laptop away.

Katarina put her coffee down. 'All okay?'

I waved my hand in front of my face. 'It's nothing.' And, realizing that she required something more, I tilted my head back, feigned unloading, confessional-style. 'I've just looked at my bank statement.'

'Oh.'

'Not good,' I said.

'Do you need me to send you something?'

'God, no. But thank you.'

Often, when Katarina had exhausted her own issues, she liked to 'discuss' – by which I mean analyse, as if from a distance – mine. She would levy accusations against me, while insisting that they weren't 'flaws at all', just 'things I've noticed'. On more loving days, I was touched by these attentions. It took a kind of closeness to be noticed, every stone turned and examined.

My issues, according to Katarina: emotional intimacy ('I'm with you, now, aren't I?'); body image ('Who doesn't?'); and, finally, money ('We're in a recession, Katarina'). I made a point never to borrow from her – even if we were standing in line for a burger, and there were only two dollars in my account. If I was ten dollars away from making my heating bill, and the apartment would be cold for us both, I would just sit on my hands, and pretend that I was 'warm-blooded'.

I believed in exact payments and repayments, in total and complete self-sufficiency. It drew me as close to moral absolution as possible. Katarina, however, thought this was 'stupid'. She did not believe in debts, not between those who cared about each other: we were more than the three dollars, fifty-seven cents we owed each other.

In the cafe, Katarina tapped her mug with a fingernail. 'I just don't get why you won't let me send you something. It's not like you won't pay it back – and even if you didn't, we're together. It's what real, adult partners do.'

I took out my phone, and logged into my bank account. I held the balance out to her. 'It's not so bad,' I said.

We sat in the cafe for a few hours, while I scrolled through news articles and Katarina typed the outline for her project. We were about to leave, and Katarina was picking up her wallet from the table, when I started to write a reply to my father: 'Looks lovely. In a town called Villa-lago right now, in Italy, on holiday. I'll send you the link to the place, if you'd like. Hope everything is well – talk soon.'

19

Though we were all there together, and Tom and Damien called us their 'friends', I wasn't so deluded as to think we were equal. For Tom and Damien, I was a supplement to the holiday – Katarina's girlfriend – someone who they thought of rarely, and only in relation to her. I liked this. In the beginning, they, too, were a kind of decoration – the couple's curiosity opened us up, and their jokes loosened tensions before they could reach any great point. It was different for Katarina; she thought about people in a different way; they were like extensions of her own limbs. Being with her meant that I was always being confronted with her good impulses, the easiness of them, and found that, after a while, I had joined in. My routine had become Katarina's, and hers revolved around Giulia, Tom and Damien, in all these moving parts. I was learning from her.

Whenever Tom became overwhelmed with the heat, Katarina would find some excuse for herself – headache, upset stomach, annoyance at Giulia – and would walk him, like a frustrated cat, around the villa. I started to join them, and genuinely enjoyed lying together – this time, in service of something good. At dinner, when Damien dropped a piece of chicken at his feet, and bent to collect it, Katarina covered the edge of the table to prevent it from digging into his side. Watching them all, soft evening light moving from the water, back to the three of them again, I realized I could not love her, without Tom and Damien getting mixed up in that, too. It helped me see them all clearly: Tom's hatred of early mornings, his lime-green iPod Shuffle, fixed to the front pocket of his shorts; Damien's fear of bugs, his ability to sense them in a room, one arm outstretched in preparation. I could find it all lovable.

But then again – anyone would, surrounded by those stones, and Giulia's meals, steaming at the dinner table. We were far from the sticky linoleum floors at home, far from the infectious stress of campus, and its constant back-and-forth between desire, insignificance and instability. This new generosity was all Villalago – and it certainly wasn't going to win any moral awards. I couldn't become better by accumulating kindnesses like a hoarder awaiting the apocalypse. And each time I helped out in the garden, folded clothes in Giulia's laundry room or stayed up late to clean out the pens, I remembered the lie, that constant uneasiness, tainting everything.

I decided to confess the next day: I would tell her everything. I anticipated her confusion – 'Why the fuck would you say something like that? What the fuck?' I saw the fleshy surface of her cheeks, brushed with anger. Disgust in her face, her words. I thought she might throw something at me – a glass plate from Giulia's cabinet; the alarm-clock from her bedside table. Or she would punch me in the mouth, and it would bleed, and I'd lose a tooth. Something appropriately hideous. But even in all these nightmarish fantasies, I would fall to the floor, freshly injured, and would be forgiven. That was just the type of person she was.

While we lounged around the river, and ate dinner on Giulia's freshly cleaned patio, I thought about telling her. I became so consumed by that moment, the eventual confession, that when I looked at Katarina's face, I could only see the twisted expression it would occupy when I eventually told her.

Dinner was not the right time. Too public, too bloated. I couldn't tell her when we were out on one of our daytime walks, either. The place was infused with romance: the walls of the piazza; the balconies overlooking the steps; the yellow stones, warm, under sandals; the river water drying on our backs. It was too beautiful, and I couldn't ruin it with something like that. Telling her after sex was just cruel, and I could not anticipate her response in that state. And so I was left with the evenings, between nine and eleven: confession time.

I found her sitting on top of her bed, naked from the waist upwards, trying to slather cream onto her back. She asked me to help; there was a spot without it, already turning red.

'Of course,' I said. It always amazed me how easily she asked things from other people, without preamble or embarrassment. As I moved the gel around, she tilted her head back, towards the ceiling. 'I can't believe there's only a week left.'

'And then we'll be back on the plane.'

She sighed. 'Back to real life.' Katarina tapped her back, to ensure that it was dry, before lying on top of the sheets. 'We haven't done much fighting here,' she said. 'Not that we fought properly before. But it's nice. You seem happier here, too.'

'I am.' I looked at her. 'I think it helps to be in a new place. I'm not as stressed.'

'And you were before?'

I smiled. 'Permanent state.'

Katarina held on to my hand. 'Maybe we should just move here.'

'God, I'd love that. We could just haunt here for ever.'

'No, but really.' She propped herself up on the headboard. 'We're almost done for the year – don't make a face – and there's nothing lined up for us. We could.'

I nodded. 'We could.'

It summarized so much of our relationship, that she expressed these words – 'we could' – with all the good faith in her body, like they were a manifestation. And I had said them, laden with cynicism and impossibility. We could move across the world, just as I could be a good, normal individual, and she could raise the dead. A fly waltzed around our heads. It was early evening, the designated time to tell her, and everything was perfect, smooth and content. I traced her left cheek, my thumbs going over a pinkish acne scar. 'I have something to say,' I began. It was the lamest of openings, so contentless: I said I had something to say.

She nodded. 'Okay.'

'I, um, haven't been the most honest with you.'

'About moving?'

I removed the hand from her face. It flailed beside me, and I realized, stomach expanding with the effort, that language had never been so deficient. I simply could not speak.

'It was just a silly thought,' Katarina said, into the silence. 'I'm aware it's expensive. And you might not even want to live together, so. I get it.'

I needed to confess – needed it with a pulsing. I can't, I'd say: I've lied to you for months, weeks. You don't know the person you're living with. Beside the bed or in the kitchen: your own stranger. 'I'd move in with you tomorrow,' I said instead.

'You would?'

'Yeah, obviously. We've already been living together, if you think about it, for months.'

'So, next year, then? That's our plan?'

'I'd love that.'

'Perfect,' she said. 'I've actually got a Pinterest board for us – I mean, if it all worked out, and we found a place – not that I thought it wouldn't. Anyway, I managed to combine both our styles there, in the board, with your more minimalist stuff, and my seventies vibe.' ('Minimalist' was a generous word – my place looked like an interior showroom, or a fresher's room, all navy sheets.)

'But,' she said, 'I think it could really work. It's going to be good.'

'So good,' I echoed, like a preacher forgetting his lines.

Katarina got out of bed and stood by the window. As she moved, I imagined that I was being carried with her. Her excitement was so strong, so sure, that it almost felt like mine. And so, when she touched my arm, and asked what it was that I had to tell her, I said that I had forgotten.

'What do you mean, you've "forgotten"?'

'I can't remember,' I said pathetically.

'Yeah, I know what the word means.' She removed her

hand. 'It sounded big. You were saying you hadn't been honest.'

'It doesn't matter.' I needed to have a handbook for them, the lies. The ones I had said, the ones I hadn't, recited for an occasion like this.

'It sounds like it does,' Katarina said.

'I'm just worried about the future, I guess.' This could have been true. 'It seems less secure for me.'

'How?'

I kissed her neck, and her jaw, only stopping to cite my problems: I was away from home, and I couldn't return, even if I wanted; the constant financial concerns (mother's money, dried up); my lack of talent, artistically speaking.

'You're the real artist in the relationship,' I said, to seal the deal. (She was highly vulnerable to compliments – I could get away with almost anything if I said them enough.)

Katarina shoved me back down onto the bed. 'Not true,' she said, smiling.

The plan, hastily concocted after that failed attempt, was to tell her after dinner. I knew, with some fortune-telling impulse, that I had to do it before we left for college. If I didn't tell Katarina then, in Villalago, I would never do it.

At the table, Giulia drank from a separate bottle of wine – 'The nice kind, for me' – and asked Tom about his love life. She wanted to know about the apps, how they were changing things, so different from 'her day'. 'I read about them,' she said, pouring out the red liquid, 'in the paper.'

Tom had the unfortunate task of being our spokesman, as the member of the group most outwardly aligned with straightness. One morning, he had sent me back upstairs to 'change', after I had appeared by the door in a tank top and jorts. 'Not very undercover,' he had said, pointing to Giulia's room.

Giulia drank from her glass until the corners of her mouth were stained red. 'Do you wait for them to send you the message first? Or do you do it yourself?'

'Well,' Tom started to button his shirt, 'you see the photos first, and swipe, if you like what you see. And then there's the chatting part.'

'You talk to her first?'

Tom looked over at Damien, who had his hands folded against his head, relaxed. He looked like he was enjoying it. 'Sometimes, they come to me.' They both grinned.

Giulia's questions became wilder the more her bottle depleted: the kind of women Tom went for, old or young; whether Katarina found a once-famous Italian movie star, strung up in Giulia's bathroom, good-looking. Giulia laughed to herself after asking them, while we became increasingly alarmed, as the joke switched hands – once about her, now about us. 'It's sad, that you are all alone.' Her elbow knocked Tom's plate. 'Well, not alone, right now, but single.'

'We're happy,' Damien said.

She ignored him. 'And there are two of you,' she pointed at the boyfriends, then at us, 'and two of you. It would not be unnatural,' she said, by which time Damien had stopped smiling, and I sat up a little straighter. 'It would not be unnatural, if you were all to find each other, here.' Giulia's smile looked off-kilter, having only just gauged the stillness of her reception. She sloshed her bottle around, and prodded Damien in the ribs with its end, telling him to 'drink up'. 'It's good,' she said. The more he protested, the more aggressive the jabs were, her face flushed, as though his refusals were designed to embarrass her.

Tom caught the end of the bottle and twisted it away from them both, placing it at the opposite end of the table. An uneasy, almost electric, charge ran through the table, the little garden lamps. It smelled like wet moss, and the cleaning spray we had used on the garden stones. Giulia looked at the garden, in the silence, and her self-consciousness: four against one.

'You have done an excellent job with the patio. And the grass. Perfect.' She looked at Damien while she delivered these compliments. 'Thank you, everyone, for joining me out here. I only talk this way,' she pressed her hands into the table, to support herself to standing, 'as it has been a long time since I have been with people like this. A very long time. I get out of practice.'

Damien led her by the arm, back towards the house, and told her to stop being silly – it was all fine. We stared at her curved back, cream cardigan sticking to her sides, as they walked down the steps. Tom stood up. 'I'd better join them.'

We waved, and stayed outside as the air became cool, stacking plates together. Katarina told me about her latest scheme: watching *The Office* in Italian, translation dubbed over the top. 'I think it's working,' she said. 'I can now say "paper company".'

From the garden, we could see Giulia's window, the light flicking on, turning the little square orange.

'I still don't understand her,' Katarina said, once we were sure she was inside, her curtains closed.

'Neither do I. But I'm so bad with people, honestly. It took me so long to even speak to you.'

'I remember. You just stood in the corner at that party in first year, saying absolutely nothing, only a "thank you".' She smiled. 'It was a little sad.'

'And then you were charmed.'

Katarina laughed. 'Not true at all. You were the one staring at me. Even before we knew each other.'

'Explain the emails, then.'

Katarina's emails started halfway through our first year, detailing events we could attend – 'This looks super helpful for our degree, let's gooooo, guys' – and general tips she had learned from the years above: commentary writing skills, the cheapest places to source paints in town. During our second year, her emails became more and more personalized, until they were really check-ins, messages designed for me.

'They were part of a list,' she said. 'I sent them to everyone on our course. You were the only one who actually responded.'

'Oh my God.' I hid my face in my hands.

'I thought it was sweet.'

'I'm reconsidering every single interaction we had together now. That's your fault.'

She folded Giulia's tablecloth, lifting my arms up to reach the corners. 'You were always so obvious,' she said. 'I think I knew how you felt before you did.'

I helped her carry the things back inside, resolving that that was enough honesty for the evening. As we walked back upstairs, we found Giulia's door open, a sliver of her bedroom visible from the hall. She was kneeling by the side of the bed, hands together, lips moving. Spit had gathered around her mouth, bubbling from the force of her prayer. I had no idea what she believed she had done.

When we left for the centre of Villalago in the morning, Giulia came with us. 'I will show you the very best,' she said, holding Damien's face. The gate swinging behind them, the boyfriends looped their arms into Giulia's as they walked up the narrow streets. Katarina poked Tom in the back. 'You're stealing her from us,' she said.

Giulia looked back at us, sweetly, and said, 'I love all my children equally.'

'I guess that makes us brothers,' Tom said. This was met with a resounding, 'Shut the fuck up' from Damien, a flick on his ear, and an expression of 'You Americans'.

We passed the ruins of a monastery, and stopped to look over the lake, where there were several pearly stones in an almost ritualistic arrangement. We crossed a stone bridge. The lake beneath us was still, blue at the centre, green at the edges. Katarina and Damien made several attempts to match the hues to their accompanying paints, while Tom looked over his boyfriend's shoulder and rolled his eyes at me. I was touched, to be included in that gesture. I knew him the least out of our group. Even Giulia and I had a few conversations, chatting before dinner, or at the sink at lunch (topics included cooking, her fascination with Instagram reels – 'So short!' – and an Italian singer my father listened to).

'We're here,' our host said.

The church – or 'hermitage', as Giulia called it – was a stone house, like the ones all over Villalago. It was nestled into a rock, or a natural cave, pitted into the side of a cliff. If anything were to be holy, it would have been that spot: arched bridge, pearly lake, the miraculously white walls of the hermitage. I whispered in Katarina's ear that, if I were allowed to stay, I might start believing in God, too. 'Free accommodation, and you're suddenly a nun,' she said.

Across from us, Giulia leaned against the stones. She placed a palm to her forehead, and said something about getting older.

'Come on,' Damien said. 'You're fitter than most of us.'

Katarina pretended to need a rest, and took off her shoes. 'I think I have a blister.' She bore her perfectly healthy feet to the air. 'Let's wait.'

Outside the four walls of the church, the steaming lake at our backs, the five of us rested. When Katarina stood up, Giulia offered a hand to her, revealing sunspots on her tanned skin, her pale forearm dotted with blue. 'You all have to come back,' Giulia said, as she was pulled from the ground. 'It is not fair for me to be alone in the house.' She nodded: we would return together; it was decided.

We all thanked her, and told her we would be there, of course we would. I held on to Katarina's shoulder for a moment too long. I knew, even then, that returning would be impossible; so many things had to remain the same. I looked at myself, and Giulia, with pity, both of us steeped in delusion: yes, we would return the following year.

I was the only one of us familiar with the narrative surrounding Catholic saints: often born in Europe, to 'great wealth', as our priest used to say; the occasional bout of sin; then a rejection of said wealth; sharing it with beggars, sinners; death; canonization. Five minutes into Giulia's description of San Domenico's first wonder – the healing of a child's fever – Katarina interrupted her. 'How do you know all this? I mean, I know my town, but I couldn't speak about it the way you have.'

Giulia shrugged. It was a much younger gesture, and I saw her at fifteen, grey hair turning to dark, skin to smooth. 'We just do,' she said. 'We're more connected. You Americans are all floating,' her hand made a loose movement in the air, 'nothing tying you down. No bigger thing. It's sad.'

Tom cleared his throat, and said, in a musical theatre whisper, that he 'didn't come here to be converted'.

Our host, immune to critiques of any kind, described the saint's other miracles. 'Then blessed water, a baby, saved from a wolf, and healing snake bites.'

'Wow,' Katarina said. It was expressed with a slight incredulity, the way a parent might, staring at the work of their child: Wow, you did it. That's really something.

Giulia dipped her hand into some holy water, as Katarina and I stood opposite another fresco. At the centre of the work, a wolf, holding a child in its mouth. The edge of the painting was fading, stone taking over. The child might have been sleeping, or dead. I asked Katarina which one she thought it was, already knowing her answer. 'Sleeping,' she said. I looked at the child's lips, almost white, cracked in stone, its limp fingers, not clasping up, but downwards, in defeat.

We walked past the church, past the arches and the bridge, down to the water. It was almost dark, bluish, the light fighting its way from the hermitage, the street lights over the hill dripping down. We stopped to watch the town.

Katarina put her hand on my shoulder, and said the yellow windows looked like stars, and laughed at herself, before I could. 'I've been reading too much bad poetry.'

Giulia insisted that we go for a swim in the lake. Our host sat down on a rock, close to the surface. 'You all go,' she said. 'I will sit here.'

We all made polite refusals – it was almost completely dark, wasn't she tired, we did not want to drag her out for long, simply to watch us. She batted a hand in front of her face, as though we were all insects. 'You start to annoy me now. First, you say I am young, in good shape, now you treat me like I'm eighty.' (She was seventy-five, according to Damien's reports.)

'Of course.' Katarina kissed Giulia's cheek. The woman blushed, and told us all to 'go, now'.

Tom and Damien piled into the water first, leaving their shorts by a rock. They were both good swimmers, and immediately entered into the rhythm of competition, all strong strokes, cutting through the water with precision. A second nature. Katarina and I stripped down to just our underwear, and Tom stopped his stroke, for a moment, to whistle over at us. Giulia shouted something in Italian at him. 'She called you an "ingrate",' Damien translated, equally as loudly.

We swam in the opposite direction to the boyfriends, hair submerged in the lake. Katarina held on to my hips under the water, the two of us treading furiously. When I was pulled down, very quickly, by the cold, by tiredness, Katarina held me up by my chin. I spat out water onto her chest.

'Sexy,' she said, and rolled her eyes.

My limbs had gone cold, and the lake water pressed down

on everything as Katarina started to swim away. Giulia waved at us from the bank. 'I think I'll go and join her.' I pointed, with a falling hand, towards the rocks. 'I'll make sure she's okay.'

'For her sake or yours?'

I splashed her, and she moved away faster, joining the boyfriends in their race. Three dark heads moved through the water, turning, slicing.

I left the lake shivering, the water slimy, like an animal. Giulia patted the rock beside her with one hand. 'Sit,' she said.

I did. Tom, Damien and Katarina were making lines across the lake, far enough that they had just become vague creatures. One would reappear as the other two went down. I didn't know which one was her, and so I became afraid for all of them, watching each dark head as though it might be Katarina's.

'Do you think they're in too deep?'

'No, no.' Giulia moved around on the stone, as though the lack of support were hurting her back. 'We were thrown in there as babies, into that lake. Our parents sat here,' she pointed between us, 'and drank. We were always fine.'

'Did you have any siblings?'

'No. You?'

'Also no. Only child.'

Giulia's eyes never left the lake, her head fixed forward. I could not make out whether this was done out of concern, or whether she was imagining herself as young, too, her head above water. 'I thought so,' she said. 'You seem like one.'

I smiled. 'Oh God.' Giulia made a tutting sound at me. 'Oh dear,' I corrected. 'That's never a compliment.'

Tom waded over, closer to the shore, to where he could stand, his reddened torso hovering above the water. He shouted for Damien to come over, and, as he arrived by his side, lifted him up, onto his shoulders. The boyfriends teetered over to Katarina like one long-headed monster.

'They're close,' Giulia said.

'They are.' Tom's hands were clasped around Damien's legs, fixing them to him. 'They're good friends. They met in first year, actually.'

I looked at Giulia, a sliver of her expression, and was surprised to find her smiling. 'You think, because I am old, I do not have eyes.' She laughed. It was the sound of a woman who had once smoked, arriving in short, painful bursts, crackling between wheezes. 'And you and Katarina? You are good friends?' Another wheeze.

'Yes.' I smiled.

'You have been very sneaky with me. Tippy toe. Tippy toe. Everywhere. But remember,' she pointed, 'I brought you coffee. The first morning you were here, I left it at your door.'

'Oh God.' Giulia flicked my ear. 'Bad habit,' I said, still smiling.

We watched the others, still in the water, and Giulia said that they would all get wrinkled, swirling her skin together, in demonstration. And then, because of our isolation from the rest of them, and that time of day, that place by the lake, draining everything out, she said, resigned, 'I'm glad you are with Katarina. And happy.'

I nodded.

'You have to keep it safe, the feeling.'

I kicked a few stones at my feet. They hit the edge of my nail, digging in. 'I don't think I'm good at that.'

'Did you know,' Giulia pointed to the space between trees, 'a boy was killed in the village, just over there? And his mother was different afterwards. They called her "the crazy woman". We saw her buying things, big bags of food, though it was just her in the house. Cans, sweet things, little blue T-shirts. We all let her.'

'Jesus. That's awful.' I looked at Giulia's lip, where the perspiration mixed with fine, black hairs.

'But if we can change for the bad, we can change for the good, too.' She turned back, towards the swimmers, those three figures in the water. 'Listen to me. Katarina is good, yes?'

'Yes.'

'And you feel good with her?'

'Of course.'

'And you want to keep it?'

I nodded.

'Then, do. Just like that.' Giulia smiled to herself on that bank, as though she had solved a great international crisis; a rearrangement of troops on the border. She clicked her fingers together, and, seeing my incredulous face, modified slightly: 'Well, maybe it's not just like that. But you will get there.'

When Katarina walked out from the water, her shoulders shaking, I held Giulia's phrase – 'you will, you will' – close to me. You will tell her this week, I thought. You will.

20

I took a call from my father after lunch the next day. I let his call go to voicemail, and walked around Giulia's garden before ringing back.

'Hey,' he said. 'I'm in the break room, so if you hear a ping, that's the microwave.'

I asked what he was eating.

'Tesco's lasagne.'

'Reduced section?'

'Of course,' he said.

My father did not believe in freezing, or expiry dates. The reduced section of a store was heaven to him. A yoghurt could be several weeks old, green fluff growing, like pubic hair, from the plastic, and he would sit down, whip the mould off with a spoon, and lick the sides of the tub in satisfaction.

'And how is American life?'

'It would be great, but I'm actually in Italy right now. I emailed you the place.'

'Oh.' A microwave sounded in the background. 'Italy?'

'Yep.' I held the phone away from my face, and let him hear the garden, the birdsong.

'Sounds lovely. How did you manage that?'

'My friends found this website,' I said, 'and you can stay

in a village – ours is called Villalago, if you can believe it – if you do a little work. Like helping around the house, the farm, that sort of thing.' This was the most I had said to him in years. I blamed the heat, and the sweat along my hairline.

I could hear chewing over the line. 'That's great. You sound good. Happy.'

'I might be.' I dipped my fingers into Giulia's pond, bringing them back to my side, dripping, clean.

'Good. Good.'

At school, I had been presented with a collection of new words, printed out on a sheet of paper, with their definitions on the other side. Serendipitous. Colloquial. Noxious. Irreverent. They were random; we received new ones each week, in order to expand our eleven-year-old vocabulary. My father quizzed me on them. He never turned to the other side, for the answers: he knew them all. I had been full of reverence ('inspiration, with an awe verging on worship'). He was smart. I could be smart. I later found another sheet of definitions, handwritten, on his bedside table. He must have said them to himself before bed, over and over. When I found out, I stopped asking for his help, and was ashamed by his hard work, his naturally stunted vocabulary – proof of our inherited stupidity. I asked my father how the job was, thinking, as the words left my mouth, that I took the wrong lessons from everything.

'Nothing too exciting,' he said. 'Though we are working on installing a boiler. It's for Moira, down the road.'

'Nice.'

'We're not charging her, so that's something.'

'Kind of you.'

'Well, you know,' he said. 'The town you're staying in sounds lovely, by the way. Please send me more photos.'

'I'll email them over.'

'Great. Great.'

We knew nothing about each other. He bought Honey Cheerios in bulk, from a colleague with contacts at the supermarket; he went to bed at nine p.m.; he called me every month, bulldozing through birthdays, anniversaries and art showings with a decisive forgetfulness. But the flesh of his life, I had no idea about.

'Your mother and I always wanted to travel. I said we'd go when we retire. Did you know we never went abroad, not even for our honeymoon?'

'I think you've said, yeah.'

'Maybe I'll take a trip soon.'

It would never happen. The man had developed a debilitating fear of flying immediately after I was born. He tried to take a plane in the early 2000s, and returned to my mother two hours later, passport and small bottles in his backpack. It was one of her favourite stories: her husband, rushing back to the house, pointing at the newborn, simply saying, 'I can't.' She teased him about it for years, asking if he was 'away to the airport' every time he left the house.

Over the phone, I told my father that it sounded like a good idea, with the same energy a parent, exhausted from a long day, might tell their child that their dog will live for ever.

'I could come out and see you in time for my birthday,' he said.

'Perfect.'

*

There wasn't even a sliver of panic, or the awareness that he might make good on his promise. When we said goodbye, I returned to the house, peaceful as ever, finding them all sitting out on the patio, where Tom was discussing 'all those mysterious calls' I was receiving.

'Seriously, though,' he said, 'do you have a whole-ass family out there?'

I looked at Katarina. 'I've actually got two kids,' I said. 'It's serious.'

Tom stood up. 'Are they mine?'

After Giulia came outside, to tell us that we were 'scaring the chickens', Katarina said, very quietly: 'You do get strange emails.'

'What?'

'I mean,' Katarina said, 'there's the spam, from that account.'

I looked around, as though someone else might answer for me. 'What do you mean, spam?'

'It has this really weird name,' she continued. 'Like "Marr Guitar" or something.'

I could barely control my face at that statement; my left eye started twitching rapidly. *GuitarzforJohnnyMarr*, founded in the early days of email, was a newsletter entirely dedicated to the Smiths member. It was run by my father, who typed away at the family computer every evening, gathering his latest titbits. *GuitarzforJohnnyMarr* sent regular updates, from photos of Mr Marr eating a pitta bread, to one of my father's more genius columns, 'Marr's Guitars', a monthly dose of his favourite instruments, played by his favourite musician. I might have found it concerning, revealing his stalker-like tendencies, were I not his only subscriber.

'I can help you block them,' Katarina said.

It didn't matter how bad I had been – I couldn't do that. Some weeks, it was the only information I received about him. 'That's okay,' I said. 'I kind of enjoy them.'

The boyfriends, having realized that the conversation would not erupt into the dramatic, tear-filled confrontation of their dreams, had lost interest, and started to clear the plates away. 'If you change your mind, let me know.' Katarina shrugged. 'Though I did see one pop up the other day, and I had to repeat it out loud to myself, it was crazy.'

'What was it?'

'*Marr's Barres are the Real Star.*'

Tom shook his head. 'That doesn't make any sense.'

I smiled at them all. I felt light, guiltless. 'I know.'

It rained the rest of the day, which ought to have been the first sign. It was a warm kind of rain, plastering our faces with water and sweat together, beginning after lunch, continuing until the next morning. Katarina ran out to collect the washing from Giulia's line, as the boyfriends fed the chickens, throwing damp grain into the air. We returned to the house, shaking ourselves out in the hallway. Giulia had provided sandwiches on the table, with a note – she would be in bed for the rest of the day.

Katarina was concerned. 'Should we go up, ask if she needs anything?'

'Let's not,' Tom said. 'Maybe she's after a day without us.'

We ate in silence, sobered by the change in our idyllic routine: no sun; no Giulia; no walk to gay paradise, the river.

In the living room, propped up against the wall, Giulia

had several DVDs and CDs, with a player accompanying them. Damien suggested we watch a series. The rest of us agreed, and the boyfriends began to argue about *Friends*: Giulia had all seasons. 'It's a useful language-learning tool,' Damien, the expert on such things, said.

Tom rolled his eyes. 'Except we know English, so all we're learning is how to tell bad jokes, and have even worse opinions.'

'Some of us don't have to learn.'

The two of them started their game, shoving each other into walls and furniture, tackling, punching. It was strange, their routine, fuelled by false anger, their pushes always on the edge of lust. Perhaps this was how they had started to date – I had visions of them meeting at a boxing society, or a softball game with a surprising twist. The beginning of their relationship, the foundation for the rest of it. I looked at Katarina. Ours could be characterized by her pity, my untruthfulness.

I started sifting through the remaining CDs: *Seinfeld*; *The Sopranos*; Italian medical shows with smiling nurses on the cover. We tried *Una donna per amico*, which appeared to be about pregnancy, and doctors having affairs. Damien got us to shout the translations of as many words as possible, creating a cacophony of 'baby', 'Oh no!', 'dead' and 'girl'.

Tom and Damien sat together, arms touching, on the large sofa; Katarina had her head propped up on the other, her legs extending out. I lay on top of her, my head on her chest. It was still raining; the Italian series continued, and I fell asleep like that, my feet by her feet, her breathing my breathing.

I woke to a plate of sandwiches, even heavier rain, and

Tom and Damien dancing at the centre of Giulia's room. A low voice was singing in Italian, and the pair were swaying, as if they were the stars of a gay Hallmark movie. Katarina looked at me, and laughed at my expression.

Tom removed his hand from Damien's waist to stick his middle finger up at us. 'Shut up,' he said. 'You shouldn't be allowed to laugh, looking like that. You literally look like my fifth-grade art teachers.'

The whole thing was sickening, beautiful. And, though I am sure we did other things that evening, said other things – had to wash our faces, scrape plaque from our front teeth, and close the door – I will always return to that moment, the peak of our stay, our relationship, sweetened and content, as I waited for the moment it would be stripped back, away from us both.

21

When my father arrived, ghost-like, rained on, in Villalago, it was three o'clock, and my face was throbbing. I told Katarina about the pain. She traced along my jaw, and asked if I had been stressed recently. 'It can get like that, sometimes. You clench in your sleep. You're doing it right now, actually.'

The weather had been bad for days. When Katarina joked that it was affecting both me and the chickens, I told her I was simply 'in tune with nature'. It was only later that I realized the pain had started the moment he stepped foot in the piazza, increasing as he walked past the cafe, the hermitage. While I lounged with Katarina, and ate pastries in her bedroom, he must have been walking up the path. As we greeted Giulia downstairs, remarking on her recovery – there he was, by the gate. I know, now, that he waited by the door for several minutes, alive with expectation. Inside, his daughter, beside him after years of absence.

He might have ducked under the porch, the rain rolling off the gutter's edge, down his neck. I imagine he knocked again, stood slightly to one side, self-consciously, as though it might be the wrong house.

Giulia answered. Katarina and I were still eating. We heard a low voice, and Giulia's increasingly high one.

'Tom?' Katarina asked.

'Probably.'

Giulia bumbled along, smiling, to pull me towards the door. It was open; we could see the outlines of a man, large shoes peeling at their edges. I remember thinking that my grandfather had shoes like that. I saw the old man's frame, folding over the hospital bed, as I looked at those shoes. And in front of the door, tired, looking older than I had ever seen him before: my father. His head was bowed, almost sheepish, like he had miraculously survived oncoming traffic, and was apologizing for inconveniencing the drivers. He raised his hands; for what, I was not sure, until I found myself being hugged.

'It's so good to see you,' he said. I blinked; he resumed his embarrassed shuffle outside the house. Flecks of dirt came with him, and he shook himself out.

'Sorry about the damp.' Droplets fell from his sleeves. 'And sorry for the surprise. I spoke with Giulia about it over email. But I've booked a different place to stay, here, just outside, so I don't change your plans.' He brought one rain-soaked hand to his face. 'It's really great to see you,' he said again. 'You look well.'

'I am.'

My father had wrinkles, in a pattern of four, at the corners of his eyes. I had not seen him in over three years. He had turned sixty-four the Sunday before. I said happy birthday, looking at his feet. Each word was not my own, pulled out against my will. But, when I looked up, he appeared pleased, and his face, which I had seen in many states – soured, terrified and resigned – smiled. He looked around. 'The place is wonderful.'

'I can't believe you got on a plane.'

My father made a little stutter from the back of his throat. 'Neither can I. God.'

Inside, Katarina spoke to Giulia. She had turned away, and could not see us. I thought, with the perverted optimism only available to the truly fucked, that she might avoid seeing him entirely, that she could remain inside, and he outside, for ever. I placed a hand on my father's arm, standing directly in front of him, like a shield.

'Shall we go for a walk?' I asked. It had stopped raining, though the ground of Villalago was still marked by it, the dirt loosening itself in chunks.

He shook his head. 'Later, maybe. But I'm dying for some tea.'

I closed the door. 'Giulia doesn't have any – she drinks coffee. There's a cafe at the centre of town, though, which does.' I held on to his hand, like I did when I was small.

His shrew-like face turned to surprise. 'Okay, then. You're the expert.'

My father carried a backpack. It was small, with no more than three days' worth of clothing inside. I gestured a hand out in panic, to take it, as Katarina walked outside, and stood beside him. 'Hi,' she said, 'I'm Katarina.'

The two of them were smiling, Katarina was tanned, my father red, burned despite the rain, the sun emphasizing the whites around his eyes. I thought about skin cancer, the charred and leathery faces from the warning pamphlets, as Katarina reached out a hand. She kept looking between us.

'It's great to meet one of Charlotte's friends,' he said. 'I've heard about you on the whole email thing, but, of course, it's different seeing you.'

Katarina stared at me again. I felt weightless, sick. There was a grain under my toe, rolling around my shoe. My father was still talking.

'What part of the US are you from? I've seen you all on TV, your *accents*,' he made the word harsh, and nasal, and Katarina laughed politely, 'but seeing you here is different.'

'I'm from Streator. It's a small town.'

'Well, we're in Lichfield, which sounds about the same.' His elbow extended out, to meet my arm, as if to include me. They both stared, waiting for an answer of some kind.

Katarina looked perplexed. 'So you live in the same area? Is that how you know each other?'

My father's head jerked back. 'Did you not say?' He stepped away. 'I'm her dad.'

'Oh,' she said, frowning, turning her body towards me, 'I didn't know you had a stepfather.'

Bless her, bless her. The extent to which she would believe me to be good. The sheer insanity of my actions, the dishonesty. And beside her, my father, halfway towards understanding. He blinked, very slowly. 'She doesn't. I'm her dad. Just her normal dad.'

Katarina stepped back, and held on to my arm. 'Is that true?'

It was a direct question. I could hardly lie, now. My mouth was strange, and heavy. I almost choked on the saliva. 'Yes.'

'I –' Katarina began. 'Sorry.' She looked at him, eyes wide.

Never before – and never again – have I felt as strongly the desire to be somewhere else.

My father, because he was there, and prone to talking, opened his mouth again. 'It's always good to check, eh? There was this woman down the road whose kid was taken, and the guy was pretending to be her dad. Awful business. Though, mind you, the girl was less than one year old at the time. Haven't heard any adult cases.' He teetered forward. 'Where they pretend, that is.'

'What I mean to say is, I'm not a stepfather. My wife and I were married for over twenty years – twenty-three, I think.' He looked at me, for a sign – to stop, to continue. I stood there, dumb. 'We would always joke, though, about who she would have married, were it not for me. The postman on Paget Close was a popular guess.'

Katarina was not smiling, and my father scrunched his nose, frowning at his reception. 'I'm sorry. I'm talking too much. Sorry.' He reached out his hand, to retrieve his bag. 'It must be the travel. I've never been on a plane before, you see.'

'No airports in London?' Katarina was looking at me.

'Plenty,' my father said. 'But it would take three hours to get there. The nearest one to us in Lichfield is Birmingham, and it's a bit of a disaster.' My father was oblivious to Katarina's increasing lividity, her face turning a strange shade of red.

'You have to go through the A45,' he continued, 'which, honestly, is not worth the hassle most of the time. The only consolation is the McDonald's on the side of the road. But they started heating the apple pies different, so. Not worth it.'

'Lichfield.' Katarina laughed. She had obviously stopped listening a long time ago. 'I've never even heard of it.'

My father continued his little shuffle – back and forth, back and forth. 'Don't worry,' he said. 'It's not well-known at all. The population can't be more than a few thousand.' (This touched on one of my father's favourite subjects – populations, censuses, and the best places to find electric guitars under fifty pounds.) 'We did get a strangling case not too long ago, which put us on the West Midlands news station. But it wouldn't have reached you. Especially not folks in "the Big Apple", like yourselves.'

'We live in Pittsford, Dad,' I said.

Katarina looked appalled, and I knew what she was thinking: How dare she, correcting him like that? I wanted to die.

She stared at me again. 'Lichfield does sound wonderful, though. I wish I'd known about it before today. Then maybe we could talk about it together.' When she smiled next, it looked demonic. 'There's a lot of things I don't know about England, I'm realizing.'

You did not have to be a master of body language to know that Katarina was not talking about England. My father wiped his forehead, which was almost a fluorescent pink. He looked nervous, shining, angelic, beyond the grave. 'It's a pretty big country,' he eventually said, looking between us.

Katarina held a tanned hand out to him. 'It was a pleasure to meet you. You seem like a wonderful person.'

He accepted the gesture, and stared at me again. She said goodbye, as I stood beside my father, watching her leave. She knew, then.

22

My father did not let me take his bag, and spent all his energy moving it from one arm to the other, eventually folding his arms over it, almost protectively. I tried not to think about Katarina, and stared at the bag instead, imagining a thin wire cutting through my head, parting the brain like dough, or jelly.

When I put his tea on the table, he thanked me twice, and picked up the bag – rucksack, decrepit, from '97 – and several euros. He placed them on the table. 'For you,' he said.

I shoved them away. 'Please, Dad, I'm okay.'

There were three twenty-euro notes, all pressed together, as if they had been sectioned out from the rest of his money, ahead of time. For me. I shook my head again. 'It's lovely, thank you, but I don't need it.'

'It would make me feel better.' He lifted up a napkin, placing the money beneath it.

'It would make me feel worse.'

'But I haven't seen you in so long. It's a gift.'

We continued like this for several minutes, each as unwilling to budge as the other. It had long stopped being about the money, but about his desire to prove his affection in a concrete way, and my desire to get away from more debts. I imagined him working in the evenings, walking up to the exchange bank, and thinking of me. It was too much, for me to have lied and to accept his kindness. And I was beyond needing his affection: it felt too much like an insult, to have it so late.

Across from me, he lifted his bag onto the table, like a bargaining chip. 'It's been years, now – maybe two – since I've sent you anything.'

'But it was your birthday,' I ended up saying, pathetically, into my lap.

'And this is gift enough.' He pushed the notes forward. 'If you take it.'

'I can't, Dad.'

'Why?' He bit into a cereal bar – it was from home, the brand my mother would get us. Orange and cashew.

'I don't want to owe you,' I said.

He used the bag to lift the money a few more paces. 'Don't be insane. I'm your dad.' He shrugged. 'It doesn't work like that.'

I stood up, to get him a refill. When I returned, he was smiling – maybe pride, maybe something else. 'You order things so well,' he said.

'And how does someone do that?'

'It's in the way you carry yourself.' His stubby fingers circled the air. 'I don't know where you get that from, but it's not from me, or your mother, that's for sure.'

My father insisted on paying for pastries, 'to take away', and then loitered near the cashier, dejected, when she told him the cafe couldn't. 'I'll just shove them in a napkin, then. A napkin,' he repeated loudly. The people around us stopped, clinked the sides of their cups with cutlery, in objection. The cashier passed him a cloth, pains au chocolat inside. He thanked her.

He wanted to go for a walk, 'just a little one'. My arms had started shaking at my sides, moving up and down like a panting dog. My father talked about the weather, and the shifts he was to work the following week: 'None too early,' he said. 'I think they're phasing me out, for retirement. Not a fan of that idea, personally.'

The people down at the pub, his sticky-handed friends, were much the same, and their marriages were in various states of disrepair. One had started an affair with a single mother across the road; another was being left, the kids moving with her. He shrugged after relaying a tale of a younger pub-goer, Riley, whose mother had died. 'We all try to be there for each other,' he said. 'Help out, listen, that sort of thing.'

He cleared his throat; we were approaching the square. 'Anyway,' he said, 'we've become better at emotions, and things like that.' He pawed at the space above his eyebrow, where the hairs had started to turn white, and the existing hairs had become thicker, unpredictable.

The whole speech might have been interesting, had I not sensed a father-style segue. Occasionally, when some facet of parenting had to be eked out of my father's body, he would talk about someone we knew first. Our Nathan, down the road, says that Janice likes women. Funny how that happens sometimes, isn't it? And that kid Maisie has a funny eating thing. (Most of his attempts were unsuccessful; they never got past the statement phase.)

Down the steps, and past the pharmacy we had visited in the first days in Villalago, my father was deploying his usual tricks. 'I feel better now than ever before,' he said. 'You know. We had a rough couple of years.'

We turned onto another via, walking at some distance from each other.

'Really rough. But we managed. And you, you're good, right?'

'Right.'

He nodded, appeared reassured, and launched into another tale of woe and decrepitude from my old town: Alfie, twenty-five, out from prison after a petty theft conviction, suicide attempt one month ago. 'He must've been a few years above you in primary school,' he said.

'I don't really remember.'

'So sad.' A head shake. 'A good lad.'

'Is he okay now?'

'God knows.'

We were making a loop around the centre of town; I was unwilling to take him back, to see Katarina again. He ran one hand over the ridges in the fence, and stopped, his little brown shoes collecting the dirt they were planted in. 'I'm saying all this,' an index finger, caught between bars, 'because I want to know how you are. Things were getting out of control, and I didn't do anything –'

'We don't have to go over it,' I said. 'I'm all good.'

He smiled. 'Even if you weren't, I would want to know.'

'All right.'

The man was already moving away, to point out a tourist

sign, finding the general direction of Giulia's house. 'Let's go back, then,' he said.

As we turned onto Giulia's drive, my breathing became strange, and all of the beauty in our surroundings – lemon trees, painted walls, dainty gardens – became insulting. My father increased the speed of his monologue, and moved from a detailed description of his latest project (broken boiler, changed water system) to his childhood. He told me that he had always wanted to leave town. The more he wanted it, and felt that pulsing, the need to get out, out, the less likely he felt it would happen. He knew he had to go. But he got scared. And so he settled into the rhythm of suburban life, the one which aligned himself with his friends at the pub, all varying shades of left behind. We waited in Giulia's garden as he told me that he felt lonely. 'But I don't blame you for going away,' he said. 'There's nothing for us back home, thinking about it.'

My feet on Giulia's patio, the others inside, it occurred to me, in a bleached, fading way, that Katarina would have to see him again.

'We could go back to your Airbnb,' I said. 'I'd love to see it.'

My father looked at Giulia's house: the hedges, the slight crack in the walls, where the ivy grew. 'It's nothing like this. You wouldn't be impressed.'

'But it's an area I haven't seen. Come on.'

He smiled, as if he knew me more than I did. 'You want to get me away from this,' he said, turning his voice upwards, as though, in different circumstances, it might have been a joke. 'You think it's too expensive for me. Your "stepfather".'

Bag at his feet, twenty-year-old T-shirt on his back, he was angled towards the villa, his hand outstretched, to knock on Giulia's door. But before he did, he turned around, and smiled at me again, as if to say: I know. I know you are ashamed of me.

23

My father was ushered into the building by Giulia, who took delight in having another guest – let alone one who was a fully formed adult. They went through the CDs together, as I stood by the door, watching. I had no plans, no lies left.

Katarina came down the stairs in a T-shirt and jeans. Her hair was up; she looked severe. I couldn't help but analyse her. Katarina wore her hair long for free days; half-up for events and trips to the institute bar; up for days in the sun, and when she was stressed, as though she could ward things off through the use of an elastic band. Katarina grabbed the back of my shirt, her breath very close. I thought about the impossibility of me not knowing her, the idea that, three years before, she had been in a bedroom, and I was in mine, and there was no link, no movement between our circles.

'I've told the others that he's your stepfather,' she said, holding on to my arm.

I started to thank her. She let go. I leaned back, towards her; I wanted the touch to be there; even in hurt, or in anger, I wanted to have it.

'I didn't do it for you,' she said.

'I'm sorry.'

'What the fuck, though?'

I stepped back, my spine against the door handle. I pressed it in further.

'Talking to him,' Katarina continued, 'was like hearing about a completely different person. Lichfield? Not London?' She laughed. 'And that's nothing – nothing – compared to the one about your dad. Do you even know how many times I've excused things for you, argued away your coldness – which makes me feel like shit, by the way – because I thought you were grieving? Are you clinically insane?'

I told her that maybe I was. I often thought about how there was a timeline, a social acceptability, for sickness, and that my designated period for denial, general craziness and pathology had already run out. I had aged out of sympathy. Most people got a year, if they were lucky. But there would come a time – in my sixties, single-bed apartment, no window – in which I could tell nobody about my mother's black and corrosive lungs, or the evenings I waited, legs cramped by the door, for her to die. Just another old face with a heaving cough.

'Well, whatever it is,' Katarina said, moving towards the kitchen, 'it's no excuse.' She stared at the print on Giulia's wall. 'And it's not my problem now, either.'

I would have liked to be the type of person who was capable of false cheer, a comedian producing jokes in the rehab centre. But I wasn't. I didn't even have the energy to lift the salad bowl when Tom asked for it at dinner.

We were all seated together: Giulia, the boyfriends, my father, Katarina. She was next to him, on the other side of the table. My father had a benevolent expression on his face, as though he couldn't believe his luck. He used the word 'wonderful' every five minutes, and changed his accent, becoming more posh, so that after every exclamation of 'wonderful' he sounded as if he were making a foray into character acting.

'This stew is really wonderful,' he said, knocking his bowl with an elbow.

Katarina did not speak, just smiled at his comments. This soundless encouragement only buoyed him further, and he continued, regaling them with tales of our hometown like a Greek traveller, forcing others to welcome him into their home. He told them about our cat, omitting its disappearance. He talked about our relative – Uncle James – ruining a train toilet with the stench of his diarrhoea, halfway through the journey to Manchester.

A particularly fond memory of his – the January of 2010, snow so thick it prevented us from leaving the house – was interrupted by Tom, who had logistical questions. 'You couldn't leave at all?' he asked, blinking.

'Nope.' My father grinned. 'We had to use what we had – do you remember, Charlotte? Trying to shovel with that big ladle your mother had?'

I poked the lettuce on my plate. 'Yes.'

'It was a right sight. The snow got up to here.' He pointed to his waist. 'Your mother was fantastic. Remember her idea: pouring the kettle all over the drive?'

There was a brief moment of silence. 'I had no idea London could get so bad in winter,' Damien said. 'It was mild when we visited in January.'

'Lichfield,' my father said, over the sound of Katarina's plate, knocking against the table.

Damien looked at my father, perplexed. 'I'm sorry?'

'It's Lichfield, where the snow was.'

Damien looked at his boyfriend, who gave an equally confused glance. The pair started whispering, and Giulia whacked them lightly with a cloth.

That woman adored my father. She extended a sun-spotted hand, and placed it on his. It was horrifying; I looked at Katarina with a pained expression, more out of habit than anything else, and was met with complete blankness.

Our host tried to encourage my father to stay after dinner. 'You can sleep in the room closest to the stairs,' she said.

It was my room. How quickly she asserted her ownership of it, how quickly it was moved – my room, back into her possession. 'You don't mind, do you?' she said.

My father refused; he had the place booked. 'I paid it all, so I might as well.'

Giulia clucked her teeth together. 'A shame.' She started walking him to the door, a hand around my waist, so that the two of us – father and daughter – were joined either side.

'Well, I'll be off now,' he said, suddenly sheepish. Perhaps it was the view of Giulia's which did it: from the back door, you could see everything: the riches, the open-plan, the antiques. He looked at the floor, and hugged me with one arm. 'I'll see you tomorrow, then?'

'Sounds good.'

My father thanked Giulia for the meal, asked her about the name of a dish – 'What's that one with the fancy meat?' – and opened the door. Giulia and I watched him leave, the rain hitting his back, the flies moving into the house in his absence.

Without him there, I was left with Katarina, and her coldness, and my guilt. I helped Giulia with the dishes in an attempt to separate myself from her: Katarina would be upstairs, above the kitchen, her feet against the carpet, as we wiped the plates. Giulia made several remarks about my father being 'a good man', as she dried a bowl with a red towel. 'He's very funny,' she said.

We washed in silence, her shoulder next to mine. She pointed to the rain slamming against the windows and said it was pretty. I gave no response. Giulia took the plate from my hands.

'Katarina is different today,' she said.

I removed the cutlery from the sink with a clatter.

Giulia took a fork from me gently. 'I think there is something wrong.'

'*Something wrong*,' I repeated, in a crude imitation of her accent. I looked at her flushed face, the patchwork of her cheeks, red coming up like a Rorschach blot. 'I'm so sorry,' I said. 'I don't know why I just did that.'

She placed a hand on my back, though when she next spoke, it was Americanized, as though she was making a great effort to remove traces of her hometown. 'You must be tired.' She tapped my shoulder. 'Sleep, now. Leave those things to me.'

All the bedroom doors had been closed. I stood outside Katarina's, knocking for a few minutes. I said her name, again and again. Neither Damien nor Tom appeared to ask about the noise, and I slumped against the wall – smooth, no traces of the popcorn texture at home – waiting for her. I told her I was sorry, from the other side. There might have been a little movement – Katarina, washing her face, a bird flying past her window. I listened for any sound of her. I wanted to be forgiven. I said this aloud. I want to be forgiven. I said I loved her, which I hadn't said before.

I went into my room, into the bathroom, which was purplish from the light outside. I googled 'how to get someone to forgive you' in the dark, and sat on the toilet lid until I stopped feeling my legs. I tried Katarina's room again. There was nothing, only Giulia's slippers dragging downstairs, quiet Italian, the static from the TV, another relic from the '90s.

I stood in the hallway, like a ghost. My head had started pulsing, warm and darkening at the edges. A grandmother of mine had been carted away to a mental institution in Ireland – 'that place', as my mother had said – her brothers taking her kicking body downstairs. Looking at the outline of the steps, I thought I could see her again, the twist of my mother's legs, her mother's legs.

The others returned, climbing up the stairs, laughing, with empty wine bottles. They had been to the river. I shivered when I looked at Katarina, her hair stuck to her shirt, as if I felt it myself, her sodden clothing against the skin. She was the first up the stairs, back into her room. Only Tom looked at me. He shrugged, and pulled Damien into him, as if to say: I still have mine.

In my room, I searched for the happiest songs possible, and played them aloud. I was sick, and felt relieved afterwards.

I spent too much time looking at my face in the mirror, the smile lines, the raised pimple at the corner of my mouth, contaminated by Katarina's skin. She liked – and I was already thinking about Katarina in past tense – a saying about faces, that they were proof that generations of your features had been loved. Something like that. I touched the glass. Katarina had failed to consider the violences across history, the woman with her rags, straining against, and away; the men in front of her; the unwanted children; sex as an exchange, or as something to submit to. Some people's features were proof of perversion. I was sure of it.

Once their laughter stopped, I went again, to her room. Her light was on, and there was a gap under her door where there was a little strip of yellow.

'Please,' I said. 'Please.' It sounded childish, as though the only words available to me were the ones I had at five. 'I didn't mean to.'

When I looked back, watching from the hall, her light was off.

I left Giulia's house at one in the morning. It was cool, dark, and damp from the day's rain. The dirt got into my shoes. I moved past palazzos and restaurants alone, barely cognizant of anything. The fact that I was moving was a comfort. My legs moved. The rest was numb; an extra dose doled out at the dentist, my limbs a free injection zone.

I walked to the river, and sat on the grass for too long. The water was black and shining, the rain hitting its surface like stones. I tried to think like Katarina: Look at the river, I imagined her saying, see the gold light on the liquid, lit up from the moon, just like van der Neer's landscape. But it didn't work. It was still me. As I touched the water, legs filling up with the river, I looked back at my things – phone, three receipts rolled in a ball – on the bank. I thought about them, more than anything. The curve of the white paper, held up tightly. The dead screen of the phone, the glass, no more messages. I dangled over the river, before I stretched out, and walked, upright, into the water.

I had been at one of those terrible ages, where I was old enough to know I was not beautiful, and young enough to think I could do something about it. My fascinations at the time included a Hello Kitty DVD player, purple body glitter and the storefronts on Bore Street, where they pressed lingerie against their windows. I would pass it on the way to school, afraid of what the shop said about my own body, and mortified by what my interest said about me. It was early December, my mother had been ill for months, making our fridge filled with purées – apples, cinnamon twist – and microwaveable mac and cheese. There was a familiar indent at the centre of her bed, and another at her feet, where I would sit and listen to her cough.

We were due to have a guest to stay for a few weeks: his name was George, he worked with my dad, and his wife was in the process of leaving him. The man was 'at his wits' end', as my father said. George's impending arrival suited the general state of the house, as our floor was littered with dried cat food, despite the obvious absence of a beloved pet. The cat was long gone, my mother only had a few more months left, and yet my father insisted on holding on to the bowls and treats.

The only respite in this strange period was my recent

casting in a school production, simply titled *Born Again*. And, while its plot suspiciously resembled the Nativity (they had rewritten Mary as 'Marie', a teenage mother), my role as a plump angel gave my parents a great deal to talk about.

I had not been cast due to talent, but rather because I was the only eleven-year-old who would, when asked, memorize lines from a poorly written script. (It really was bad: 'Marie' talked about the dangers of abortion, and sang the opening bars of an Elton John song, which had confused me, even then.) The other candidates for the play were either preoccupied by hanging around their older siblings, who drank on the green (led by Tracey, fourteen), or in detention, having set a seagull on fire in a school bin (Peter).

I asked for money from my father, telling him that I had been invited to Tracey's party, and needed an outfit. I took the train to the shopping centre, and found a white slip dress: satin; sticking to my skin with a decisiveness. I ordered a halo, a pack of slimming gum, and a make-up palette from the family computer, under my mother's name. I looked like an inflatable. But, in front of the mirror, the overhead yellow lights on, I felt clean, and pure. Dragged up, I could have been a model – not high end, of course, I wasn't deluded – but one who could pass on the cover of an Argos catalogue. A normal woman. I was proud.

On the way back from the first performance ('Marie' started laughing halfway through, and later refused to come back onstage), my father asked to stop at the local pub. He appeared tense, and ripped tapes out from the car player, one bar of music for another. I was silent, and assumed that his general mood could be traced back to a fault of mine.

He hit both hands on the steering wheel, pulled a face, and turned up the volume control. 'Well done, by the way,' he said. 'You were the best one there.'

I rustled around in my outfit – white polyester shift, no bra, heavy burgundy lipstick. 'Thanks, Dad.'

He told me that he would be stopping by the pub for a few minutes, to 'check up on George', who was due to travel back home with us. 'He's in a pretty tricky spot,' my father said, turning into the gravel car park. 'Would you like to stay or come in?'

'I'll come in.'

Pub-entry privileges were fairly new – a rare benefit from my mother's lung cancer. The new routine: sitting at the back of the room, with a Diet Coke, eating a bag of KP Nuts.

We walked inside, as I moved my dress around. I sat towards the front, where the men leaned over the bar, moving their heads towards each other's ears, to whisper and spit words out. My father was on one of the bar stools, his legs resting on the silver poles. And George – colleague at Dad's work, known for his ability to keep facial hair, and his inability to keep his wife – was beside him.

I felt alive, adult. Beside the heater, I watched other people without shame, half of my face sweating, scorched, the other side cool. My father cried in his seat. George patted his back awkwardly, great big slaps, almost violent. I could not hear them, but I knew, just as I knew that the things on the bottom of my arms were hands, and my mother would be dying soon, why he was crying. I looked across, into the mirror at the side of the room, as if my curved nose and the over-lining of my lips might protect me.

The next few moments are unsure, as if, in my bored, mindlessly insecure brain, I might have fabricated it all. But this is what I do know: I left them both, George and my father, to go to the toilet, a tiny, piss-smelling room which was always warm, even in winter. I stayed there for a while. I do not know how long. I walked back into the main room, where the Carpenters were playing through the speakers, and my father was not there. I leaned over the bar, feeling on the edge of something – true independence, terror – as I asked where my dad had gone.

The barman shrugged. He had a moustache, and told me to 'try outside', which I did. At the back entrance of the pub: no father, but George instead, smoking. I felt as if I needed to say something. I was infused with a new kind of energy. It was raining. The surface of my dress became darker, cream splotches decorating it roughly. George asked about the play, and my mother's health.

'It's all good,' I said. 'The next run is tomorrow.'

'Impressive. You're a proper star.' He stood very close, as if I were to be punished through his exhales, the grey breath catching mine.

I blinked. 'Do you know where Dad is?'

I felt as if I had touched a live wire, and some animal, almost maternal, thing wanted me to get out. I looked at George's chin, where hairs, like blackheads, stretched out. He held on to my wrist. I remember thinking that I had to eat more; that no person should be able to pull it so deftly, without effort of any kind.

I found my father sitting in the car, entirely recovered. My cheeks were red, and his were clear. I opened the back door.

'Sit here, with me,' he said. 'Or I'll feel like a taxi driver.' He patted the seat beside him and watched my face. 'Is everything okay?'

'I don't like George,' I said.

'What? Our George?'

'Yes.'

My father frowned. 'He's a little rough around the edges recently, after his wife. That's all.'

My legs were shaking. They kept hitting the glove compartment, where my mother kept her apple gum. I told him that George had 'done something bad', as we waited for the man himself to arrive, to drive him back to the house. 'I don't feel good,' I said.

My father touched his eyebrow with one finger, the other on the wheel. There were lines on his face, purplish skin. 'He's all right,' he said. 'He's only staying for a few days; we'll be well shot of him soon.'

When George appeared five minutes later, several bags of peanuts in his hands, 'as a thanks, for putting up with me', my father asked if I could get out of the car, to sit in the back seat again.

I complied. The kind of child I was, I would have done anything – lied, stolen, cried, knelt by anyone's side – if it meant I would be liked. I had a complete inability to question anything; any command made of me was justified, and, if my faith could stretch to a man being swallowed and saved by a whale, it could certainly extend to something else. So, over the next four days, when George walked over the carpeted floors, checked the already closed blinds, and told me to lie down, I would do so. This habit of his lasted each night, and would continue months later, if he ever stayed for dinner, and found himself far too drunk to drive himself back home.

It was never just once, and was always in plain sight. Later, whenever I saw young children, young girls, specifically, I thought: How impossible. That my parents, when confronted with this particular hurdle, had taken the easiest option. Had maintained the silence in our house, as George danced from the downstairs sofa into my room. It's easily underestimated, the desire for a normal, uncomplicated day. That, when given the opportunity to confront something terrible – to say, This should not happen, and will never again, I am sorry – we will take a nice, quiet life, over everything else. Of course, it was hard for my father, specifically, to reckon with any of it. Firstly, that it was his friend; secondly, that I was his daughter. But both of them knew – my mother and father together – and yet they could not find it in them to walk upstairs, look me in the eye, and talk.

24

The river water had reached my shoulders when the song started – and, by that time, I'd already had enough. I was heading off to my death, not thinking of the vastness of time, held in a grain of sand, the endurance of love (and so on), but the opening bars of 'Barbie Girl'. Talk about undignified.

I picked up my phone from the bank, and started to make my way back into town, dripping everywhere. I arrived in the hallway of my father's bnb an hour later, arms and legs pricking as I stepped inside. I saw him in the doorway; his stomach, which began at his ribs, jutting out. Beer belly, shining from the light at the end of the hall. He stepped closer, and I shut my eyes. It was pitiful, to be so old, and in this state, returning to him like a child, stewed in old bathwater. He touched my shoulder.

'A bit of late-night swimming, then?'

His expression was so sweet, and the joke was such a kind attempt, that I started crying again. 'I'm terrible,' I said, half of my face thick with mucus.

My father left, and came back with a blue patterned jumper. He threw it; I failed to catch. He knelt down, and pressed it into my hands. 'Put it on, please.'

'Okay.' I wiped at my face with a hand. He stood opposite

me for a minute, and then nodded to himself, having been reassured that I looked warmer. These were new heights of mortification.

We walked into the room beside his – a blue-painted library with a sofa, and no curtains. He offered tea, and then cut in again before I could answer. 'It's not really a question. You have just been dunked into a vat of water – or dunked yourself, I don't know.'

'Self-dunking.'

He stepped forward, as if in a bid to hug, and then retreated. 'Right.' A hand was waved into the air. 'You were saying something about being terrible?'

'Yes.'

He sat down, and pulled on the edge of his pyjama bottoms with a severe expression on his face. They were red, and had dancing snowmen.

When I got to the specifics of the lie – you, Dad, dead of a heart attack – his left eye twitched, as did his knee. But when I finished, he started to laugh.

'I'm almost glad,' he eventually said. 'I was so sure you had committed a murder on the way over here.' He leaned forward in his chair. 'You looked how they're meant to look, from the TV shows. All white and crazy.'

I blinked. His movements had returned to normal, had lost their jolting, haunted quality. He stood up and rummaged around the windowsill. There, he pulled out a single cigarette, and a black lighter. 'They have a policy, here.' He opened the window. 'The woman who owns this is nothing like your Giulia, and she caught me this afternoon, so I left one here.'

'Did Mum know?'

'About this?' He waved the lit cigarette in the dark. 'If she did, she hid it very well.'

'The English way.'

He smiled. 'It does seem unfair, now, that she went the way she did. Health conscious, and all that. And me –' He stubbed it out on the ledge, and let it fall out of the window with a shrug. 'I understand,' he said, 'why you lied like that. I wanted me gone, too.'

His face looked pearly in the light, and we could both still taste his cigarette from the grey air. I closed my eyes, found my head shaking. 'Please don't say that.'

His hands were raised upwards, palms facing the ceiling. 'What do you want me to say, then?'

'That I'm insane, and I should be carted away. Probably for ever.'

'I *do* want you to come home, if that counts.'

I was under a drunken trance – half cold and wet, half warm. 'I want you to say that I'm sick, or something. And that you don't want to see me again.'

The man, and his snowman pyjamas, leaned forward. 'I can't do that, come on now. You're my daughter.'

Another fact of life: the Fibonacci sequence; Newton's apple; hamsters eating their young. And I was crying again. Between those sputtering, aching breaths, pulled out from the diaphragm, I had settled on a phrase, as if to prove my insanity further: I'm bad. I'm bad. He stood up, and came over to hug me again. I watched the red blur of his movements, and tried not to be touched. He reached me anyway. What a shame, for him to have raised this. He started patting my head, and said that I was his daughter again, as though that might remedy everything, every evil. That stuffy room, with its thick heat, was confessional-like, warm and close. Later, when searching for a quotation for a painting – little dots, like raisins, on the edge of the work, childish fingerprints – I would find a passage, and think of him, and that tentative hug. He who created you, he who formed you: Do not fear, for I have redeemed you.

Some pretty words.

The next morning, it was hot again, the air pushing down on us, and Villalago. I was ashamed. Other embarrassments – tripping over, the announcements of failed crushes, incomplete hook-ups, my naked body over Katarina's – all came back, pooling over, as if to remind me of the extremity of the most recent one. I had developed a rash from the river. The skin around my neck was doughy and wet, like a peeled peach.

My father returned in the morning with a yoghurt, not a trace of the day before anywhere, not a single word turning to anger or disdain. There was only a slight relaxation in his face, as though my sins had allowed him to let go of his hold, his stiffness. He asked questions like he had never before, with true patience, and an intensity which suggested he genuinely wanted to hear the answers. And he was fascinated by my landlord: something about the man's single, shuffling nature (those shoes!) interested him. 'And you're saying he lives alone?' He opened the window a little wider.

'Yes. He has a son, but they don't talk. Or he's ill, or in a different state. Either way.'

My dad shook his head.

'He doesn't say much at his inspections,' I continued. 'Just puts on his slippers – he has outdoor ones, too – and walks around, in silence.'

There was a stack of Italian board games in the room, and empty biscuit wrappers in a trail across the floor. He was used to being the only one to see it, his mess. And he was still interested in the man.

'How often does he visit?'

'Every month. He sends an email before he does,' I said.

'And you talk to him, offer him tea?'

'He's probably a coffee drinker.'

He cleared his throat. Having changed out of his pyjamas, he appeared more dignified in the light, and raised his head. 'I know I haven't said anything about yesterday, and I won't, unless you want me to. It's forgotten.' This was expressed with no huge sense of levity, only a little embarrassment on his part, and a great deal on mine. I was sure that I was red. 'We're probably too old for this, now,' he gestured between us, 'and it's beyond me to tell you to eat your peas, and go to bed at a decent time each night.'

I smiled.

'I wish I could. Do all that. But I do think, now we are where we are, that you should be a little kinder to people you think aren't worth it.'

I started to speak, but he only said, 'It's a dreadful thing, Charlotte,' and left, returning ten minutes later with two glasses of orange juice.

When we arrived back at Giulia's, the others would not look at us. Tom and Damien rearranged their collars, occupying themselves with their hair. Katarina's skin was peeling;

there was an ashiness, white flakes. She blinked in the sun, and her eyes moved from the point between her sandals to the bottom of Giulia's patio. The four of us remained outside – my father had gone with Giulia. Damien said something about the weather; Katarina agreed, too loudly. Tom left first – 'I've forgotten a bag.' His boyfriend watched him leave, and turned to us with a look of apology. He had to help Tom – the man couldn't handle that sort of thing, packing.

It was impossibly uncomfortable, the silence between us, though neither of us made any attempt to break it. I wanted to shake her by the shoulders, a wronged mistress. I know you, I would say.

Katarina started stacking Giulia's chairs, though there was no sign of rain. She caught the tip of her thumb between the wood, and swore. 'Fuck,' she said, looking at me, and then away again.

'I'm sorry,' I said.

She continued to stack, her mouth even, features as neutral as possible. I had seen that once before, the time we watched a sad French film together, the schoolmaster leaving his children behind. Her face had smoothened out like that, heavy blinking. Now, hunched over, collecting the last chair, she was attempting an unperturbed air which did not suit her. 'What are you sorry for?'

'You know,' I said.

'I don't. What are you sorry for?'

'Almost everything.'

Katarina made a crude sound, like a barcode being rejected: wrong item. She kicked the edge of her new pile. 'I'm done, now.' She looked back at her work. 'I'm going inside.'

I watched the house, the grooves in its walls, the picturesque setting – rolling hills, humid vineyards, the church, the river. Through the window, Damien and Tom stood together, their foreheads touching. Tom said something, and they both laughed, flashes of American teeth, lined up in their gums. My father was inside; Katarina, too. How strange that they could all occupy the same space. I thought about that for a while – the different origins of everyone: Katarina, roads in the Midwest, her ageing parents; Giulia's town, the swimming; my father, his kitchen in disarray, his dead wife. There was another laugh – Katarina's – and I walked back towards the house. We are drawn to others' enjoyment, even if we cannot participate in it ourselves.

Our flight would leave in four hours. My father had already gone. He had said something kind – that it was good to see me, and that I should call more often. He then asked me to come home. I smiled, thought about the popcorn walls, my mother's discounted perfume, half-empty, and said I would.

Katarina was packing, her door open. She stopped only once, to look out of her room, where she caught me, presumably red-faced, watching her. She opened the door wider, and I saw her face, the fullness of it, and, even in her anger, I loved her.

'Taken to spying now, too?'

'It got you to talk to me.'

'You're actually insane,' she said. 'I can't believe I didn't see it before.' Katarina held on to my arm, pulled me in, and closed the door. She looked terrible. Her shirt was open, as though she had been halfway through changing, and had decided against it. My wrist was slippery from the sweat. 'Just tell me what to do, to make it okay again,' I said. 'I'll say anything.'

Katarina shook her head and threw a striped shirt at me. 'It's yours,' she said. 'Don't want to get it mixed up with the rest of my things.'

We packed separately, quietly, before Giulia drove us to the train station. When we arrived, Tom and Damien jumped out to collect the luggage. The boyfriends said their goodbyes, pulling Giulia into a hug by the side of the road. She insisted that she ought to stay outside the station. 'I will just wait here,' she said, hovering by the concrete like a fable, the woman trapped by a geographic line. She told us to travel safely, and to 'come back next summer', nodding to herself. 'I'll see you all then. Not long.'

And before we boarded the two o'clock train, the flight into Rochester, and the train from Louise station to Monroe, there was the back of Giulia's silvery head, and the opening of her car door as she drove away, returning to the house.

25

We did not speak for the next two weeks, though I often walked around campus, spending money in the hope that she might be behind me, hidden between sweaters, or yarn, or tins of fish. I sat in parks, read straight romance novels where ice skaters, lawyers and dubious British royals found love. I found comfort in their predictable cadence, and always cried when they married at the end. I moved in a half-drunk state, aware of only my legs, as though the rest had been severed off, somewhere across the Italian coast. I left voicemails, apologizing over and over; I lay in my bed in a stew, windows shut, the sweetened, rough smell of myself getting everywhere.

Old habits returned, sliding back so quickly it was as if they had always been there. Without Katarina, there was no need to make my life beautiful, to decorate it with chequered tablecloths, two-dollar flowers or the breadcrumbed mac and cheese she loved. Not only was it excessive – two hours of preparation, soapy liquid running over the plates, then dried, then dirtied again, ten hours later – but it felt cruel, having to keep up this performed happiness, without her. I ate once a day, spooning grey gunk straight into my mouth, and took over-the-counter pills to avoid stomach aches and indigestion, resulting in a perpetual bloat, which I carried around like a small child. Then bed, where I picked at my hair, strands plucked from the scalp like perverted elastic. The human body was used to only so much inaction – it developed gangrenous sores, and hair could grow mould in a matter of weeks. I read articles about people much worse off than me – those bed-bound, comatose bodies – until it became a fantasy.

Tom and Damien seemed to vanish, and I thought I had imagined them – and perhaps her, too, my lovely fever. Matthew doubled in his communication, as if to make up for it all. I suspected that one of them had sent him to check up on me, which gave them too much credit, and Matthew none at all. His primary method of 'checking-in' was through email links, mostly with no text. There had been links to a site which claimed to 'align your throat chakra', an online PTSD questionnaire, and a forum called 'lonelybrits' (which, after investigation, happened to be a fetish website). The most recent email was more substantial: 'There's this thing tonight,' it read, 'maybe you'd like to go.'

Matthew and his group of new-wave-utopian-socialist-anarchists were protesting outside Starbucks. At the bottom of the message, in a rushed paragraph: 'Heard that you and Katarina aren't a thing any more. Ik we don't talk about that stuff but it's got to be rough.' Matthew had attached a meme: a small cat, with a squashed nose, in a birthday hat. I cried about it for hours, though I think it was meant to be comforting. I sent him something back at random, from the suggested bar in my phone. He asked to meet the next day.

*

Matthew was much brighter than I'd seen him before, his life arranging itself neatly: relaxed Saturday job; refurbished bathroom; minimal contact with his father. That last fact was a particular point of celebration; Matthew found his parents' bourgeois sentiments intolerable, and called his father 'the enemy of progress'. (This was something he actually said, over his cafeteria muffin.) Forty-five minutes into seeing him, I laid a hand on his back for too long.

He moved away, like a startled animal. 'Are you doing okay?'

I told him I was, and mentioned a new painting I had not started yet. 'It's going to be massive, from here,' I gestured to a point in the wall, 'to here.'

Matthew nodded.

'The theme's water.'

'Sounds interesting.' He bit into the side of his muffin, and moved his chair closer to the door. 'I spoke to Katarina the other day, by the way.'

'You did?'

'Yeah. She said a few things.'

'I bet she did.'

'I think she's just nervous to talk to you in person. You can be a little stressful. But she's not bad.'

Matthew still had a childishness about him: he found things to be simple, 'good' or 'bad', and assumed that other people had the same cocktail of damage and innocence as he did. 'I think Katarina's overreacting,' he said, as we walked onto the street, blinking to accommodate the light.

'That's nice.'

'No, seriously, dude, I mean it. You've obviously got

stuff going on, and this,' he made frantic circles with his hands – 'this', meaning me, meaning her – 'is obviously a distraction.'

'Thank you,' I said, and he smiled. 'I had no idea – absolutely no clue – that you had become a fully qualified therapist, Matthew.'

I sounded so much like my mother, then – I had her half-sweet, half-bitter tone, the one used for street salesmen or Protestants – that I couldn't even enjoy Matthew's expression. I thought about asking him where he got his psychology degree from (classic), and looked at his head, which fell, as if the act of transporting it was too great, and stopped myself.

We waited outside the apartment (he still liked to call it this, despite its resemblance to a five-person family home), as Matthew continued his therapist's plight. 'I don't think she realizes – Katarina, I mean – how humiliating it is, just to say nothing, and ghost you. There's literally no communication from her.'

He was inches away from pulling me into a hug, and performing an 'it's not your fault' ritual on me.

'Like, okay,' he continued, 'lying is bad. But a relationship should be unconditional, not I-do-something-a-little-off-and-it's-out.' He blushed, aware of the stupidity of his speech, the reference to 'a little off', his mysterious 'unconditional' relationship, more like a fantasy, or a prison, than anything real. 'Anyway,' he said, 'I'm talking too much. Tell me how you're doing.'

Cars passed, and drivers spat out of their windows, others throwing cigarettes onto the pavement. While

Matthew frowned, and flicked a stub off his shoe, I stepped towards him. 'Do you want to have sex with me?'

His head jerked away, towards the traffic, as though I'd hit him. He made a few high, embarrassed sounds from the bottom of his throat. 'What?'

'Do you want to?'

'What are you talking about?' He laughed, less sure of himself. 'Is this some kind of performance art thing?'

I shook my head. 'That was last semester.'

'Can you stop it, then? You're stressing me out.' He lifted his arms, in a yawn. His shirt moved upwards, showing the bottom of his stomach, a trail of hair. 'I thought you were a lesbian now,' he said.

'I guess.'

'What do you mean, "I guess"?' He smiled. 'Was sleeping with me for a few weeks not enough to find out?'

'Come on.' I pulled my hair forward, to the front, as though that might add to my allure. A group of first-years walked past, and Matthew smiled at them, his face shifting maniacally between myself and the students. 'Let's go inside,' I said.

Matthew did nothing, and appeared more interested in the group than ever before, waving, almost obsessively, while they looked away, at their phones.

I touched his hand. 'Why not?'

Matthew shook his head. 'You don't want to.'

'What, like I've never seen your dick before?'

'Funny. Funny. I just think it would be bad,' he said. 'I think it would be bad for you. And I don't mean the actual thing itself,' he blushed, 'but mentally, or whatever.' There were muffin crumbs near his collar, and he had a society meeting in an hour: things to take down, establishments to disestablish. 'I also honestly don't want to.'

'Please.'

'No.'

My eyes had started to water, my face was warm, drenched. 'Please,' I said again.

Matthew moved closer, as though the tears had eroded a previous radioactivity, and placed tentative arms around me, in a hug. He patted the back of my head. 'Don't worry,' he said, his voice high, 'this is better than anything I could have done, sex-wise.'

I walked back while it was still light, and the schools in Pittsford were closing for the day. Mothers held their daughters, all bobbing ponytails. I thought they could all see the embarrassment on me. I looked at the ground.

When I got back to the flat, Matthew had texted. 'hope ur back and all is ok.' I felt terrible.

26

All was, sadly, not OK. It had only been two weeks, and the highlight of each day had become the walk through Victor Road, where I visited the 24/7 drugstore. (It was not, in fact, 24/7 – but it shut at ten p.m., which suited me just fine.) At the drug store, they had to talk to me, as per their job contract, and I spent most of my time there making furtive eye contact with my favourite worker, a young woman who always wore a cap. She might even have been bald; the cap went so far as to cover most of her forehead. I'd go there in the afternoon, when I woke up, to the 'by the seaside' alarm, which did a good job of reminding me that it was another day, and I was cursedly, terribly, alive.

The place smelled like artificial strawberries, and it had strip lights along the aisles, like an airport runway. I would spend over an hour there. Some days, I got it to an hour and thirty, just pretending to look at air pressure socks. They were as far away from 'digestive health' as possible, which was perfect, as it gave me plenty of time to wander over and buy things: loperamide; or dextromethorphan, for a bit of variety.

The bald woman smiled at me when I reached the checkout, punched the tablet boxes into her machine, then handed them back. She had painted eyebrows, too dark for the rest of her skin. I thought about buying a make-up pencil for her, in the right shade – mahogany, or even taupe – handing it over, watching her brows move upwards, like a mime.

'Have the best day,' the woman said, once I had paid. (She always said that.)

In the evenings, I joined Subreddits, and voted on whether people were assholes. Most of the time, they were not. This was frustrating – the only reason they'd posted at all was to hear the resounding applause of their goodness: 'it's not you, I promise'; 'they're just horrible'; 'don't beat yourself up'. Whenever this happened, I commented that they were, in fact, the asshole. 'Totally on you,' I wrote, constipated, having taken three loperamides. 'You should always specify which colour the bridesmaids need to wear.'

After I received a text from Katarina – it was remarkably bland, as though she wanted to Etch-a-Sketch me out of her life – I found a new forum. It was for children seeking answers from 'internet parents'. Teens visited to discover how to wash up properly, how to navigate college. I sorted through for hours, reading their insane, domestic dramas. Katie from Arkansas was unsure how to talk to her roommate, who had decorated the space in tapestries, and 'waved a stick crystal around'. Animalluvver603 had their first interview, and didn't know if they should cover up the My Chemical Romance tattoo on their forearm, or, 'fuck it', because, if they valued him as a worker, the company shouldn't give a shit about that sort of thing, anyway.

And the responses piled through: heretohelp!34, mothermakescakes2nite and idrisforeverr used words like 'honey', 'darling' and 'sweetie'. The 'adults' told the posters not to worry; they recommended a pants and shirt set from Costco; they masqueraded as mothers. (Perverts sent the occasional links, as they always did.)

I made a fake username, and found someone asking a particularly lonely question: 'I just don't know what to do, what if im like this forever, im just stuck, and there doesn't seem to be a way out, im too tired now to care.' This continued for several paragraphs. My response was filled with platitudes, and I wrote about the certainty that she would 'find her crowd' from my bedroom. I did that for a while, typing as 'linda73mathewson'. I drank coffee, took the thin, blue pills from the pharmacy packets, and sent a dry message back to Katarina: 'Nice to hear from you, everything is fine, thank you. Hope it's all going well your end.'

At six in the morning, when the channels turned to daytime television, I watched a show about a family of rabbits. When the mother rabbit, distinguishable from the father due to her apron, tucked her son into bed, my face got very hot. I opened the window, and looked down. There was nothing but yellowish grass, and a can, glinting back.

Ordinary humiliations kept coming. I had to visit an institute 'adviser' in one final meeting before the project deadline, 'to check my engagement' with the course. On my way to the building, I thought I saw Katarina, and watched the back of her head bob through the institute grounds, the flick of her hair in the wind, tripping on the pavement the very moment she turned around, to reveal a man with a dishevelled beard.

In the meeting, my adviser spoke about his ex-wife, a

Michiganian with an awful – 'really awful' – slot machine addiction, and Hyacinthe Rigaud. He had written about the portraitist in the '80s, and had never quite recovered from the strength of his dissertation – 'eighty-seven, unheard of, even back then'. His office was covered in prints, all seventeenth-century men in rounded hats. I called it 'pilgrim-chic' to his face. He coughed, and sat down.

'We're waiting for your final submission,' he said, clicking his mouse. 'And graduation is approaching.'

I nodded.

'If you miss the next deadline, which the course organizers have already kindly extended for you, you will have to retake the year.'

Another year in Pittsford, at the institute: more seminars, more tepid weather. 'I'll submit on time.' I smiled at him. There was a cut on his chin, and a piece of toilet paper at its centre. It had started to bleed.

'Good,' he said. 'We don't like failing people here.'

'I know.' (The previous year, a student had turned in a pig's head for their final assignment. Other legendary works included: de-shelled M&Ms; a bathroom selfie series; a felt-tip drawing of Jeff Buckley.)

'I've looked at your other submissions,' he said. 'Circles, squares, things like that. Modern. It's not my specialty, as you know.'

The adviser had several non-fiction books on his desk: *Rigaud and Regard*; *Laughing Cavaliers: Rigaud and Seventeenth-Century Politics*; *The Man and His Portrait*. He ran his hand over them and breathed in, as if touching sacred works. There were no photographs, no smiling graduation certificates from children, hand-drawn crayon portraits of deranged, centipede-like dogs. This was it, his life. I wanted to ask him, then, whether it had been worth it, whether his singular, archaic life, dedicated to this nobility-loving man, felt justified; if he held on to his papers at night, thinking, over and over: marriage to Chastillon, six months, annulment; complete failure. It was only there, sitting in the adviser's office, that Katarina's obsession with her professor made sense. We shared a need for guidance, reassurance that this life wouldn't go wasted, on stale ideas and dead men.

The adviser's hand was still over his book. 'It's generally none of my business,' he said, 'as I'm sure you'll graduate.' He looked at his wall, and back towards me. 'But I'd really appreciate it if you tried this time. Out of respect, if nothing else.'

The problem was that it was difficult to begin, after having committed myself to artistic laziness for so long. It was a 'bit', as Katarina used to say, smiling: 'you and your bit'. But it had lost its texture. And so I began working in earnest.

I started to do all sorts of things which I rationalized as being part of the 'process'. I walked to bars, ordered rum, or vodka, or both, and drank. I watched documentaries about artists other than Andy Warhol, and listened to them talk about their art problems, humming along to their words, as if they were a form of hypnosis. I put off laundry, considered talking to a priest. I unfollowed Katarina, then requested her back again. A month before the deadline, I attended institute seminars with headphones in, and cited sensory problems which I did not have. Each day became a stream of 'I's. I couldn't get away from myself – and I believed that getting away from yourself was the point of all lives, generally.

I befriended a student librarian (there were such majors at the institute), who allowed me to print off as many inspiration photos as I liked, on the unspoken condition that I listened to her issues with physical intimacy.

'It's like I can do almost anything,' she said, opposite the *War* section, 'besides have sex.'

I asked if she might be gay, and she lit up, as if she had carefully constructed the conversation to reach that very conclusion. I waved at her on my way out. 'It's great to see you again,' I said, holding several printouts of painters I admired: Goran Djurovic, Peter Brown.

A series of sketches followed, from a squatting position on my bedroom floor. A strange, impossible heat moved through me as I traced the work. I followed their figures: standing at the centre of an open window; bodies flung over staircases. There was a cosiness, a decided intimacy, in Brown's work; an abject remoteness in Djurovic's. I scoured the internet for interviews, articles, as though proximity to their talent might, by virtue of knowing, lead me to my own, and after a few hours, I had a figure of a woman, eked out from cheap oil paints. But I was jealous, not a genius.

As the deadline approached, I became viscerally afraid that Katarina might die: a shooting; too many drinks, liver failure on Willowbrook Road. That she could have died, without anyone telling me, or thinking to call. It felt inevitable, her early death. I would panic reading the headlines: mass-shooting in Church Street; physical assaults in the only 'gay-friendly' bar in the county. After listening to the television static of the news, and seeing Streator – her hometown – appear at the bottom of the screen, I called her. There had been a fire, or rather, several fires. A suited presenter made comments about the 'civilian toll' from the screen, in a clipped tone. Behind him, buildings vomited out black smoke, while civilians ran from their homes, carrying bulldogs and charred photo albums. I closed my eyes, and imagined Katarina walking on screen, covered in sulphur, like Sodom's angel.

She picked up the call. That was the first surprise – that she had accepted. I wondered what my name was in her contacts.

'Hi,' she said, 'is everything okay?'

'I saw the news.' A pulsing had started at the centre of my chest, as a young boy, grey-faced and tear-stained, was lifted into his mother's arms.

'What news?'

'The stuff about Streator,' I said. 'The fires.'

'What?' Her voice was low, as though she had just woken up. 'What's going on?'

'There was a fire,' I said. 'I'm just checking you're okay. Which you are.'

'You're making no sense.'

I ignored her. 'Are you at home?'

'No, I'm at the apartment,' she said. 'Please, just tell me what's wrong. You're scaring me.'

'Are your family in?'

'They're in Boston, visiting my brother.'

'Perfect. Okay,' I said.

'Is that it, then?'

I often thought about the things I wanted to tell her. It

was a dark, reddening feeling, to discover that all the minor frustrations of our lives – of mine, and hers – would go unwitnessed, until they died out. 'That's it,' I said.

'Good. Please don't call again.'

I hung up the phone, and sat on the sofa, listening to the residents of Streator cry, as the houses gave way, blistering, against the smoke.

I visited Matthew in his apartment-house-complex the next day, mostly to apologize for my earlier insanity. Had the conversation been a corporate email, the subject might have read: *Potential sexual harassment, discussion pending*.

'You can come over,' he had said, 'but only if you send me proof of signing up to this system.'

The 'system': I had expected another union or a freelance political group. Instead, it was the student counselling service. It claimed to give 'free, non-judgemental access for all institute members'. On the website, they included an image of a woman in a suit, with a few quotations encouraging students to 'live your best life'.

'I'm the happiest I've ever been,' one testimony said. 'I wiped away my finals stress with just a few sessions with Jennifer.'

'Hahaha,' I replied to Matthew. 'Excellent one.'

'I'm not joking,' he typed back.

When I arrived at his flat, I handed over a gift – *Steal this Book*, a pamphlet on the importance of anti-capitalist theft, from a stall on campus. They had charged me seven dollars.

I stood several feet away from him. Matthew talked about anarchy, and the development of the Starbucks strike. He accepted the pamphlet, and asked no questions, which felt a little bit like love. I breathed, very quickly, into my palm, as he walked around the room. His face burned; he sat down and stood up again. It was almost beautiful, watching his feeling – true feeling – for the ideas he discussed. None of it was new information (capitalism bad, poverty bad, sickness bad), but it seemed to cleanse him, energize him all the same. What would happen, when he aged, and the feeling gave way to something else?

'Do you agree?' he said, pointing at his new pamphlet.

I nodded. I did not know what I was signing myself away to, but I did it anyway.

'Good,' he said.

I took his narcissism, the fact that he needed little input from me, as a kindness, and sat on his sofa for two hours. A third of that time he dedicated to YouTube, searching for lecture clips, which became a stream of academic words in my head: dialecticism, analogous, clinical.

I excused myself to go to the toilet once the *Rick and Morty* video essay began. Matthew had decorated the space in Post-it notes, little squares above the loo-roll holder, one water-stained note on his tap. Moving through his house, I started to notice the rest of them: bed frame; door handle, little neon accents. Each one contained a frenzied statement: 'STOP CONSUMING', scribbled on his laptop screen, 'BE KINDER, FUCKER', beside the salt shaker, 'DO SOME GOOD PLEASE' on his sofa.

'EVERYTHING MIGHT BE FOR A REASON' touched me, in particular. The 'might' was hesitant, angling to the left, crammed in. The note sat by the window. What an insight into his brain. I was sure he had everyone he knew categorized in that way. (Orange square, 'LOOK AFTER HER', mine might have said.)

I left him a new one by his carpet, stealing a pen from his desk. 'You're doing a good job,' I wrote, complete with a smiling face.

Matthew asked about my plans for the next week as I was leaving. We made an arrangement to see each other in a few weeks, at a party he was hosting. Matthew tapped me on the shoulder before making a little shoo-ing gesture. 'Just go to one session, dude,' he said, before he shut the door.

Then the pharmacy again, and a walk back. The air had a strange texture, almost grainy. The woman in the cap asked if I was buying tablets for a friend. I shook my head, and told her I was looking after a man in my building. 'It's informal care,' I said. (I might have invented the term.) 'He can't afford a proper nurse.'

It must have been convincing. I didn't look like someone who would be abusing store-bought drugs. I still did my hair in the morning. I put tinted lip balm on, teeth-whitening strips on Wednesdays. Either that or the bald woman was several hours deep into the shift, beyond caring. I looked at her tag: Laura.

I went back the next day, and waited for Laura to turn away, to get some sleeping tablets, while I left a sandwich and a blue energy drink on the counter. I scribbled her name out on the back of a receipt, and walked out of the pharmacy before she could say anything. It made me feel good, for a while. Like the space after laughing. It was nice.

*

Matthew stayed true to his word: by the following week, I had completed half of the painting, and we hadn't met up once. 'I'll see you once you go to your first session,' he typed back, after I sent a particularly vulnerable text, begging to come over.

'Never,' I responded.

By morning, I had a slot booked in. One hour with their therapy service, at the centre of campus.

27

The sessions were held in a rectangular building. It was several storeys, and the brightness of the lighting, and the pink sign – 'Campus Therapy' – felt both interrogatory and demeaning. I was not a good mental health patient, primarily due to my insistent belief that I was more intelligent, and thus more capable, than anyone I might be opposite. On the day of the session, I walked up to the front desk, where a young woman smiled prettily, purplish lipstick moving up and down. Her beauty was disconcerting, and I imagined her laughing at me the moment I turned away. There was a poster opposite her, with 'Embrace the Real You' attached in Arial font.

After a few minutes, a woman appeared, called my name, and led me to a room with no windows, a pre-emptive box of tissues and a stock image of a friendship group on the wall. The woman closed the door, and waited for me to choose a chair.

'Sit wherever you like,' she said.

I hovered, expecting her to relent and choose one first, the result of which was several minutes of hedging silence, her vacant staring and my increasing awkwardness. 'I guess I failed that test, then,' I eventually said, taking the seat closest to the door.

She blinked, false lashes following the movement seconds later, delayed. 'There's no exam, here. No right or wrong. I'm really here to see how you think, and offer alternatives.' Her first lie of many, then: that there was no right and wrong, that we existed in a place completely disbanded of good or bad. A terrifying thought. The woman asked me how I felt, 'entering the room'.

'Like the way I walked in?'

'More the way you feel today, in the space.'

I wanted to point out that her use of 'more' suggested that there was a better thing, or meaning. The stock image on the wall bared its teeth at me. 'I'm good,' I said. 'Yeah, good.'

She folded her hands on top of her legs and smiled. 'That's fantastic to hear,' she said. 'Though I'm sure that if that were the case, you would not need to be at our session.'

'Perhaps this is a hobby of mine.'

The woman leaned to one side; her lashes bobbed. 'Do your hobbies tend to cause this much discomfort?'

'I'm not uncomfortable,' I said.

'It would not be strange if you were. It's our first session together, and, as you say in your form, your first visit here in general.'

'I've been practising, though. I also watch far too many Robin Williams films, so I've got the whole therapy act nailed.'

She was having none of it. Her face remained in its alabaster form, her little frown and insect leg eyelids her only distinctive features. 'This only works, I'm afraid, if we are honest with each other.' She nudged the box of tissues with a finger. 'So much of our speech, day to day, can be protective. I can try to decode, and really try to understand what you mean, but I worry that it might take us far too many sessions. And I'm sure, from your reluctance today, that you'd rather avoid that.'

The woman cleared her throat. 'In other words, it's important for you to tell me the truth. It might be the only place you can talk,' she gestured around her, 'without worrying about the consequences.' When she stared at me, her body tilted towards the edge of the chair, and I thought she might fall over, crashing into the carpet.

I decided to give her a show. I felt bad for her. She must have been bored, with all the crying trust-fund children and their B minuses.

'My mother died a few years ago,' I said (bold opening). 'And then, when I moved here, I lied about my father being dead, and got into a relationship. When she found out, she essentially dumped me.'

The woman blinked. 'That sounds – that sounds very challenging.'

'Sure.'

'And it sounds like we're working with several things here, and we have,' she looked at her watch, 'twenty minutes left. Which part of that would you like us to look at together?'

'You mean, dead mum, lying or break-up?'

'Yes.' Her face was unreadable. They must have taught the expression in college.

'You choose,' I said.

I had been to a makeshift therapy session in secondary school, with a woman not unlike this one, same shoulder-length haircut and thin upper lip. The first question of the day: 'How are you doing?' I told her I was great, by instinct, and then had to commit the remaining fifty-eight minutes to my answer. The new therapist, unknowingly copying the other in her wardrobe choices, frowned. 'Again, I can't help noticing that there's this abdication of responsibility.'

'Okay.' I pretended to look hurt. But I was enjoying it. I liked being told things about myself – it didn't matter if they were negative.

'Are you often uncomfortable with making decisions?'

'Not consciously.'

She smiled: a win for her, then, pulling that subconscious out. Freud was smiling down at us both. She leaned forward, and her stomach bulged through her trousers.

'I mean,' I continued, 'I do sometimes prefer it. Less room to go wrong.'

'Wrong,' she repeated, with a smile. 'There's this tendency we can all have, separating ideas into different categories. Good, bad. And I know you understand this, rationally, at least, but life is far more complex.'

'Of course.'

'So, for you, being told what to do is safer? Or it seems safer?'

'It was just a throwaway comment.'

'Of course,' the therapist said, repeating the words back to me. She looked at her notebook, which had been bookmarked with a receipt. 'Just looking at the things you've already told me today – thank you, for feeling comfortable, and sharing –'

'No problem.' I waved a gracious hand in the air.

'I'd like you to rank them in order of how much you think about them.'

'As in, amount of time?'

'Yes.' She raised a finger to her upper lip. The overhead light made flecks of yellow appear on her nail varnish. 'It's unconventional, but it can be a useful tool, when unpeeling layers of repression.'

'I'm not repressed.'

The therapist retracted her lips. She looked like a peeved capybara. 'I'd like you to complete the exercise, please.'

'I guess I miss Katarina. I think about that a bit.'

'Your ex-partner?'

'Yes.' I watched the therapist nod and write something down.

My hands were warm, and I found myself noting the changes in my body: slippery hands; pain at temple; forehead sweat, migrating down the face. I could taste my own breath, it was so quiet. The box room had a remarkable dampening effect on any reluctance I had to speak. She was right – in no other environment could I say the things I knew I felt, immoral and as horrendous as they were. The therapist had such a low opinion of me, anyway, that there was nowhere to go.

'I'll see something in my day,' I said, 'and think I could tell her about it – like, I don't know, the bad pun the smoothie shack man made – and will actually think, Katarina will love that. I mean, she'd go to town on the stupidest stuff – babies falling over, things like that. But then, you know, I'll go back home, and it's just me.'

'This is common,' the therapist said, smiling, 'and I see it so often in my clients, old and young.'

This did not make me feel better.

'I'm aware it doesn't help,' she continued, 'but processing your emotions, here, will.'

'Okay.' I was yet to complete the woman's little exercise. Her birdish face waited for an answer. I did not want to disappoint her, and all her goodwill, and tried to summon all the honesty I could bear. 'I think about Katarina the most,' I said. 'Even though I should never have lied about my dad. But it's like, once I had done it, it was just who I was, the sort of thing I'd do. And, after a while, it truly did feel as if he was gone. And then their questions, and Katarina's sympathy, felt strangely appropriate.'

I looked at the woman, white paper moving with her breath. 'Is that insane?'

'I don't tend to use that word here.'

'So, yes.'

She allowed herself a small laugh. 'I can see how, after maintaining this performance for so long, you might believe it. The brain makes all kinds of tricks for ourselves.'

I nodded. 'And I never really thought of myself as a good person, anyway, so adding this to my list of sins didn't have much of an effect.'

'That's interesting.'

'Thank you.'

She frowned, and I could just see her reprimanding herself, the mental note which followed – client must not be allowed to obtain validation through interest. The woman coughed into her hand, and held out the other for me to shake. 'We're booked in for next Thursday,' she said. 'Looking forward to continuing our chat then.'

Over the next week, I sat on the floor by the window, holding cheap wine from the liquor store. I purchased a paint-by-numbers set, completed an image of a log cabin, and considered turning it in to the institute. I ripped it up a second later, to ensure that I couldn't. On another day, I gathered the few cooking ingredients I possessed (cinnamon, paprika, bought during a rare productive spell), added water, to make a paste, and splashed it onto the paper, in a turd-inspired shape. Then, I sketched my adviser, standing in a grey cell. He looked like he had emerged from *A Clockwork Orange*, or one of those wartime prison-escapes my father was always watching. It was too cruel to hand in. I imagined the adviser's little disappointed frown, the books lined up on his shelf, and blamed Katarina for the emergence of my conscience. Before her, nobody had a context. She had opened me up to it, to the idea of the man's twin bed, his daily teeter over to the sink, fluoxetine prescription in his cabinet. I found it hard, slipping back into my old ways – I'd lost the reflex for it.

It had stopped feeling indulgent, the loneliness. And so, when the next appointment arrived, I was strangely excited. I believed that, if anyone had the power to fix me, this woman could. It was the words she used, as if from the pages of a thesaurus. It took so little to sway me, in those days. I almost walked inside a Scientology building on my way into campus, simply because the woman on the door had good eyebrows.

Back in the box room, the therapist had exchanged the stock image for a portrait of the Eiffel Tower. It was an aesthetic nightmare, the type of print which would be strung up in a two-star hotel.

'I preferred the other one,' I said.
'I'm sorry?'
'The painting over there. It used to be different.'

'So it did.' She pulled at her cardigan – this time it was purple, and reached past the waistband of her jeans. 'I don't really have much control over the interior, I'm afraid.'

'What would you have, then, if you could choose?'

The woman was flattered. She stood up. The wrinkled parts of her arms sagged with the movement. 'Places like this,' she said, 'should feel homely – it lowers the inhibitions. I'm thinking books, all around here,' she pointed to the left wall, 'maybe a CD player on the shelf, for guided meditations.'

'I like it,' I said.

Realizing who she was opposite, the therapist frowned, and her face became smooth, like an effigy, as she made the odd transition from authenticity into corporate civility. 'We talked, last week, about the thinking space certain events and thoughts occupy.' She flicked through her book. 'You mentioned your ex-partner, Katarina. And then we touched upon your lying to her, briefly, about your father's death. Or, should I say, non-death.'

'That's funny.'

'Thank you.' She smiled. 'I do think, though, that before we look at your ranking as a whole, we should touch on why you felt the need to lie in the first place.'

'There's not much point,' I said. 'It's over.'

'You know as well as anyone else that nothing is ever fully complete. We carry it here.' She pointed to her chest. 'And here.' A general gesture across the rest of her body.

Despite the years between them, she looked so much like Giulia, then, that I almost felt the sun on my back, the suncream on Katarina's neck. It took a few seconds to absorb her words. 'Is that really true?'

She shrugged. 'Perhaps not. But humour me anyway, Charlotte.'

The use of my name was an excellent touch. I found my mouth opening. 'I guess I just wanted,' I said, 'her to listen to me.'

'Who, specifically?'

'Katarina.' I looked around, for a visual escape. The artless Eiffel Tower, rainbow at its back, stared back.

'Your primary motive was sympathy, then?'

'Yes.' I remembered her face, on the day I told her, turning to horror. I felt sick. 'I think that was it, initially. But then I really knew her, and I didn't want any of that any more. Just to be near her.'

'It's interesting to me,' the therapist touched the spine of her notebook, 'that you decided to lie about your father, as opposed to simply telling the truth about your mother.'

There was nothing to say about that.

'Can you think about why this happened?'

'I don't know.'

Some things were not done consciously, though the woman's vision of therapy hinged on the idea that everything, from taking a maple ham and cheese sandwich in the cafeteria to a fascination with tinted lip balms, was an insight into the soul. That we could be unspun, and they could hold up our parts, saying: Look. This is what you are made from. It was comforting, the idea that there might be a driving force, a clear explanation, for all sorts of cruelty: the lie; the way I prioritized my immediate comfort over Katarina's happiness; my parents' silence, and the young girl's suffering. How comforting, how stupid. Some things just happened.

My silence disappointed her. She looked as if she was on the cusp of a revelation – hands eager, mouth wide – and had been pulled from the precipice, back into the real world. 'Perhaps we could try,' she said.

'Go for it.'

The therapist held her hands to her face, catching a cough before blinking at me. Her eyes watered. 'Of course, I can answer my own question,' she said, wiping her left eye, 'but I do think you'd benefit from trying it yourself.' She waited in that room, ripe with my sweat and her dismay, for a response. When none came, she continued, in a higher pitch. 'In unpredictable environments, we might seek control above all else. And I believe you decided to use something you could not confront – namely, your mother – and twisted it into something controllable.' The woman tilted her head, like an auctioneer judging her next price. 'How true did that feel?'

'You make me sound so calculating.'

'How would you rather sound?'

'Insane.'

'That word again.' She smiled. 'I've talked to many people over the past few years, many, I'm sure, you might label, using that word. And trust me, you're not one of them.' The woman flicked through her book. It was littered with tiny black words, scribbles just out of reach. 'You look disappointed,' she said. 'Why?'

'It's nothing.'

'We have,' she looked at her wrist, 'ten minutes remaining. I'd like us to discover more than nothing.'

It was her easy, chiding nature which did it in the end – so close to the kind of mothering I knew. 'I almost want to be mad,' I confessed. 'I think it would make everything easier. I want to be blameless. But I don't know how to move past, like, anything.'

She let us both settle in that thought. I could taste the salt of my phlegm, its steady beating against my throat.

'Which brings us, finally,' she said, 'to the ranking I asked you to do in our first session. And I couldn't help but notice that your mother did not appear there – that you do not think of her, it appears, at all.'

'That's not true,' I said weakly. I did think about her. For a very long time, I thought about murder, quite intensely, every time I heard someone cough. That sound, either of wet or of dry hacking, provoked some bodily, knee-jerk reaction. Initially, I assumed I had been carted off with the plague in a past life, or had been animated from one of those creepy schoolchildren in a 'Ring o' Roses' cartoon. When Katarina got sick in winter, I left her a bowl of chicken soup, a short note, and did not return for several hours. I got a taste of that brief freedom I imagined that husbands, upon leaving their wives, received; the slap of the wind against my face, getting out of Monroe, towards Orange County, where there would be no coughing, only the complete silence of the road. The sound itself was not the issue, of course. It was my mother. Always her – in the back of the cinema, three rows away; in the lecture hall, hacking up blood. I'd be sitting with Katarina at a restaurant, and would hear choking from a nearby ramen bowl, and would listen out for its aftermath, the quick and devastating sounds of someone bringing up their lungs.

It got so bad that I would sometimes play coughing sounds to myself, through my headphones. When I was kind to myself, I framed this as a form of exposure therapy; in more honest moments, it was a round of self-punishment. That was where I found her: my mother, on the subway, on the wintry streets of the institute, or in the mouths of children, their constant, and open-mouthed, propulsions of spit. But I couldn't help it. I missed her and despised her in equal measure. This, I knew, was something the therapist would not be able to fix; it was part of the sonic landscape.

The therapist was staring. 'You can take a moment,' she said.

I imagined her pointing the pen at her chest, digging it, nib first, into the skin below her collarbone. Ink and blood combining at the wound's gummy centre. Her pen – facing the paper, now – tapped along the notebook's edge. Surely, we were reaching the end. Her ten-minute warning felt deliberately misconstrued.

'Typically,' she said, 'I get my clients – or students, when I am working for the institute – to do physical exercises. Tapping their arms or their legs. We call them somatic exercises. When we experience something distressing,' she shook her head at my expression, 'the mind makes an attempt to sever itself from the body, typically for the protection of both.'

I looked at her – single curl, grown-out roots, dark at the centre of her parting. As her lip folded in on itself, flipping back out again, I wondered if she had been attractive at my age, had married a flawed yet capable man in his thirties – too early, of course – moving into her career, into this building, with the weight of someone who knew who she was.

She buzzed on in the background, talking about 'deploying tools' and 'grounding techniques' with one hand raised in the air. 'You have to want to be happy,' she kept saying, minutes before the session ended. Perhaps she knew I would not be returning. 'You have to want it,' she repeated. I remember telling her I didn't need happiness. Honestly, and very simply, I just wanted my mother back.

That week, I would fall asleep when 'working' on the painting, palettes smeared everywhere. The bedroom became terrible, disgusting. I became fixated on a brand of ramen, which I left, in its red packaging, around me. 'Trash', as Katarina would call it, trailed from the bedroom to the kitchen. But I had a routine: each time I finished a section of the painting, I would treat myself to a packet of Indomie and a lit candle. It wasn't good, the work. Even calling it 'work' felt insincere. My mother had believed that anything less than manual labour did not count, and the older I became, the more I agreed with her. Most institute careers were invented, nouns plucked at random ('director of the curatorial studies centre', 'quant portfolio management'), and involved meetings to organize the next meeting, ushering in a generation of children who could only say, when asked, that they 'honestly had no idea' what their parents did.

Though I had an appointment booked with the therapist – Wednesday, three p.m. – I told myself I was too busy. I sent her a short email, thanking the woman for her help so far, but that I would not be requiring any more sessions. Her office forwarded an 'out of hours' message back immediately, which I took as a sign in favour of my decision. An hour later, Matthew decided to break his silence in support of the few therapy sessions I managed to attend. He waltzed into my apartment, dodging ramen packets, and asked, in a sing-song voice, if there had been 'any revelations'.

'No,' I said, handing him a stale brownie to shut him up. (It worked. He was a simple man.)

I painted, while he 'made tweaks' to his CV. I watched him move bullet points ('summer intern, the *Art Digest*') on his laptop. When it got dark outside, Matthew ordered pizzas for us both. He ate less than half of his portion, and packed the rest away in my fridge, 'for tomorrow'. I had to turn away, then.

'Dude,' he kept saying, watching my hands cover my face, 'dude, don't worry about it.' Once he had gone, the apartment felt musty and sweet, like a brewery, and I could smell his kindness in the takeout boxes he had neatly arranged in the kitchen.

I went back to the canvas. My elbow kept dipping into the paint. I started with the vague outline of a woman, realized that she was beginning to look like Katarina (same bulbous chin, fleshy cheeks), and painted over it with a dark yellow. Still, her features poked through. I went over it again. A clean slate.

Having eaten Matthew's leftovers, I visited the library, where the usual librarian sat behind her counter, placing pink Hello Kitty stickers around her desk. I waved at her, and, less than five minutes later, she was describing – in great detail – the curve of her boyfriend's penis.

'It's a condition,' she said. The woman pressed another sticker – Hello Kitty on a bike, Hello Kitty in a frog hat – to her blazer. 'It's called Peyronie's disease, apparently. I got him to see someone about it.'

I pretended to look sympathetic, as I picked books from the 'Biography' section. 'That sounds tricky.'

'It is, honestly.' The woman blinked. 'That's not even the worst part. He doesn't seem to enjoy it, whenever we're together.'

'Is he older?'

'He's my age,' she said.

This was so far out of my area of expertise. I counted the seconds until I could feasibly exit the conversation, books in tow. I had applied too late for a library card, and this was my punishment: listening to the woman's drivel, in the hope that she would let me leave, carrying those hardback tomes.

This time, I suggested that it was her boyfriend who might be gay.

The woman sighed. 'You're probably right. God.' She hugged me, and her hand touched the back of my bra. I added another book to my bag. 'Thank you for being so honest,' she said.

I was sent through the library gates, five minutes later, with a Toulouse-Lautrec biography by my side. A rare win.

Henri de Toulouse-Lautrec, the only surviving child of French aristocrats, seemed to be a lonely child. He made that seamless transition into a lonely young adult, when, at sixteen, he stopped growing entirely, at four feet, eight inches. This was partly due to a congenital health problem (first-cousin parents, à la royal family) and his unhealed broken femurs. The affliction seemed to hang over this man. All the biographies, 'the facts', lavished on the image of Henri, permanently on the tips of his toes, staring at something always just above him. And, as he moved into Paris, taking a studio in the 18th arrondissement, he searched for people to paint, people to love. Throughout his short life (he died at thirty-six – alcoholism), Toulouse-Lautrec aligned himself with the sex workers of Paris: Henri felt as if he, too, had been lumped with a fate he could not rail against.

I found him fascinating, his paintings breathtaking. The woman at the library had allowed me to use three dollars of her printing credit, which I dedicated to reproducing his work. In each printout, *La Toilette*, *Gabrielle the Dancer*, there was a vulnerability. Some subjects looked caught, aware that they were being watched; others looked wistful, enjoying a bliss which might be interrupted at any moment.

Le Lit – The Bed – was the best, the one which had pulled me in. I had seen it the year before, and had forgotten its name, as someone might forget a book, returning to it later, an old woman, when they needed it the most. In *The Bed*, two women, both occupants of a late-nineteenth-century brothel, lie in bed, faces inches apart. Where other painters might have included their nakedness, or a sense of judgement, Henri instead depicts the lovers as quiet, understated, sleeping under the covers. They could be anyone, in any period, going unrecorded.

I had four copies, and I cut them into sections, and studied each square, staring at each tuft of hair, the heavy indents in the white pillows, skin folds mimicked outside the body. I traced over Henri's lines, again and again each morning, until the women started to shift under the light.

The more I watched, and played with his image, the more I felt his world becoming real, the headboard above their heads like my own, the movement of the red blanket like the one by my feet.

Two days before the deadline, I had something – oil paint on a large canvas, bigger than myself. I stepped back. It was the best thing I had ever done. The best thing, I thought wildly, the best thing. I couldn't look at it for too long. I brought out a long black coat from the cupboard, and covered the canvas, not caring whether the paint had dried. What could I do, now that I had tried – truly tried – and this was it: the early-morning sweat, my childhood delusion, coming to its fleshy head?

That evening, I opened all the windows in my flat, and heard the extractor fan downstairs – my landlord had the same idea. I leaned over the windowsill, until the man's mutterings reached me. He was talking about his dinner in a soft, lilting way, the way someone might speak to a child. He ran through his itinerary for the week, aloud: 'Talk to old office' – a short clang of a pan – 'then pick up meds on 21st Street' – another rustle – 'no heart attack today, Tony.'

This was the landlord's name, then. He had never introduced himself to me, merely nodding and stepping into the apartment. As Tony ran through the rest of his list – 'collect the rotisserie chicken at Market 32, doctor's appointment on the 17th' – I found that there were no names on the itinerary besides his own, and felt incredibly sorry for him, until I remembered that my schedule, if said aloud, would be the same. And, as if answering this thought, Tony stopped speaking. A button was pressed, and guitar sounds began to pluck quietly, just reaching my apartment, travelling above the cars.

As the song swelled, and the men sang wistfully, I found I knew it. We had been cleaning out the basement, in one of her seasonal attempts at turning the house into an 'after' image from *Grand Designs*, when my mother found a CD in a brown envelope. She had lifted it with an attempt at mysteriousness and theatricality, only revealing, once I had sorted the clothes into piles, that the track belonged to an old boyfriend. I was frightened – by her playfulness, and by the knowledge that she was not thinking about my father, but a man I did not know, evidence of a life before mine, a life which might have been her real, true, one. Now, years later, I read Katarina into that moment, even though she had no business being there, until my mother's longing for the unnamed man, and mine for Katarina, mixed together and became impossible to separate. And when the strings arrived, it summoned all of us: Katarina; Tony; Matthew; the old friends in the song; my mother, too.

Once it ended, I opened my laptop, and started writing an email to Tony, where I thanked him for the apartment, and the rent, 'which had helped me out during a difficult time'. I told him about the song, and what it had meant, ending the email with an offer to collect his shopping at the supermarket. It felt right, different. How many times had I leaned against my bedroom wall, tired, alone, as he had been doing the same, mere feet away?

I sent the email, and prayed, with everything in me, that it wouldn't become evidence in a true-crime documentary in ten years' time, my limbs chopped up under Tony's floorboards.

28

Matthew was beautiful, popular, the kind of person everyone believed was their best friend, only to be surprised later, as ten other people claimed the same title. He had described his party as 'small' and 'nothing to worry about, really', though, as I walked towards it, I could tell that there would be over a hundred there, all sweating and stinking in the dark. It was the end of term, our submissions had all been handed in, and this was our reward: 'free drinks free people free fun' (Matthew's words, texted, en masse, two hours before). I could hear the music from the street, the French rap reaching the main road, in little vibrations on the concrete.

He opened the door, looking behind him, as though he was already making an escape, cigarette in hand. 'Dude, it's crazy in there.' He started to take off his jacket, hot, overwhelmed. 'I had no idea I knew so many people.'

I smiled. There was something unavoidably good in Matthew: he waved at people, remembered names. He was immune to social hierarchies, and was surprised when anyone else subscribed to them. Half of his face was bathed in dark red, from inside, the other blue.

'Thank you for inviting me,' I said.

'Shut up. Obviously I was going to.'

'But – you know. I'm not the most popular right now. So thank you.'

It was a thank you for his insistent company, the pressurized coffee – 'Dude, come on, I'll meet you at four, I don't care.' His refusal to sleep with me, and the fact I knew – just as I knew he would never bring it up to me, not even jokingly – that he would never mention it to anyone else.

'Thanks,' I said again.

Matthew squinted, and moved his head closer towards mine. 'Have you taken something?'

'No.'

'Are you sure?'

'You're the one running away from the party,' I pointed to the house, the drunk renditions of musical numbers from the building, 'and you look high as hell.'

He hit me on the back. 'Good chat,' he said, smiling. There was a gap between his two front teeth. 'See you inside.' Matthew walked away – my one social tether, gone – to smoke by a tree.

Inside, I talked to an older man called Frank about his favourite painter, Frans Hals, until the tips of my fingers went cold from the glass. I wondered how much of Frank's love for the artist was due to their phonetic similarity, as if, by praising one (which he did repeatedly – 'Frans is a marvel, ahead of his time'), he could transfer some of the virtue over to himself.

Two people, touching at the hips like conjoined twins, asked where I got my outfit. I was honest. 'H&M,' I said. They were disappointed, and spent the rest of the conversation pretending they weren't.

Near the kitchen, Matthew's high school friends had gathered, all wearing vintage tees. They socialized in a circle, heads turned inwards, in an almost sweet, protective measure. One of them pointed across the room, screamed 'It's you!' at me, jubilant, drunk, and returned to his beer.

I had seen him at the centre on Elmwood Avenue, when visiting Matthew, post attempt. I used to visit on Wednesdays and Sundays. Each time, I'd bring a copy of the obnoxious *Nova Ars* and dark chocolate. And each time, I would pray that Matthew might send me away, or that he might say something sufficiently passive-aggressive to justify my not coming back. But he never did, and so I took the number 11 bus, and then the 14 towards Saginaw, finding him sat up in bed, in the blue T-shirt he always wore.

At the party, Matthew walked back into his house, where the people inside gave a little cheer. He waved a hand – 'Stop it, guys' – and went to the corner of the room, to pour out two drinks. One for himself, one for me. The others, buoyed by their sound, started chanting, and they ran around in a circle, bodies flinging backwards towards each other. Matthew spoke about an American snack I had never heard of, his breath hot and low against my neck. I thought about thanking him again, in the red light, on the thrumming floor, sticky tongue.

'I thought I should tell you,' he said, touching the corner of his eyebrow, 'that Katarina might come tonight.'

'What?'

It was possible that, through the shouting, and the bass, I could have mistaken her name. It felt like being kicked.

'Katarina's coming tonight.' Matthew blinked, very quickly. 'I saw Tom yesterday, at the water fountain thing, outside campus. He asked if I was doing anything, and I felt so bad, dude, that I invited both of them. Because he wanted her as his plus one, and I said sure, whatever, bring her.'

'Fuck.'

'I completely forgot.' His eyes looked as if they were moments away from watering, and he patted my left shoulder anxiously. 'But she might not come. It might just be him.'

Matthew's friends from high school – $47,000 per year – raised a speaker in the air. They turned the volume up ceremoniously, jagged mouths grinning. 'I'm sorry, dude,' Matthew said, shouting now. Technopop ran through our limbs. 'I just didn't think. And you have to see her at some point, anyway.'

He was enveloped by the ex high schoolers, and lifted up, bar mitzvah style, thrown against the ceiling. I only saw flashes of him for the rest of the evening: his back; the side of his face, leaning in to speak.

Without any alternatives, and unwilling to be alone when Katarina arrived, I talked feverishly with a couple in fur coats. They wore eyeliner on the bottom lid, and loved complaining. He was a poetry masters student; she a 'human development' artist. The boyfriend scrolled through his phone. When I asked what he was looking at – an attempt at sweetness, interest – he said, 'My list,' imperiously, and nothing more.

We spent the next minutes in silence, until the man, upset at his reception, explained: 'It's my ins and outs list of the semester.'

'He does it every few months,' the girlfriend said.

He nodded. 'Currently,' he kept scrolling, 'feminism is in. Champagne is out. And complaining is definitely in.'

The girlfriend scratched her neck, and touched her beloved's elbow, interrupting. 'Sorry,' she said.

'Catacombs: in. Romance novels' – I had mentioned them to him, in a panic, when he had asked what I did all day – 'definitely out. So is acid.' The boyfriend's ideal date night must have involved a virtual-reality audience, a podium made of pixels. 'Black Lives Matter is out, done. The Harlem Renaissance, however, is in. Other ins: mojitos; The Cave; bamboo. And calling your parents.'

His girlfriend nodded. Her skin was pale; her life-blood had presumably been sapped out through prolonged exposure to her partner. 'That's so real,' she said.

From the side door, at the back of the kitchen, more people were arriving. It was Katarina. I knew this without seeing her: I felt as if I could find her anywhere. The boyfriend continued his tirade as Tom and Katarina poured drinks. She saw me – between the kitchen counter and the carpet of the living room – she saw me. She waved. I did too, then looked back at the couple as they began on the subject of eggs, and gave them a smile which they did not deserve.

'I used to eat them all the time,' he said. 'So they were very in. Fried, and with ramen. The best.'

'You can't just get them anywhere, now,' the girlfriend said, in her longest contribution of the evening.

Katarina's family had owned a chicken farm. Every Saturday, at eight, they would go to the market on Main Street, where she would take her brother away from the meat stall to look at bracelets together. Beaded ones: two dollars. Gold: five. Her parents would stand at the back, by the chickens, and their metallic smell would make its way over to the jewellery stand. She hated that section of the square, hated their little white tent. There, the carcasses would be strung up by their legs, and their skin always looked cold, prickly, far too human in the morning light. They reminded her of naked women, their legs pointed up, at the sky. It helped, that these chickens were not *theirs*. They were the Baileys', or the Fullers'. Her family just collected the eggs. It was one unpleasant Christmas, when Katarina, teetering in her snow boots, discovered the origins of her dinner that night, and the night before: her father, standing over the metal pot, plucking away at the dead animal's feathers.

What could we do with all the things we knew about each other? I could feel that moment, excavated from her life as if it might have been mine. There were things she knew about me, too – and we could never get any of them back. I looked at her side of the room. Katarina stared in the opposite direction. I tapped the couple on both shoulders.

'I dated that girl,' I said, pointing towards her, like an aged Hollywood star dragging out their glory days. The couple blinked. 'We were together for a few months, actually.'

'Wow.' The girlfriend pulled her lips over her teeth, like a horse imitating a human.

'You can add seeing exes at a party,' I elbowed the boyfriend, 'to your *outs* section.'

The statement was not well received.

*

I walked over to her first, holding a vodka-water as if it were a prop. The glass was mostly empty, and I had started to find the whole thing very funny.

She stood in the corner, staring into another person's phone. She laughed without any sound – it was politeness, then, more than anything else. When Katarina liked something, truly enjoyed it, she looked ugly. Her face would look bloated, and her double-chin would be on show. But this laugh was all prettiness. I smiled, wildly, on the way to the corner. Thoughts arrived in abstract, telling me that this might not be the smartest of decisions. They left, after a while, and became a low hum. I stood on the edge of the group, their little faces blurry, with the back of Katarina's head as clear as anything. Tom saw me; he waved, and said my name loudly, nudging Katarina as he did so. A warning. There was a pain in my throat, and the side of my stomach, like something needed to be emptied, some fibrous thing lodged between organs. I wondered if Katarina would visit me in hospital, even reluctantly, even if I had to beg her. I started speaking to her, in Matthew's orange-hot room, with everyone else there. The others looked away, and stared at each other. The place was thick with embarrassment.

Katarina placed a hand on my shoulder – and I knew that hand well, and here it was, touching with such impassiveness, such remove. I almost shook her off.

'You don't even know what you're saying.' Katarina pulled at the bottom of my top, and dragged it downwards, in an attempt to cover my stomach. 'Go home,' she said.

I told her I loved her. 'And sorry about the call the other day.' I leaned onto her side, as though we were old friends, as though I were catching up with a colleague at the water stand. 'I saw something on the news – see,' I pointed at her face, 'I'm not completely terrible – and I thought you had died.'

A few seconds in, I realized that Katarina was moving me, by the arm, towards the bathroom. There was a pressure in her hold, the arm wrapping around my back, as if I were being scooped out, and removed. That's nice, I thought. Katarina pushed me towards the wall, and left me there, like a deserted fish, flopping away, to push open the bathroom door. Inside, the couple I had spoken to earlier were making wet, sucking noises. Their faces became one mass of flesh.

Katarina pointed at the couple. 'Out.' She pulled on my arm. 'We actually need it, over here.'

The boyfriend – the 'ins' man – wiped his mouth with toilet tissue, and pointed between us. 'Doesn't look like it. Only takes one to piss.' He and his girlfriend laughed together, mouths like little black wounds. Perhaps this is what we had looked like, when we were together, Katarina and I. Utterly detestable.

Katarina swore at them. 'If you want to deal with vomit for the next half an hour,' she looked at me, 'then go ahead.' They moved aside, and we walked in, a pair of revolving doors. The bathroom locked on the inside, and the room smelled of Katarina's mango spray and salt. I felt waves – both nausea and terror, all the things I had said, and the fact that she was there, just one step away. The pain began in the lower stomach, then rose up with each terror, moving to the throat, gnarled and closing.

She was watching me. The very top of her eyelids had been doused in silver eyeshadow, and the sparkles moved in the light. 'Here.' She pulled my wrists towards the sink. She turned the cold water tap on. 'This should help.'

'That's kind,' I said, instead of, I love you.

Katarina had a new spot at her temple, above her eyebrow. She got them from holding her face in her sleep. She held on to my back. 'Do you think you'll be ill?'

I shook my head.

'Are you sure?'

'No.'

She stood at my back, the softness of her pressing on my spine. I felt the graininess of my skin, the cool wrists turning to mush under the water. I leaned back, stepping on her toes. 'I'm so sorry,' I said. The tap was running. 'I don't know why I did it.'

Katarina said nothing.

'Maybe you'll find this funny, considering, but it was actually my mother –' Katarina brought my wrist back under. 'It was actually my mum –'

She waited for me to continue.

'I think there's something wrong with me,' I said. It was the kind of statement which, once said, was immediately known to be true. 'I don't know what to do.'

'Just keep it here,' she said, pulling my wrist closer, the water trickling down both of us.

There were several banging sounds at the top of the door. Katarina kicked it back. When I turned to face her, arms dripping, and leaned closer, to kiss her, as I had done so many times before, she shook her head. 'I don't think so,' she said.

We walked back into the main room together, the lights new, fresh, a baptism. She talked to Tom, who held his phone up to me minutes later, to tell me that an Uber was arriving soon. I made a joke – it was like being in the secret service, the black car pulling up, to take me away – but he did not respond. He just looked at me with wide eyes, as though I were in a foreign, and dangerous, animal exhibit. Then a hand was on my back, and I was being moved into a car, knowing that I was embarrassing myself again, yet I was incapable of changing it.

In the morning, I thought about Katarina, standing on the steps of Matthew's house, watching the street. Her expression had been so distant, then, that it summoned many others – Katarina, outside the pharmacy in Villalago; her leg bleeding in the back of the car; Katarina, laughing at one of the many exhibitions – so that they all became one long expression, from love to respect and back to indifference again. I can still see her now, nodding to herself as the car drove away. Watching us stop at the lights. Looking, with each second on the sidewalk, as though she had finally paid off her debt, one kindness for another.

29

The last time I saw my father, we were in Pittsford, for the 'graduate showcase'. He gave me weeks of warning, as though he could shake off the unpleasantness of Villalago through advance notice. 'I'm taking the plane to Rochester, the 7.40 a.m. one,' he told me, over text, 'then the bus to the transit centre then the 11 into St John Fisher.' He had attached several screenshots of his tickets. 'Looking forward to it and are there any snacks from the UK you fancy as I have forgotten. Dad.'

We discussed his plans over the phone, how we might get him across Atlantic waters. New seas, an eight-hour flight, and crippling aerophobia. 'I'm an old man,' he kept repeating down the line. 'An old man, now.'

He was to get in on 2 September, for the institute's showcase the next day. It was dedicated to recent graduates – our final exhibition, a strange, yet characteristic, goodbye for our cohort. I'd told him the visit was unnecessary. But he simply repeated his age back at me, his final say: 'I am sixty-four, I'm not getting any younger. I've always wanted to go.' His pressing sense of time, life miles unused, trumped everything else.

I made a sign for him, in a rare and remarkable moment of sincerity. It was cardboard. On its surface, I drew 'Dad' in bubble letters. It could have been the work of a six-year-old, but I took it anyway, turning the lettered sign towards me as I sat on the bus, then walked to Union station.

I could not find him at first, and waved to several men over fifty. After a particularly close encounter with a late middle-aged specimen (stray man in grey jumper), there was a tap on my shoulder. He was pale, presumably still queasy post-flight. We hugged, as around us, shoes squeaked against the marble floors.

He looked at the sign, smiling. 'It's lovely.'

'I held it up for hours. I think I looked like a right idiot.'

'Not possible.' He placed a hand on my head. He smelled like my mother, and our old fabric softener. I stared at him as we walked through the exit signs. The green light changed his face, and he looped an arm through mine. He nodded to the taxi rank, where white flecks of gum and 'USA'-branded stickers had settled on the floor. 'This is it,' he said.

When we arrived on campus, he pretended to be impressed, complimenting the shape of the trees – 'Are those fern? And in such good condition, too' – the yellow path to the institute gallery, the concrete slabs of our classrooms.

'It's okay,' I said, 'you can tell me it's not what you imagined.'

I was convinced his visions of the place involved light snow, jagged buildings and the orange haze of sky. Woody Allen's New York: bodegas, Gershwin and humid activity. Not the steady mediocrity of Pittsford, where the largest building was a small office 'tower'. It had taken me several months to convince him that I was not in 'the big city', though I knew he liked to tell people at the pub I was there, suspended between the MoMA and the Rockefeller Center: 'My daughter, in the Big Apple.'

I dropped his bag at my flat, where I had arranged a small bed for myself on the sofa. We argued – as I had anticipated – for half an hour, my father peppering his case to take the sofa with compliments about the apartment – 'This lamp, was it free?' His chest heaving with the effort of both travel and speech, he gave in.

'Thank you,' he said. He stood under the window. The sky, the ground beneath, the walls, his face were all greyish. I felt as if time was accelerating, that, if we both remained there, I could watch him waste away like burning plastic. I looked at the top of his head, which had become shiny, the ghost of previous hairs giving his hairline a V-shape. My mother's head had become like that: bony and fleshy simultaneously, distended like a rotting thing given too much water. My father watched the street serenely, oblivious to his visual deterioration. He laughed to himself as a man dropped a briefcase in the street below. 'It's so flashy here,' he said.

I hadn't the heart to tell him the man was, undoubtedly, another student, dressed for a photoshoot. Suit from the costume department, tie from the thrift store. I nodded. 'It's wonderful, isn't it?'

My father smiled as the man picked up the case and walked away. His private victory. We ought to have said more – broached a conversation about his future, or even mine; retirement plans, health checks; his wife, his loneliness. I might have forgiven him, for the baths I had to drag my mother into, alone, and all the meals I left by his feet.

But I needed to hate him, just a little. The most terrifying thing about the dead is that they take the site of your resentment with them. So I needed him to live, be well, so that I could continue my charges.

He asked if I was nervous about tomorrow.

'Very,' I said.

'You'll be grand.'

My mother used to say that. I looked at the fridge, the groceries I had bought for his arrival, third-rate meat. I started to prepare dinner, slicing onions vertically on the chopping board.

'You were seeing someone,' he said, while I added the mince, 'when I popped by last time.'

I separated the grainy strings with a spoon. The pink turned greyish in the silence.

'She had a funny name. It was Polish, or something.' He paused. 'I do remember things, you know.'

'Katarina,' I said.

'Yes. That girl. I thought she was nice. Kind face, and all that.'

My parents, for the most part, did not believe in lesbians, although my father could understand, on some level, desiring women – but for my mother, it was alien, slippery, almost monstrous. I was doing terrible things with the femininity she had given me, bastardizing it – that was the idea, anyway. My father's admission of Katarina's 'face' looking 'kind', then, was the strangest thing of all. I did not understand him.

'I wouldn't mind meeting her properly,' he said. 'I'd actually quite like to see her again.' He leaned back in his chair, at peace with his act of great magnanimity.

'We're not together any more,' I said.

'Oh,' he said. 'That's probably for the best.'

In the window, outside blacked out, I could see myself, posture hunched, a child. 'What do you mean?'

'Nothing bad, now.' His skin was flushed. 'Nothing about any of that. I just think that you're better off without her.'

'Of course.'

He nodded to himself, checking the conversation off: polite love life enquiry, brief allusion to homosexuality – done. 'You know,' he began, 'Ethan's sister from Manchester broke up with her partner not too long ago.'

I placed his bowl in front of him. He looked up at me. And, before he launched into the tale of Ethan's sister from Manchester, token gay of his life, he stared, eyes watering, and opened his mouth to speak. It is impossible now, of course, to say what those words might have been. In weaker moments, I like to think it was a declaration of love, bubbling up to the surface. But I try not to allow that illusion for too long.

We walked to the gallery in the morning. My father wanted to 'check the area' ahead of time, as if it might disappear in the hours before the event. He heaved himself up the path, stopping every so often to comment about the statues – 'Is that a young woman? Or an octopus? I can't tell. Is that the point?' The man was severely overdressed, and looked as though he was attending multiple events at once – he wore a green jacket from his (actual) '80s wardrobe, a pair of camouflage trousers and sandals, which seemed to have alligators stitched onto their straps. It was a sight to behold.

We took the bus back, my father having his fill of

campus sights: a library used for the charging of laptops; a gallery space with Hershey's vending machines parked outside. Back in the flat, he looked at the red indicator on the oven every few minutes, and brought out his phone – smashed screen, over five years old – from his pocket. He did so clumsily. The phone fell on the floor.

'Is everything okay?' I asked.

'I'm trying to time it right.'

'Time what, Dad?'

The air around him smelled medicinal, and bitter. In the light, his eyelashes were blond, almost non-existent. 'I've got an outfit change ready for tonight,' he said, 'and I want to get clean, and shower before then, and save enough time, so we're not late.'

'That's okay. You look perfect now.'

Plain T-shirt, camo trousers: his uniform. It was considered 'inauthentic' to dress up for institute events: if you must prettify yourself, the motto went, it should be within the parameters of everyday plausibility. It was a way of weeding out the pretenders, those who looked stiff in designer clothes – in other words, the non-trust-fund students. My father got up from his seat and left for the bedroom. On the bed, he had left a suit, still in its packaging, and a white shirt.

'Look,' he said. He was immensely proud.

'It's wonderful.'

'I bought it specially for this evening.'

I watched as his hands smoothed over the creases, again and again. It made a crinkling sound over the plastic.

'You didn't have to do that,' I said. Or, rather – I wished that he hadn't. The man would radiate difference. I imagined someone asking if he was a security guard, and winced.

'You don't like it?'

'Of course I do. I do. It's a lovely suit. And it must have been expensive.' I bowed my head, as he placed a hand on my back, clapped it heavily, and teetered towards the bathroom to get changed.

The two of us – man in a suit, daughter in black jeans and a T-shirt – left for the exhibition an hour in advance, at his request. The walk was anticlimactic. My father hummed the final bars of a hymn. It seemed to be a nervous habit of his, part of his single routine: 'Jesus be with you' at the washing machine, the sweet cadence of the final amens, folding his shirts for work, the supermarket, the pub.

'Sorry,' he said, finishing the song. He pulled at his sleeves when we reached the top of the hill, where groups of students were already outside, chatting wildly, holding champagne. He looked like a chauffeur, or a stale butler. I stood close to him, as though I might protect him, or myself, from them.

Tamsyn and an older sibling (a parental guest, for her, would be decidedly uncool) were in matching shades of lipstick. I had to fight the urge to run away and slam the bony part of my skull against the concrete, innards spilling out like a watermelon. Tamsyn waved at us, a hand around her sister.

'She seems friendly,' my father said.

'That's Tamsyn. She's a bit of a nightmare, actually.' Lord, praise me for the understatement. 'She said I was talentless not too long ago. Dead serious about it, too.'

'Bastard.'
I smiled.

We accepted brochures from the gallery entrance, and my father traced my surname with a fingernail, before folding it in half and putting it in his pocket. The first room, shining from the hall, featured an arrangement of flower lamps and giant light bulbs. We nodded politely, reading the placard, which described the exhibit as 'A trip through visual time, from Edison to IKEA'.

The next section of the exhibition was darker – a welcome respite from the retina-blast of the previous one – and featured Jules's work. Designer shirts were stapled to the walls, pinned by the collar. A few had been cut into strips, the cotton trailing to the ground. Others were multi-coloured, like a dip dye gone wrong. My father blinked several times, standing opposite a strip, where the word 'society' had been printed on its side.

'It's so conceptual,' he said, nodding. 'So conceptual.'

The following room was split in two – the first half involved the arrangement of decapitated Bratz dolls lined up next to a cheese grater. On the other side, a student – a live one – lay on a mattress. My father used the word 'conceptual' again, while I waved at the student on the bed. Her right hand jerked in response, though the rest of her remained rigid. It was an impressive performance, judged by stillness alone.

In the hallway, we were handed a pair of flimsy glasses, paper, the kind from old 3D screenings. This cheered up my father immensely. He beamed at a student, who wore a half-shirt, half-dress concoction, and asked if 'there's a film on, like *Jurassic*'.

'No.' The student frowned.

'*Avatar?*'

'No.'

'Not even *Kung Fu Panda*? They do this thing, with the animation, and it all goes big, in your face.'

The student did not believe that worth an answer. My father looked at me, while the affronted genius made exasperated faces at the other attendees.

'That's a shame,' my father said. 'I'd honestly just love to sit down.'

Glasses in hand, we were pointed in the direction of the next room, where the door had been replaced by several stringed beads, reminiscent of a fishmonger's, or a tarot den. The student put one pale arm in front of us, blocking our entry. 'Glasses on,' he said.

Our view obstructed by the strange, blacked-out lenses, we walked towards the centre of the room. My father held on to my shoulder. 'Can you see anything?'

'Nothing.'

'Strange.'

'This might be it,' I said.

I reached my hand out, to scrape along the edge of the wall, to find something. The tips of my fingers touched an almost shiny material, smooth and soft on the outside. I could hear the student talking outside, elated, ushering in his next set of visitors. I reached for the wall again. I already had my suspicions. Removing the glasses, I was confronted with a line-up of rainbow dildos, the silicone fixed to the walls, and arranged in a circle on the table.

'Oh my God.'

My father tapped my side. 'Have you taken the glasses off?'

'You don't need to. This is it.' I started to manoeuvre him away from the room, parting the wooden beads. 'It's a commentary on blindness,' I said, as I read the exhibit's title: *An Unfortunate Surprise*.

We walked through the other rooms, watching the carousel of projects. Tamsyn had painted a series of portraits of the guests in a housing cooperative upstate. There were five, all in various stages of perceptibility. Some figures were blurred, loose strokes of the brush, others almost photorealistic.

'The visibility of each portrait,' the placard read, 'corresponds to the amount of time Tamsyn Saunders had a meaningful conversation with each sitter. She wishes to suggest that, although we might assume we know someone on looks alone, reality is more blurred.' I imagined Tamsyn writing her own description late at night, coffee in hand, and smiled. She had called the work: *SEEING*.

'She got a lot better at the whole painting thing,' my father said, pointing between the first portrait and the last. 'Your school taught her well.'

On the way to the next room, I saw the artist herself, discussing her hour-long hypnosis routine in the gallery hall, rocking back and forth on the balls of her feet. Her sister stared down into her phone, not listening to a word.

'I loved your portraits,' I told Tamsyn, before she could say anything. 'Well done.' I expected a snide comment back, or a smatter of derision. To my surprise, she hugged me.

'Thank you,' she said. 'I was so worried. Genuinely, thank you.'

'You're welcome.'

The next section of the gallery, the one I longed to see the most, was not mine, but Katarina's. The room had been lit softly, turning the room a faint yellow. I knew that she had arranged this ahead of time, her particulars. I half expected it to smell of the peppermint diffuser in her bedroom, though, of course, it was just like the rest of the gallery – wood and fresh paint. Other people moved through the section quickly, to get to other sections, celebration parties and restaurants downtown. I looked up – there was a large canvas, split into sections at the centre. Radial symmetry, it was called. Katarina loved this idea, the convergences between nature and art.

In each section of the canvas, Katarina had painted a different scene, all in a different shade of yellow: her bathroom; her room in Italy, morning; the institute cafeteria; what I imagined to be her childhood bedroom. They were all joined by a single point.

My father pointed a large finger at the Italian scene, hovering inches from the church she had painted, just visible from the bedroom window. 'We've been there.' He circled around Villalago, the loose brushstrokes. 'She's good. I like it.'

'Me too.'

I could not say any more: he had summarized it perfectly. I liked it. It went beyond intelligence, my love for it. Like everything she did, it had the ability to hold me down, so that I would look, and keep looking. It was arresting, and there was something so bleak about all these rooms, entirely devoid of people. While we had been together, Katarina had been learning about the politics of 'painted bedrooms'. She was fascinated by Marlene Dumas, and I had bought several books in order to understand her better. I still read them sometimes.

30

Last week, I saw her again. I could not believe it. She rarely came up in conversation: there were no Katarinas on the news, on the front of T-shirts, on billboards. There had been several years without seeing her anywhere at all. And now – there she was, her name in the shop window, a gift, or a curse, shining in Arial font.

I leaned in, towards the glass. Yes, there it was – her full name. The same Katarina, now an artist with an exhibition that evening: Gladstone Gallery, 24th Street, 7 p.m. I looked back at the poster, as though it might have been a mirage, a hallucination – a Catarina, the wrong surname – but it wasn't. It was her. I thought about walking back to the office, forgetting about the whole thing. Arriving on 39th, a quick hello to Janice at reception, taking the lift, watching the red numbers increase, walking back to the fifth floor. But it felt like a waste. I'd be no use at the desk: I'd only be able to think about her.

And so I walked up and down 23rd, grateful that I hadn't thought about her in months. When I did, it was the sweet things I remembered, smiling at her intensity, her moral certainty, wondering if she might be embarrassed by it all now.

It was autumn, and I still couldn't shake the first-semester anxiety, the cool, expectant feeling which seemed to stick after graduation. Even as I reached the building, I thought it impossible, that she might be there. She had only seemed alive in the institute in Pittsford or in Villalago, and her hometown felt invented, something we'd made up together, half-drunk in her room. It was also possible that she might not recognize me at all, that I'd just be somebody in a black blazer and patent shoes.

At the desk, a young woman asked to see my ticket.

'I'm sorry, I don't have one,' I said. 'Could I buy it now?'

'Sure.' She punched the computer. 'Is it just the one?'

'Just the one.'

I walked past the reception, ticket in hand, and the gallery was so familiar, with its wooden scent and dark brown floors, that I felt as though I were back at the institute. Everything after her – the office, my apartment in Inwood – seemed to fall away and shrink. I turned around, half expecting my father to be standing beside me, waiting to walk into the next room. I remembered, then, how I had led him to the painting of my mother, aged, in her bed. I had been excited, expecting praise, an outburst of grief: tears, hugs, the works. Instead, he had stopped, blinked at the canvas, and said, 'You've got the nose wrong.'

'What?'

'The nose,' he had said, 'it goes out, like this.' A little gesture, as he traced his face, extending it out. 'You've got it all wrong.'

I heard her first. I stepped into the room, the walls a wash of blue paint. I was afraid that she might look different – and it was true, she did look different, her hair had been cut short, above her jaw – though she smiled the same, exposing a thick layer of gums.

'Oh my God,' she said. 'Charlotte?'

I was completely awkward: I stood below the door frame, stupefied.

'Oh my God,' she said again. 'I can't believe it's you. I had no idea you were around.'

'I can't believe it either. I just saw this ad – I really did, I promise – and I thought I'd say hello.'

'This is insane.'

'The exhibition is beautiful,' I said, not looking at it once. Her skin was entirely clear, almost reptilian, smooth under the light. 'Just perfect.'

'Thank you.'

Katarina pointed at the window, where there was a vague shadow, a woman, waiting outside for her. 'That's Charlie,' she said. 'I'm heading out with her, back to the apartment for a bit, but we'll be back before the place closes.'

I blinked. It was so strange, hearing her again. I even felt, looking at her, as though I were hiding something, though I knew it had all been laid out. There was nothing more to confess.

'I'm so happy you came,' she continued. 'It's so weird, seeing you.'

'A good weird?'

'A good weird.' She looked back at the window, where the woman was rocking on her heels. 'Fancy coming back with us?'

Back with Katarina, with Charlie – back to witness their

beautiful place, green sofas and Tiffany lamps. I was happy, of course, that she had someone – I had expected it, too – but visiting their apartment, and appearing, like a little dark cloud, in their kitchen, would be too much. 'That's so kind,' I said, 'but I think I'll stay.'

'It won't be strange, I promise.'

'That's all right.'

'Come on.'

I just shook my head: No thank you.

'I forgot what you're like.' She laughed. 'That's British for, I'd rather get shot.'

'It is kind of you, though, to offer.'

'But you won't actually stop by.'

'No.'

I smiled, as she said, 'Well, then.' She gave her usual goodbye, that little wave, before she walked outside, to join the woman. Katarina kissed her once, quickly, and slid a hand into hers.

When they turned onto 23rd, becoming a blur in the purplish light, I started to run out of the gallery. I passed exhibition rooms, vending machines and the reception desk, shoving my ticket back into my pocket. I was terrified, as I tried to catch up with her, that I might forget her kindness – that, with each year, it would seem unlikely, or laughable, that I could ever be like her, and instead, the old impulses would come back. For so long, I'd held on to the idea of a chance encounter, and now it had happened, I had done nothing wrong, proved my mild health, and sanity, in front of her. It was gone – and I thought the one motivation I had, for being better, had gone, too.

But, as I stepped out onto the sidewalk, I saw it all: the

sweet, damp air; the lights from the brownstone apartments; the children rushing past, laughing, swinging between their parents' arms. I waited for it all to go away. For some brutal shout, a cry, a twisted wrist. Instead, there was only the soft light, their ponytails, bouncing in the wind. And, as I stood at the end of the street, only a few minutes away from Katarina, I looked back, towards the gallery. The building was beautiful, shining, and I could see the canvas through the glass, great stretches of blue across the wall, flecks of white, blinking back like light on water. I turned away from her. Enough now, I thought. Enough.

ACKNOWLEDGEMENTS

Thank you to Ella Harold, the most wonderful editor, who advocated for this novel from the very beginning, and to Emma Leong, my incredibly talented agent. To Penguin's 'WriteNow' programme, and to everyone at the Fig Tree imprint – I am unbelievably grateful.

Thank you to Leah Boulton, for her beautiful work on the formatting, and to Natalie Wall, for all of her assistance. I am also incredibly grateful for Alison Tulett's copy-edits, and to Annie Lucas, for her guidance throughout this process.

Thank you, too, to my first reader, Pollyanna Jackson, and my beautiful friends: Rhona Bowie, Nora Rowser, Nina Coetzer, Ella Holdway, Amelie McKay, Jess Kennedy and Brooke Jessop.

I am also hugely indebted to far better writers than myself, without whom this novel would not exist: André Aciman, Brandon Taylor, Garth Greenwell and K Patrick.

Finally, thank you to my sister, Evie Murray, and my parents, for everything.